£12
(NCU)

The
Arthurian
Formula

The Arthurian

Formula

Legends of Merlin, the Round Table,
the Grail, Faery, Queen Venus & Atlantis
Through the mediumship of
Dion Fortune &
Margaret Lumley Brown
Edited, with introductory commentary by

Gareth Knight

Additional material by
Wendy Berg

Thoth Publications
Loughborough, Leicestershire

A CIP catalogue record for this book is available from the
British Library.

Cover design by Bob Eames
Printed and bound in Great Britain

Published by Thoth Publications
64 Leopold Street, Loughborough, LE11 5DN

ISBN 10: 1-870450-90-6
ISBN 13: 978-1-870450-90-4
Web address: www.thoth.co.uk
email: enquiries@thoth.co.uk

Contents

Foreword
Gareth Knight

The Arthurian Formula, which began as a series of trance Communications received by Dion Fortune between April 1941 and February 1942 formed the corner stone of the inner work of the Society of the Inner Light for the following twenty years, senior members being involved in practical work upon the archetypal principles enshrined in the Arthurian legends. The original scripts were supplemented by Margaret Lumley Brown, a remarkable gifted psychic, who became the channel for much of the post war teaching of the Society from 1946 until 1961.

In the presentation of these scripts, Dion Fortune's original work appears as Part One, and Margaret Lumley Brown's as Parts Two and Three. In addition I have included in appendices a series of extracts that, whilst not part of The Arthurian Formula, add relevant material from similar sources, along with some fascinating new light on the faery tradition in Arthurian legend by Wendy Berg, abstracted from her full length manuscript *Red Tree, White Tree*.

Channelled communication is not an exact science, even at the hands of those as gifted and experienced as Dion Fortune or Margaret Lumley Brown, and apart from whether we are prepared to take on board commitment to traditions as mind bending as ancient lost continents, faery lovers and ladies of the lake, and dynastic theories embracing Merlin, Arthur and the Knights of the Round Table, the scripts do show some inaccuracies – a certain confusion over the role of troubadours and trouvéres for example. Without being officiously intrusive I have endeavoured to draw discrete attention to any lapses in this respect but have refrained from censoring or correcting the original script. Otherwise the material is as it was issued to members of the Society of the Inner Light at the time. The chapter headings are, however, my own.

Certainly I have found a hidden power to reside within the scripts, and in *The Secret Tradition in Arthurian Legend* I endeavoured to present a general overview of them, with additional material drawn from various academic and esoteric sources. The time now seems to have come for the original work to be released to a wider public as it stands. May it have equally powerful and inspirational effects upon all who now receive it as it has ever had upon me.

Introduction
Gareth Knight
The Glastonbury tradition

Dion Fortune's concern with the Arthurian legend begins and ends at Glastonbury. Here she settled in 1922, building a group of chalets at the foot of the Tor, at Chalice Orchard, which remained her country retreat for the rest of her life in addition to her headquarters in the west end of London. Her body now rests in the municipal cemetery at Glastonbury, close to that of her friend, financial supporter and general factotum, Charles Thomas Loveday.

She celebrated her long standing love of Glastonbury and its legends in a little book called *Avalon of the Heart*, which she first wrote as articles in her house journal *The Inner Light Magazine*. This was published in volume form in 1934 and remains an evocative guide book to the esoteric side of Glastonbury, albeit with a number of minor factual inaccuracies. At the time of writing, with an enormous workload of writing, lecturing and organising, she had little time or opportunity for checking facts but wrote straight from the heart. In this however lies the strength of her little book, which is still in print to this day[1].

In her review of the Glastonbury legends she cast her net wide, as a selection of some of her chapter headings reveals: the Avalon of Merlin, Avalon of the Graal, Avalon of the Keltic Saints, the Holy Thorn, Glastonbury of the Monks, the Tor, Avalon and Atlantis. The tone is set in her opening paragraphs:

There are many different roads leading to our English Jerusalem, "the holyest erthe in England". We can approach it by the high-road of history, which leads through a rich country, for there is hardly a phase in the spiritual story of the race in which Glastonbury has played no part. Its influence twines like a golden thread through the story of our islands. Wherever mystical forces make themselves felt in our national life, the voice of Glastonbury is heard; never dominating, but always influencing.

Or we can come to Glastonbury by the upland path of legend. In and out twine the ancient folk-stories, full of deep spiritual significance to those whose hearts are tuned to their key. Arthur and his knights come and go. The Graal shines in the night sky above the Tor. The saints live their quaintly beautiful lives amid its meadows. The poetry of the soul writes itself at Glastonbury.

And there is a third way to Glastonbury, one of the secret Green Roads of the soul – the Mystic Way that leads through the Hidden Door into a land known only to the eye of vision. This is Avalon of the Heart to those who love her.

It is with the eye of vision and poetry of the soul that Glastonbury was well known to Dion Fortune, and which led eventually to her dictating *The Arthurian Formula*, as the amanuensis of her principle contact and inner teacher.

Her earliest recorded glimpse behind that Hidden Door was, however, twenty years earlier, in the presence of her mother and Frederick Bligh Bond, the architect who had begun to excavate the abbey ruins in 1907 but who had become the centre of considerable controversy when it was revealed that he had been using psychic sources to help him, although Dion Fortune's association with him came some time after this. On the evening of September 25th 1921, using powers of mediumship that she had newly developed under the guidance of Maiya Curtis-Webb, an old family friend and her superior in the Hermetic Order of the Golden Dawn, she received a communication that extolled the uniqueness of Glastonbury[2]. Soon afterwards, Bligh Bond departed for America, but Dion

Fortune met her future colleague C.T.Loveday in the grounds of Chalice Well, and with him formed a small group that was to develop into the Society of the Inner Light.[3]

Her subsequent esoteric interests covered a broad spectrum, Christian, Therapeutic, and Hermetic, which she wrote up in various articles and books, but it was *Avalon of the Heart* that expressed her love of the Arthurian traditions. Parts of it were based upon her own inner contacts but at the end of the book she acknowledges some external sources that, she recommends, "should be in the scrip of every pilgrim who takes the road to Avalon."

These were *Glastonbury, the English Jerusalem* by C. L. Marsden and *The Glories of Glastonbury* by Armine Campbell, two slim contemporary books on local history and legend respectively, together with an evocation of the spirit of such holy places, *The Priest of the Ideal* by Stephen Graham, a semi-fictional mystery tour of the British Isles, including Glastonbury, Iona and Lindisfarne, that was published in 1913, and in retrospect seems as if it might have been a rallying call for the group soul of the nation about to be plunged into the first world war. To these she added two classic poetical works, *The Ballad of the White Horse* by G. K. Chesterton, and Tennyson's *Idylls of the King*, along with Fiona Macleod's *The Immortal Hour*, Rutland Boughton's musical version of which mightily impressed her when she attended a performance at Glastonbury in 1920[4]. However, most important of all in light of her general interests was *The Mysteries of Britain* by Lewis Spence, whose contents she considered, "touch the very roots of our island tradition".

The Atlantis tradition

Lewis Spence was a popular anthropologist with a sympathy toward esoteric traditions, who had also produced a series of books on the Atlantis tradition, and one of the elements in *The Arthurian Formula* that is likely to startle any conventional reader is the evocation of legends of the lost continent of Atlantis.

Some hints of this are already to be found in *Avalon of the Heart*. Indeed, in the chapter *Avalon and Atlantis* she advances what she describes as her own theory, based upon "many threads that have never been unravelled and pieced together," in support of which there is "a steadily increasing body of opinion which is inclined to view the mythical lost continent of the Atlantic as offering the solution of many of the problems of pre-history".

She asserts that the data is to be found in many books, and although she does not name them, from other articles of hers[5] it is apparent that they include *Atlantis: The Antediluvian World* by Ignatius Donnelly (1892) and the series of titles by Lewis Spence published during the 1920's, which include *The Problem of Atlantis*, *History of Atlantis* and *Atlantis in America*.

The 1920's, when Dion Fortune was cutting her teeth as a developing occultist, was a decade quite sympathetic to a revival of ideas about the lost continent. The ground had been laid by Ignatius Donnelly, who was not, as Dion Fortune assumed (perhaps on account of his name) a Roman Catholic priest, which indeed she found somewhat odd! He was in fact an American politician, a Republican congressman for the State of Minnesota, and an intellectual pioneer in many senses of the word.

He had studied law but preferred poetry, set out to build a city on the west bank of the Mississippi, and on becoming tired of politics, turned his attention to various off-beat topics that happened to attract him. The first of these was the Atlantis tradition, after which he turned to other speculative pastures, including the theory that Francis Bacon wrote the plays of Shakespeare.

He died in 1901 but many of his ideas lived after him and his work on Atlantis set the tone for most subsequent debate. Starting with an assessment of the probabilities of Plato's story in the *Timaeus* and *Critias*, he went on to consider whether such a catastrophe was geologically possible, and compared the deluge legends of various nations along with similarities of flora, fauna and human culture on both sides of the Atlantic. On publication, his theories were taken seriously enough for the British Prime Minister, Mr Gladstone, to seek government funds, albeit unsuccessfully, to send a ship to test some of them out.

He certainly inspired Lewis Spence's series of books and presumably also the explorer Colonel P.H. Fawcett, who embarked upon an ill fated expedition into the Amazon jungle in 1925, encouraged by the novelist Rider Haggard, in search of remains of a majestic civilisation perhaps 10,000 years old, ante-dating Egypt, that held the secret of a mysterious light, possibly based on knowledge of atomic energy, and familiar with astronomy. We have an interesting sidelight on this in that he was in correspondence with Margaret Lumley Brown just before he left, who had written to him on account of a series of dreams and visions that seemed to be related to Atlantis.[6] Whether or not they shared all these speculations, the expedition was sanctioned by the Royal Geographical Society and the American Geographical Society. Unfortunately Colonel Fawcett never returned, although there remained considerable psychic interest in his fate, particularly as he had arranged to try to maintain psychic contact with a small band of clairvoyants during his journey.[7]

A more esoteric strand of traditions about Atlantis stems largely from Madame Blavatsky's *Isis Unveiled* of 1877, elaborated to a considerable degree in *The Secret Doctrine* of 1888, supplemented by the clairvoyant researches of W. Scott-Elliot in *The Story of Atlantis* (1893) and Rudolf Steiner in his somewhat more abstract *Atlantis and Lemuria* (English translation 1911). Dion Fortune was familiar with all of these, and the outlines of this line of tradition, which became part of popular theosophy, were replicated by her in *The Esoteric*

Orders and their Work, an elementary textbook which she wrote shortly after founding her esoteric school in 1927.[8]

Here we find the general metaphysical background of Root Races, when other species of human beings existed prior to humanity as we know it. That the Atlantean period saw the development of the individualised concrete mind from a more general subconscious level of mentation, but that this brought about a crisis of self oriented free will, which had to be mitigated by spiritual beings contacting the more advanced individuals of the time to re-link them with divine origins. This was said to be the beginning of schools of initiation. It eventuated in a great Sun Temple in the City of the Golden Gates in the latter days of a civilisation which had lasted over thousands of years. In the last days there was a series of great cataclysms accompanying each of which an emigration came east, the last of which crossed North Africa to reach its zenith in the civilisation of ancient Egypt, which forms the basis of the Western Esoteric Tradition.

Dion Fortune, like Anna Kingsford before her, parted company with the Theosophical Society's emphasis upon the wisdom of the East, and found support in the works of Lewis Spence and in particular his book *The Mysteries of Britain* (1928), which stimulated her interest in any lines of investigation which might provide a link to pre-Roman civilisation in Britain and the Druidic cult.

It is of course another great jump to consider that elements of ancient Brythonic myth, picked up and developed in the oral traditions of the Celtic tribes, should originate in even older emigrations from a mythical west. However Dion Fortune would have found a certain hint of academic support from a much well thumbed book in her library, *The Morte D'arthur of Sir Thomas Malory* by Vida D. Scudder (Dent & Dutton, London & New York, 1921), in which we find:

> *As the study of Arthurian romance proceeds, the variety and scope*
> *of it becomes more and more impressive. Every decade unravels a*

little further the interweaving of the stories, penetrates deeper into the region of origins, and appreciates more clearly the reactions of historic circumstance. The most fascinating work is the investigation of sources. It leads back and back, till behind Geoffrey's Arthur fighting the giant of Mont St. Michel rise all mythic heroes who have slain monsters of darkness, and the traits of Morgan le Fay are explained by her kinship to the Valkyrie, or the Irish war-goddess, the Morrigu. It is in Celtic myth and legend that the richest suggestions are found; yet the mind is impelled to peer toward yet farther horizons: Guenevere borne away by Meliagrance may be own cousin to Persephone in the courts of Hades; Gawain, waxing in strength as the sun mounts the sky, certainly suggests the large family of sun-heroes; and Perceval, dumb and puzzled as the Grail passes before the bier of a king dying yet never dead, may assist at the mystic burial rites of an Eastern god of vegetation. Who shall say indeed that faint recollections of lost Atlantis may not gleam through the stories?[9]

It is, moreover, a scenario that appeals to the popular imagination, as demonstrated in J. R. R. Tolkien's evocation of Numenor in *The Silmarillion*, which could be regarded as Atlantis under another name. And in psychological terms we find Dion Fortune, as early as 1922, suggesting that clairvoyant investigations of the akashic records should not be dismissed out of hand, in light of Jung's theories that the collective unconscious may contain deep racial memories.[10]

Lewis Spence however, for all his flirtation with occultism over the years, drew the line at accepting clairvoyant evidence of the lost continent very seriously. In his last work on the subject, *The Occult Sciences in Atlantis* (published c.1941), he states quite unequivocally that he found it impossible to make practical use of any material professing to be communications from the Otherworld. After careful examination of all that had been sent to him by interested persons, he felt compelled to reject the entire body of witness, as he found that not a single one agreed in its circumstances with another.[11] This perhaps need not be all that surprising in respect of a civilisation allegedly lasting over such a huge expanse of space and time. Whilst his other criticism, that the communications were often couched in a high handed and hieratic manner might well square with a civilisation that was on the point of self destruction through overweening pride.

Neither Dion Fortune nor Margaret Lumley Brown were averse to making their own clairvoyant investigations on the subject, whether or not they ever tendered them to Lewis Spence, and a selection of their findings is provided in Appendix 2.

The Faery Tradition

Apart from Atlantis, another major culture shock to the conventional reader of *The Arthurian Formula* is likely to concern the assumed existence of the Faery race.

Not that this is necessarily a stumbling block to academic research, in that a major characteristic of the Arthurian world is its lack of minor gods – the over-riding religion being ostensibly Christian, if of a somewhat unorthodox brand. This suggests that any seemingly Faery beings were originally pagan gods who are in process of being humanised yet have not yet quite made it. Or were originally prominent human beings, perhaps local kings or queens, partway emphemerised into becoming deified. However, this academic "middle way" overlooks or subverts a very prevalent and longstanding tradition of Faery as having a perfectly valid existence in its own right.

A classic work in the field is *The Fairy Faith in Celtic Countries* (1911) by W. Y. Evans Wentz. This marked a step forward from the anthropological orthodoxy represented by Frazer's *Golden Bough*, which assumed that world wide and age old traditional beliefs were merely misapplied logic, naive attempts to explain natural phenomena. Evans Wentz, in his field work in five Celtic countries, found, at any rate to his own satisfaction, that faery beliefs and traditions appeared to contain elements of a pre-Christian religion, namely the Druidic, which, as Kathleen Raine points out, Pythagoras himself in ancient time considered to be custodians of esoteric knowledge.

Whilst he favoured a psychological theory to account for sightings of the faery world (and it has to be remembered that he was writing an academic thesis in pursuit of a doctorate at the University of Rennes) Evans Wentz nonetheless rendered accounts that might be more in keeping with psychical research, rather than fantasies of superstitious country folk. In a fulsome joint dedication to the poet W. B. Yeats and George Russell (author of the mystical classic *The Candle of Vision*,[12] under the pseudonym AE) there is a broad hint of where his sympathies lie. Indeed in later life he went on to produce some major works of mystical scholarship on Tibetan Buddhism and, posthumously published, a work on traditions surrounding sacred mountains. One interview in his fairy book of which he was particularly proud was with George Russell, reporting his experience of radiant visions of beings of the Celtic Otherworld.

Both Dion Fortune and Margaret Lumley Brown bore witness to similar experiences in very different locations and circumstances. Dion Fortune recalls how at Whitsun 1926, when walking upon Glastonbury Tor, she and her companions were suddenly taken up with a feeling of ecstasy that set them whirling in an impromptu dance, during which a repetitive chant seemed to beat through into consciousness which they afterwards set down and treasured as "The Chant of the Elements".[13] She also provides a considerable amount of faery lore in her Dr. Taverner stories.[14] that she claims are derived from practical experience. Margaret Lumley Brown, as an exceptionally gifted natural clairvoyant, left many accounts of her visionary experiences, including drawings of various elemental and faery beings.[15]

For a modern and consistent coverage of the Faery tradition however we are indebted to the Scottish writer, musician and composer, R.J.Stewart, who in a series of books,[16] spells out in unequivocal fashion a demonstration of the faery tradition, and bears witness to a species of living beings who, out of a wide range of spiritual beings traditionally described, lie close to the human race.

Stewart has buttressed his written work with a series of experiential public workshops and finds that the subject fascinates all kinds of people, including the hard nosed sceptic and the open minded. All are generally surprised to find that they are not involved in a vague and cosy event about little beings "with gauze wings and frilly knickers" but are confronted with visions of human size or greater, in imaginative techniques based upon traditional themes and images that have the effect of expanding individual and group awareness. This initial encounter can lead to a deeper awareness of the faery realm, in the more advanced stages of which a dialogue and relationship may be developed in which human and faery beings act in an alliance that is gradually extended to other orders of living creatures.

This is not necessarily a recipe for developing schizophrenia as cautious critics might assume, but a perfectly natural process that abuts the highest flights of the creative imagination – as has been hinted at, each in their way, by William Blake and Samuel Taylor Coleridge. The one as cleansing the doors of perception, and the other as the development of the secondary imagination, as complement to the primary imagination that is our vehicle for apprehension of the purely physical world.

How does this marry up to relationships with faery beings in Arthurian legend as suggested in *The Arthurian Formula*?

Celtic myth is unsurpassed in world mythology for its recognition of the world of faery. The Irish folk soul in particular is permeated with it and it lays before us, just as it did the knights, a series of symbols, challenges and encounters with guardians of many thresholds between the worlds, often encountered guarding a ford or a bridge. Whilst it is often the sharp tongued and challenging women, ostensibly appealing for help, who lure the knights onto their quests and test them thoroughly upon the way by word or by deed. In fact it is arguable that women play a part in the dynamics of the Round Table and Grail traditions that is at least as important as the more prominently featured knights.

Sir Yvain meets and marries a faery queen who sits beneath a tree beside a magic fountain, which leads to an almighty battle with the guardian of the land beyond and husband of the fée, whose place he is then expected to take. Whilst his mother, Morgan, is a richly composite character who contains aspects of various ancient sources, from the great queen of Irish legend, to the Morrighan who hovers over the battlefields as the black birds of death, or the Washer at the Ford who oversees the rites of passage between the worlds of the living and the dead, yet who also has a reputation as a healer, and finally appears as one of the mourning queens in the barge that takes the mortally wounded Arthur off to Avalon. One of the difficulties modern readers have in coming to terms with the various actions of Morgan le Fay is that much of the time she is acting as a goddess and initiatrix, testing and challenging her heroes, whereas in the medieval context that has come down to us, having lost her supernatural status, she tends to appear simply as a gratuitously spiteful and vengeful woman. It is little wonder, therefore, that she is somewhat ambiguously cast into a kind of halfway house, half woman half fay, or as Malory bizarrely puts it, "was put to scole in a nonnery, and ther she lerned so moche that she was a grete clerke of nygromancye!"

Then there is the Lady of the Lake, in her various forms, completely autonomous, a queen in her own right, moving between the worlds with a strange freedom, like Merlin. Suddenly arriving in a story and then returning in different guise a little later on, returning to the Lake or simply fading from sight, who has the reputation for taking and fostering

children, as with the infant Sir Lancelot and his cousins Bors
and Lionel, to bring them up and educate them in her faery
world under the Lake, before they are returned to the human
world to take up their lives and destinies.

Igraine, the mother of King Arthur, who in *The
Arthurian Formula* appears in the guise of an Atlantean princess,
has a hardly less likely role in Chrétien de Troyes' *Conte del
Graal* where she appears as queen of an otherworld Castle of
Maidens, a place of ancestors and matriarchs, situated upon an
island in the centre of a lake, in which there are great wonders,
including a Perilous Bed upon which Gawain is attacked by
mysterious archers and a ferocious lion, during his quest for
the lance that is associated with the Grail.

The most prominent instance of the Faery problem, or the
dual role or multi-faceted aspect of characters, is to be found
with the figure of Queen Guinevere herself. In *The Arthurian
Formula* she tends to be cast as a rather pathetic human
spouse who has little chance of gaining Arthur's affections
in competition with faery lovers, but alternative readings are
possible, including seeing her as a faery being in her own right.
Her name derives from "white shadow" or "white phantom"
and the *wen* or *wyn* element in her name suggests a being who
is not human but comes from the world of faery.

What could lie behind a marriage between the two races?
Between a Faery being whose dower, arranged by Merlin, is the
Round Table itself, and the human Arthur, bearing the native
royal blood of the Pendragons and the clairvoyant Atlantean
blood of his mother Igraine? Arguably Arthur's kingship
would need to be ratified by his union with a representative of
the inner land - and who more appropriate than a faery being?
An inner mating in which the human king was initiated into
the deep wisdom of the land by a faery representative of the
great Earth goddess, who withdraws once her task is done?
Once Guenevere is seen as a faery or inner world being rather
than a fallen woman, much that is otherwise unsatisfactory or

inexplicable falls into place.

Beyond that, she bears strong indications of having been a Goddess of the Land, embodying the principle of Sovereignty, who bestows her favours only onto the best champion, and so it is not without significance that Lancelot is lauded as being "the best knight in the world".

Whatever nuance of meaning we choose to put upon it, the incontestable point is that Arthur, Lancelot and Guinevere exist in the hearts and minds of different generations as guides and representatives of inner truths, whether consciously perceived as so or not. They remain firmly rooted in consciousness to serve us now, as they have served our predecessors, as functioning archetypes of inner and outer relationships.

The triangle between Arthur, Lancelot and Guinevere may be reinterpreted by each generation according to its own lights. Indeed Dion Fortune's script is plainly related to what she called her Isis work - her mission to reform contemporary sexual and marital attitudes of the 1930's, which was largely the theme in her later novels[17] as well as a series of articles entitled *The Circuit of Force*.[18]

The Merlin Tradition

Much the same multi-layered dynamics apply to the relationship between Merlin and Nimué. To match the Victorian feeling of pious disapproval of Guinevere's adulterous behaviour Tennyson's portrayal of Nimué was as the wily minx Vivien who beguiled and imprisoned a besotted old man who was pestering her. Yet the reasons for Merlin's withdrawal into the earth in company with a fée are considerably more complex and elevated in meaning than that.

The Arthurian Formula, whilst on the one hand depicting Merlin almost as a Manu of the 5th Root Race, or at very least as an Atlantean high priest, also seems happy to accept the less flattering scenario of the magician, asserting that "he also failed for a time, and like Arthur, had to sleep and wake again, and then make up for the time he had lost…became an instrument of mere sensation for a time…lost the deep impersonality that was the greatest part, if rightly understood, of the religious side of the Atlantean Priesthood."[19] And although account is taken of varying traditions about his birth, Part One asserting that he was born of "a virgin and a high Elemental" whilst in Part Three it is of "a great Atlantean High Priestess and a Lord of Flame," such paradoxical variations need not deflect from the validity of much of *The Arthurian Formula*, in whole or in part, for we are dealing not with a simple history but with a great complex of traditions, some them of very great depth. One might note, in this respect, a certain *cri de coeur* from the communicator, "There is so very much to dwell upon in this great racial power that I myself am at a loss to wield the power enough to bring it into some kind of whole which can easily be handled. At present we can only take certain parts, developing these bit by bit."[20]

It should be apparent then, that the Arthurian tradition is like an archaeological dig of very considerable antiquity, at a complex cross roads of human cultures, and one that has been turned over and considerably mixed up by different generations throughout the centuries. Nonetheless it is this that indicates its value and provides its challenge and fascination.

Even the more obvious and available roots of the Merlin tradition have tended to be overlooked, that were first developed by Geoffrey of Monmouth in his *History of the British Kings* of 1135, which incorporated the *Prophecies of Merlin,* and was swiftly followed up by the *Life of Merlin*. R. J. Stewart has been a tireless pioneer and perceptive commentator in putting this to rights.

When he first approached the *Vita Merlini* he assumed, along with most of us, that it was a random jumble of old folkloric and magical remains mixed with medieval political prophecy. Only when he began to examine the themes in greater depth did he realise how intimately two streams of

Celtic legend and classical or post-classical philosophy had been merged, curiously and cunningly fused into a mixture so rich as to suggest a third source beyond them both - that of the mysterious Otherworld upon which the ancient Mysteries had been founded.

As he has demonstrated in his books upon the subject[21] we are dealing with an essentially oral tradition, for the material set out by Geoffrey of Monmouth is not a biography but a collection of traditional tales, images, poems and loosely related themes woven around the central figure of Merlin, by means of which we have been provided with a virtual time capsule containing the basic lore of an oral wisdom tradition. In this role Merlin is a spiritual being, transformed from the human state into a higher mode of consciousness yet remaining human, whose powers are not magical in the trivial sense but related to the energies of the land, cyclical, mysterious at times as the prophet himself, a symbolic model of transformed consciousness, whose actions and utterances are highly amplified, exaggerated, archetypal. His periods of apparent madness are different from our concepts of insanity or mental unbalance, and are a stage through which he passes in the arousal of inner energies, for his relationships achieve a harmonious relationship with feminine principles, until, the epitome of a pagan seer, he grows beyond the supernormal powers of seership and achieves an integrated understanding of the universe as the mantle of prophecy passes from him.

Looking into the origins of Merlin is thus more than a literary exercise, and there are traditions of Merlin quite apart from the Arthurian legends. Esoteric tradition suggests indeed that there has been more than one Merlin, each incorporating the power and wisdom of his predecessors. *The Arthurian Formula*, in going so far as to suggest that Merlin is linked to lost Atlantis as a carrier of wisdom to new horizons from a corrupt and dying civilisation, is harmonically linked to Geoffrey of Monmouth's theme of Britain being founded by

Brutus, whose ancestors fled from the sack of Troy. Historical correlation is irrelevant in these matters, all falls are the fall of Atlantis, they are harmonically, magically and psychically the same event.

Merlin, regarded as an archetype, typifies wisdom from a source that is not human or personal yet which can be applied to humanity both individually and collectively. At another level we may find the prototype of the tribal king who becomes attuned to the land, becomes one with it by voluntary sacrifice. R. J. Stewart has recorded something of this dynamic in his report of experience at a well preserved and recently excavated prehistoric tomb at Les Monts Grantez, Jersey in September 1978.[22] This would seem to be the ancient truth behind the medieval legends which have him enchanted by a female power, to go beneath the ground or into a crystal tower or merge into a flowering thorn.

The Troubadour Tradition

Another stratum in all of this, which is itself a complex mix of heterodox sexual, social, philosophical and religious ideas, is to be found in the troubadour minstrelsy, which spread from southern France in various forms. Whilst some important elements of it were stamped out in the Albigensian persecution of the early 13th century, others flourished into what ultimately became the flowering of high medieval culture in Dante's *Divine Comedy* in 14th century Florence, when a virtual worship of the feminine was brought into a cosmic Christian context.

There is no certain knowledge as to where this form of poetic sensibility came from but a strong argument can be made for Arab dominated Spain. What is more, the original Moorish invasions extended far north into France before being stemmed at the Battle of Poitiers, which later became, under Eleanor of Aquitaine, a centre for the tradition of the Courts of Love, and perpetuated by her daughter, Marie of

Champagne, the patroness of Chrétien de Troyes, the first Arthurian romancer, and of Andreus Capellanus, who wrote a virtual textbook on *The Art of Courtly Love*.

Early troubadour poetry at Poitiers, through its most influential practitioner, Marcabru, was concerned with moral and philosophical questions as the basis for certain definitions of behaviour. *Fin amors* was a love that unified physical and mental desire with spiritual aspiration, and could be outwardly expressed in *cortesia* (courtliness), which included youthfulness of spirit (*jovens*), the quest for happiness (*jois*), and various other qualities. In short, love could be an enobling and purifying passion and the basis for a civilised and courtly life expression.

At its height this could reach metaphysical levels wherein physical and divine love are barely distinguishable, and in one line of development led toward the cult of the Virgin Mary. Although it should be said that troubadour poetry had a very broad base and some of its examples were quite bawdy or downright lascivious, and there was also a tradition of female troubadours. However, the classic courtly relationship promoted in troubadour love songs stressed three things:

a) the supremacy and aloofness of the lady;
b) the need for total subservience in gaining her love;
c) the enobling power of ideal love.

It was a literature written primarily for an aristocratic society, and usually assumed that the troubadour's lady was married, and so in practice involved a fantasy based on an idealisation of this adulterous relationship. Indeed one celebrated ruling concerned whether love was even possible between man and wife.

This reflected a social reality of the times when most aristocratic marriages were made for dynastic reasons. In addition to this, general standards of behaviour were pretty brutal. We need to realise that life at the time was not all a matter of "perfect gentle knights" in the romantic pre-Raphaelite image, all behaving like Victorian Christian gentlemen with the sporting ethics of the playing fields of Eton.

In a relatively brutish feudal society ruled by a warrior class, with women classed as chattels, or bringers of dowries, it seems no surprise if a desire for flights of fancy break through and ladies of the court found stories based on Celtic legends so appealing. They could find release in having their imagination stimulated by the otherworldly summons of a Celtic King of the Underworld; or a faery mistress calling to her human lover, sat by her magic fountain, or her secret garden of abundance or upon a magic island.

In the hands of poets of the calibre of Chrétien de Troyes, we find a combination of troubadour love interest, and dynastic stories drawn from Celtic myth and legend, to produce a literature in which the knightly civilisation of the time could find an idealised representation of itself, with authority derived from the ideals of chivalry as exemplified by King Arthur's court, whose heroes were patterns of virtue.

In this respect the Arthurian stories are played out by archetypal ideals rather than actual humans, even if half remembered historical events, or very ancient mythic dynamics often break through.

The Queen Venus Tradition

Another element in the 12th century elevation of the status of the feminine was an influx of heterodox religious beliefs and ideas coming back with the soldiers, pilgrims and various travellers, returning from the Holy Land and Byzantium during the crusader period, many of whom passed through southern France via the port of Marseilles. It is perhaps not without significance that it was in southern France that Mary Magdalene was said to have ended her days.

In the ministry of Jesus the figure of Mary of Magdala (or of "the tower of doves") comes and goes, always in the background, yet playing some undefined yet crucial role. Her anointing him with the fabulously expensive spikenard leads directly to his denunciation by Judas, (who by his actions and sympathies, seems closest to Jewish orthodoxy). She is the first to come to the empty tomb on the day of the resurrection, to be angelically commanded to take the news to the other apostles, and who on the way encounters the risen Christ. In the apocryphal gospels she has a clearly authoritative role, rallying the faithful and being a source of wisdom to the other apostles – a feminine wisdom figure. The apocryphal Gospel of Philip declares that Jesus loved her more than all the disciples and used to kiss her often on the mouth. The Gnostics went so far as to call her Mary Lucifer, Mary the Light-bringer, before the medieval church demonised the name, and in the Nag Hammadi scrolls Peter acknowledges that Jesus had a relationship with the Magdalene that surpassed his own. Thus in the two hundred years before the canon was finalised it appears that several groups took it for granted that Mary of Magdala was in some sense the partner of Christ and first among the apostles.

In *Polarity Magic: The Secret History of Western Religion*[23], Wendy Berg and Mike Harris examine these factors, including the resonance with Celtic Christianity, wherein women apparently also served at the Mass, and wherein the goddess/saint Brigid/ Bride takes on the role of foster mother to Christ, with a centre at Glastonbury, with a chapel at Beckary, which before its dedication to Brigid was held to be sacred to the Magdalen.

Further to this, in his description and virtual gazetteer of *The Cult of the Black Virgin*[24], the Jungian psychologist Ean Begg draws attention to the survival of the goddess in the form of black images of the Madonna. The great age for these was also the 12th century, although legends about them hark back to the beginnings of Christianity. The land of the troubadours was also that of the Cathar heresy, a seemingly rigidly puritanical and earth denying sect in some ways, yet which at the same time appeared to be in agreement with the troubadours in acknowledging a woman's right to take a lover – not that they particularly approved of the practice but simply thought it no worse than the formal conjugal bond.

There is such a complex tangle of traditions here that it is not our purpose to try to unravel, even if it were possible, and there has been no shortage of speculative and highly popular books on various elements of the Cathars, the Templars, Rennes le Chateau, and so forth. As Ean Begg points out, the cults of the great goddesses, particularly Isis, Cybele and Diana/Artemis, retained their old prestige and fervour in many places all along the Mediterranean, whilst there is evidence of worship of the Triple Mother and of Epona, the mare goddess throughout the Celtic world. This is the general line of tradition that *The Arthurian Formula* refers to in the portmanteau term of "the cult of Queen Venus".

The Modern Mystery Tradition

It is very much with the dynamics of the Cult of Queen Venus that Dion Fortune was concerned when she was promulgating the semi-public performance of her Rites of Isis, that had their apogee in 1938, and which is back of much of the drift of Part One of *The Arthurian Formula*.

With the Second and Third parts of *The Arthurian Formula* we come to the period from 1946 when Margaret Lumley Brown, working closely under the direction of a new Warden of the Society of the Inner Light, Arthur Chichester. The quality of her work is evident in here in addition to a remarkable quantity of communications on many mythological, psychological and cosmological subjects.[25]

The nature and purpose of the inner work of the Society from the time of the reception of *The Arthurian Formula*, through to 1961, when a new phase was instituted, was basically along Arthurian lines. All new students, of which I was one at the time, were expected to have read Malory's *Morte d'Arthur* from cover to cover, as a back-up to their meditation discipline and general course work. The deeper Arthurian work was however confined to the Greater Mystery grades.

Arthur Chichester was largely responsible for composing the Holy Grail Rite that is mentioned in the script and which formed a regular part of the higher level ritual programme. It was based upon the early scripts that Dion Fortune recorded at Glastonbury, with a representation of the symbols that are generally known as the Grail hallows – Lance, Cup, Sword, Stone – and evoked a vision of Merlin welcoming the Grail as it appeared before the Round Table fellowship. Allied to this was a regime of personal discipline wherein senior members identified with specific Arthurian archetypes, in a spiritual intention regarded as "the redemption of the archetypes".

This notwithstanding that the Arthurian mythos is basically one of failure. Ultimately the Round Table is dispersed, only Bedivere appears to be left to accompany the wounded King after the terrible last battle, a few stragglers are allegedly to be found in monasteries or nunneries, whilst the Grail has been removed to an inner kingdom of Sarras – the outer world not being good enough to retain it. Obviously then, a somewhat more complex operation is involved than the more familiar one in magical or religious circles of dedication to a particular god form or saintly paradigm. In a system where the powers are not so much gods but relatively flawed heroes and heroines one can see the logic in a caveat by R. J. Stewart: "If any individual or group dares to take upon themselves the archetypal images and patterns of the Arthurian myths they will polarise and amplify each and any inherent weakness or corruption within themselves." Certainly for the time it lasted the degree of dedication that was expected from, and expressed by, those concerned was of a very high order.

As might be assumed from the very popularity of the tradition over centuries there are very powerful dynamics at work within it, but fortunately there are many less demanding ways of working with the tradition than that required of senior initiates of the Society of the Inner Light half a century ago.

The key lies in the practical use of the pictorial imagination, which can be aided by reading aloud from any of the texts. Reading aloud comes particularly into its own when working within a small group that is visualising the scenes described. But even when working on one's own it is far superior to the modern habit of reading silently. It slows things down to a more effective pace for assimilation, and the human voice as vehicle of the word has a certain magical quality that is seldom realised.

This has been brought home to me on various occasions when conducting seminars when simply reading aloud from a text as apparently commonplace as Tennyson's *Morte D'Arthur*, from *Idylls of the King*, or a translation of Chrétien de Troyes' *Yvain – the Knight of the Lion* has resulted in memorable inner experiences and even synchronistic happenings. It is largely of course, all in the imagination, as any sceptic will tell you. But when applied with sincerity in the right company and circumstances, and with the right dedication, the imagination may hold dynamics that the sceptic little suspects.

The literary resources

It was plainly part of Margaret Lumley Brown's function, particularly in the third part of *The Arthurian Formula*, to bring through additional material upon the archetypes that might be helpful to the group, individually and collectively. This was plainly an attempt to supplement one of the first pleas made at the beginning of *The Arthurian Formula*, of the need for more informed scholarship upon the legends.

Although the legends have never entirely lacked for that, in 1941, when *The Arthurian Formula* was first commenced, comparatively little work was published on the Celtic origins of the Arthuriad. Indeed there was a strong tradition in the academic world that no such Celtic involvement existed, or if it did was quite minimal. The positivist school of academic thought refused to countenance the existence of any manuscript that was not physically available – let alone give credence to any possible oral tradition, and thus chose to ignore the claims of major writers such as Geoffrey of Monmouth, Chrétien de Troyes or Wolfram von Eschenbach, that they were indebted to older sources. Things were perhaps not helped by the speculative work of Jessie L. Weston, who in *From Ritual to Romance* floated the idea of the Grail being based upon an ancient fertility ritual. This has since been reckoned not to be sustainable, although it is conceded by the more generous at heart that the spirit of her enquiry and her intuitions were pointing in more or less the right direction.

However, the plea for more systematic and readily available work upon the origins of the Arthurian legends was answered by a spate of important books in the post war years, largely under the aegis of the American scholar Professor R. S. Loomis. We conclude therefore with a series notes of a number of them, which are little short of essential reading for anyone who seriously intends to come to terms with the traditions contained within *The Arthurian Formula*.[26]

Texts

The Arthurian Formula mentions that Malory is quite adequate for general purposes and versions of his classic work are available in many editions, but we would recommend getting as sumptuous a one as possible, rather than a cramped student text or paper edition. One battered old favourite that we still use has illustrations by Arthur Rackham, but almost as evocative is the three volume Oxford University Press edition of the Westminster manuscript, (that was discovered only in 1923), and is edited by Professor Eugène Vinaver under the title *The Works of Sir Thomas Malory*. This uses the original spelling, which may take a little getting used to, but is particularly rewarding when one has. The change of title from Caxton's

Le Morte d'Arthur is on account that it seems probable that Malory did not intend one comprehensive volume, but a series of smaller independent ones. Hence the anomolies between certain sections. But all this is largely academic and the text is much the same as far as the general reader is concerned.

Also highly recommended is a recent edition of the Caxton version, running to a thousand pages, and profusely illustrated, edited by John Matthews.

Malory's *Le Morte d'Arthur* is, in origin, a free translation of a number of French works, generally referred to as the *Vulgate Lancelot*, a vast medieval rambling soap opera of a text. The main parts of it are largely available in paperback student editions, translated by modern scholars, under titles such as *Lancelot of the Lake, The Death of King Arthur, The Quest of the Holy Grail.*

The first Arthurian romancer was Chrétien de Troyes, translations of whose verse tales, apart from his incompleted Grail romance, have been published as *Arthurian Romances*, and it is interesting to compare his stories with parallel ones to be found in *The Mabinogion*, translated from the Welsh, and which appear to share a common source.

Going back yet further is Geoffrey of Monmouth's *History of the Kings of Britain*, who seems to have kick-started it all with this Latin work of 1135, whilst free renderings of it into Norman French by Wace (who introduced the Round Table) and Middle English by Layamon (who introduced the elves) have been published together in English translation as *Arthurian Chronicles.*

Other important Arthurian themes are those of Tristan and Iseult of which there are two versions, one by Beroul, available in translation as *The Romance of Tristan*, and one by Gottfried von Strassburg, translated as *Tristan*. In the Grail tradition there are, from the French, *The High History of the Holy Grail* and the German Wolfram von Eschenbach's *Parzival*, which was the inspiration for Wagner's opera cycle.

Academic Guides

R. S. Loomis

We are indebted to Professor R. S. Loomis for a life time's work researching the Celtic origins of the Arthurian legends. Two works aimed at the general reader give an overview of the whole tradition. *The Development of Arthurian Romance* and *The Grail: from Celtic Myth to Christian Symbol* (both Columbia University Press, 1963).

He is also responsible for two more heavyweight texts, *Arthurian Legend and Chrétien de Troyes*, (Columbia University Press, 1949), which provides detailed research into the Celtic sources of the works of the first writer of Arthurian romances; and *Wales and the Arthurian Legend*, (University of Wales Press, 1956) a collection of journal articles written by him tracing Celtic roots to the Arthurian legend.

The virtual bible for Arthurian studies is however, a work edited by him, *Arthurian Literature in the Middle Ages*, (Oxford University Press, 1959) a comprehensive work by a number of scholars ranging from early Welsh verse and oral traditions right through to Sir Thomas Malory's great English classic *Le Morte d'Arthur*.

D. D. R. Owen

A work inspired by the work of Professor Loomis, *The Evolution of the Grail Legend* (Oliver & Boyd, Edinburgh, 1968) traces the transmission of a body of legendary material, from Ireland through its growth and metamorphoses until it came into the hands of Chrétien de Troyes, the first Grail romancer.

Alfred Nutt

A scholar from a previous era, but whose *Studies on the Legend of the Holy Grail* subtitled *With Especial Reference to the Hypothesis of its Celtic Origin*, first published in 1888, is so useful and comprehensive, giving handy summaries of the various Grail stories, that it still merits new impressions. The one is my possession is by Cooper Square Publishers, New York, 1965.

F. R. P. Akehurst & Judith M. Davis

A modern scholarly guide to the whole Troubadour tradition by two American professors *Handbook of the Troubadours* (University of California Press, Berkeley, 1995).

L. T. Topsfield

A much loved Cambridge don whose two works are a superlative guide to their topics: *Chrétien de Troyes: A Study of the Arthurian Romances* (Cambridge University Press, 1981) and *Troubadours and Love* (Cambridge University Press, 1975).

Esoteric Guides.

However, more importantly for practical students of the esoteric tradition within Arthurian legend, is a series of books written during the 1980s and 90s, not by academics, nor by hack popular writers, but by intelligent and well read practitioners within the esoteric field. Some of these have already been mentioned, and include R. J. Stewart, Caitlín and John Matthews, Marian Green, Mike Harris and Wendy Berg apart from my own modest efforts.

These works provide valuable lines of investigation in not being hog tied to intellectual academic disciplines but practically experienced in imaginal techniques. They are thus able to fill in yawning gaps that exist between the lines of the basic texts and the academic approach to them.

It should be said that the titles listed below do not by any means, include all the works of the writers mentioned, but simply to those that most directly pertain to practical elements within *The Arthurian Formula*.

Caitlín & John Matthews

Caitlín Matthews: *Mabon and the Mysteries of Britain* (Arkana, 1987).

At one level a literary guide to the mythological patterns which underlie *The Mabinogion*, and at a deeper level a practical exploration of the archetypes and mythical themes from these medieval stories that descend from proto-Celtic oral tradition.

Caitlín Matthews: *Arthur and the Sovereignty of Britain* (Arkana, 1989).
Subtitled *King and Goddess in the Mabinogion* provides a full commentary on the stories showing how the Divine Feminine has always been a primal facet of British mythology, and as Lady Sovereignty has become both subsumed and elevated in mythic consciousness.

John Matthews: *Gawain: Knight of the Goddess* (Aquarian, 1990).
The result of more than 20 years research investigates how and why Gawain, once the most important knight at Arthur's court, was diminished in character as the popularity of the romances grew, representing him almost as a villain rather than as a Champion of the Goddess.

Caitlín & John Matthews: *The Ladies of the Lake* (Thorsons, 1992) .
Portrays nine women in Arthurian legend, Igraine, Guinevere, Morgan, who are Arthur's kindred, Argante, Nimué and Enid, who bring the wisdom of the otherworld, and Kundry, Dindraine and Ragnell, who manifest the compassion of the Grail, demonstrating them as Ladies of the Lake in whom the ancient Celtic goddess is fragmented and reflected.

John Matthews & Marian Green: *The Grail Seeker's Companion* (Aquarian, 1986 and [Updated] Thoth Publications, Loughborough, 2005)
A guidebook to places, people, stories and theories surrounding the Grail. A reference book including history, ritual, meditation, advice and instruction. In short, everything

you are likely to need before you set out on your own personal Quest.

R. J. Stewart.

His important works may be listed under two traditions, that of Merlin and that of Faery.

Merlin Tradition

The Mystic Life of Merlin (Arkana, 1986).
The original text of the *Vita Merlini* is given in an edited English translation, accompanied by a set of illustrations depicting the psychology, cosmology and magical and mystical concepts it embraces.

The Prophetic Vision of Merlin (Arkana, 1986).
The Prophecies of Merlin are embedded within Geoffrey of Monmouth's *History of the British Kings*. Drawn from Welsh or Breton oral tradition they form a manual of psychology and metaphysics that describes the methods of inspiration employed by seers of the Celtic cultures.

The Way of Merlin (Aquarian, 1991).
A practical guide book and series of exercises for inner development based on ancient traditions associated with Merlin.

Faery Tradition

The UnderWorld Initiation (Aquarian, 1985).
A powerful system of altering consciousness in a dynamic and far-reaching manner, the central symbols of which derive from songs and ballads whose roots are in the Celtic and pre-Celtic past.

Earth Light (Element, 1992).
Examines the traditions of the Faery realm as a source of transformation and enlightenment, through powerful

techniques of visualisation and imagination, leading to true healing and regeneration, both of ourselves and the Earth.

Power within the Land (Element, 1992).
Exploring our oldest and perhaps most neglected spiritual tradition – the Underworld – takes the reader into the deepest levels, focusing on contact with energies and spiritual beings hidden within the land itself.

The Well of Light - The Mystery of the Double Rose (Mercury, 2005).
This book concludes the above comprehensive series that has been developed over the last 20 years.

Robert Kirk, Walker between the Worlds (Element, 1990 and Thoth Publications, Loughborough 2007).
A new edition in modern English of Kirk's 17th century *Secret Commonwealth of Elves, Fauns and Fairies*, with comparisons between ancient rites and powers of the Faery tradition and second sight with those of shamanism, native American tradition, Celtic myth and legend and perennial magical arts.

The Living World of Faery (Gothic Image, 1995, current edition by Mercury, USA).
A more general book on the Faery tradition revealing the living reality behind it and demonstrating that the subjects are not romantic bygones but represent themes that are deeply significant for modern humanity, including second sight, distance contact, meetings with faery allies and co-walkers, and extracts from a previously unpublished 18th century journal.

Mike Harris & Wendy Berg

Mike Harris: *Awen: The Quest of the Celtic Mysteries* (Melchior, 1999 and updated by Thoth Publications, Loughborough 2007).
Celtic bards laid the foundation of inner wisdom that has come down to us as the Arthurian tradition. "Awen" is a Welsh word often translated as "inspiration" but in its fullness it is untranslatable as a single word, comprising a kind of irradiation

of the soul from paradisal origins. Shows how the Celtic bards provided a bridge that leads to a very ancient world, preserving much of the traditions of the Bronze Age beaker people, and beyond them the Neolithic and, some believe, even more ancient wisdom.

Wendy Berg & Mike Harris: *Polarity Magic: The Secret History of Western Religion* (Llewellyn, 2003).
Explores the hidden traditions in the Western mysteries, focussing on the Divine Feminine and the sexual dynamics of magic. How polarity magic lies at the heart of the Western Mystery Tradition, constituting the core of all mythology and mystery teachings, featuring ancient historical and mythological couples such as Isis and Osiris, Taliesin and Ceridwen, Arthur and Gwenevere, Merlin and Gwendydd, Akhenaten and Nefertiti, Mary Magdalene and Jesus.

Gareth Knight

The Secret Tradition in Arthurian Legend (Aquarian, 1983, Weiser, 1996)
A book developed from the hints and instructions given in *The Arthurian Formula.* How King Arthur is a living contemporary archetype, not an ancient dead king. Shows how the Arthurian legend may be structured into a workable mystery system, comprised of three primary grades of attainment. The first of the powers of Arthur – of loyalty, dedication and service, enshrined in concepts of chivalry. The second in the powers of Merlin, bringing knowledge of the invisible forces that are the true roots of causation in the material world. The third the powers of Guenevere, for those who work with power based upon the forces of polarity within the aura. Beyond that lie the Greater Mysteries which open awareness to higher spiritual forces and the Grail.

Notes

[1] Currently published under the title *Glastonbury – Avalon of the Heart*, (Weiser Books, Boston/York Beach, USA)

[2] The complete script is given in Appendix 1.

[3] Details of this development are to be found in *Dion Fortune and the Inner Light* by Gareth Knight, (Thoth Publications, Loughborough, 2000).

[4] Currently available as a double CD by Hyperion Records (CDD22040) with a booklet containing Fiona Macleod's libretto. An esoteric interpretation of the work by Dion Fortune's friend Netta Fornario (Mac Tyler) is contained in an appendix to *Practical Occultism* by Dion Fortune, edited Gareth Knight (Thoth Publications, Loughborough, 2002).

[5] Specifically *Books on Atlantis* in the series of *Inner Light Magazine* articles *The Literature of Illuminism* (c.1929/30) reprinted in *Practical Occultism* by Dion Fortune, edited Gareth Knight (Thoth Publications, Loughborough 2002).

[6] This was some 15 years before her association with Dion Fortune's Society of the Inner Light. Details of the correspondence are reproduced in *Pythoness: the Life and Work of Margaret Lumley Brown* edited by Gareth Knight (Sun Chalice, Oceanside CA, 2000; Thoth Publications, Loughborough 2006).

[7] Geraldine Cummings, *Exploration Fawcett* is an account of Fawcett's interests, arranged from his manuscripts, letters, log books and records, by his son, Brian Fawcett. (Hutchinson, London, 1953). See also Geraldine Cummings, *The Fate of Colonel Fawcett*, (Aquarian Press, London, 1958).

[8] Currently published by Weiser, York Beach, 2000, with introduction by Gareth Knight.

[9] Chapter 1, pp 6 – 7.

[10] Writing under her baptismal name of Violet M. Firth, wearing her psychologist's hat, in an article *Psychism and Occultism* in the *Transactions of the British College of Psychic Science*, edited by F. Bligh Bond.

[11] Be this as it may, neither Dion Fortune nor Margaret Lumley Brown felt inhibited from indulging in work of this nature, and a selection of their findings is included in Appendix 2.

[12] First published in 1918, latest known edition *The Candle of Vision: Inner Worlds of the Imagination* (Prism Press, Bridport, and Unity Press, Lindfield, NSW, Australia, 1990)

[13] The circumstances and the complete chant are given in *Dion Fortune and the Inner Light* by Gareth Knight (Thoth Publications, Loughborough, 2000).

[14] *The Secrets of Dr. Taverner* by Dion Fortune, first published as stories in *Royal Magazine* from February to July 1922, published in volume form 1927, latest known edition Aquarian Press, Wellingborough, 1989). Refer also to *The Magical Fiction of Dion Fortune* by Gareth Knight (Thoth Publications, Loughborough, 2007) for descriptive review of individual stories.

[15] Refer to *Pythoness – the Life and Work of Margaret Lumley Brown* edited Gareth Knight (Sun Chalice, Oceanside, California, USA, 2000) and Thoth Publications, Loughborough, 2006.

[16] *Robert Kirk – Walker Between Worlds* by R.J.Stewart, (Element Books, Shaftsbury, 1990) and Thoth Publications, Loughborough 2007 incorporating a new edition of *The Secret Commonwealth of Elves, Fauns and Fairies* by Robert Kirk (1644-97) foreshadows a series of practical books, based on practical workshops he has conducted, *The UnderWorld Initiation* (Aquarian Press, Wellingborough, 1985), *Earth Light* (Element Books, Shaftesbury, 1992), *Power within the Land* (Element Books, Shaftesbury, 1992), together with a more popularly oriented overview *The Living World of Faery* (Gothic Image, 1995).

[17] *The Winged Bull, The Goat-foot God, The Sea Priestess* and *Moon Magic*.

[18] *The Circuit of Force* by Dion Fortune, with commentary by Gareth Knight (Thoth Publications, Loughborough, 1998). Originally published in *Inner Light Magazine* February 1939 to August 1940.

[19] See page 95, paragraph 3.

[20] See page 96, paragraph 3.

[21] *The Mystic Life of Merlin* and *The Prophetic Vision of Merlin* (Arkana, London, 1986).

[22] *The UnderWorld Initiation*, by R. J. Stewart, (Aquarian Press, Wellingborough, 1985) Appendix 1; also reproduced in *The Secret Tradition in Arthurian Legend* by Gareth Knight, (Aquarian Press, Wellingborough, 1983 and Weiser, York Beach, Maine, USA 1996) Chapter 15.

[23] *Polarity Magic: The Secret History of Western Religion* by Wendy Berg & Mike Harris (Llewellyn Publications, St. Paul, MN., USA. 2003).

[24] *The Cult of the Black Virgin* by Ean Begg (Arkana Penguin Books London, 1985 and 1996).

[25] See Appendices 2 & 3, and also *Pythoness: The Life and Work of Margaret Lumley Brown* edited Gareth Knight (Sun Chalice, Oceanside, Cal. 2000 & Thoth Publications, Loughborough, 2005).

[26] We have given publisher details where we can, but in the case of specialised small edition academic or esoteric works, books are liable to go out of print for indefinite periods, perhaps to be taken up by another publisher at a later date. Nowadays, one's best resource in searching for books, whether currently available, or second hand, is undoubtedly via the internet.

The Arthurian Formula – Part One
Dion Fortune

Sources of the Legends

There is no waste of time in considering the bearing of scholarship upon the study of the Mysteries in general and, in particular, the Arthurian legends of which the Grail forms a part.

The same type of story can be traced through many a mythology and scholars collate them, tracing the common factors in widely diversified schools and traditions. This is valuable because knowledge is never without value. There is the question of collating legends first with one another, and secondly, with other traditions.

Take the Grail or Wounded King. There are many versions of the Wounded King within the Arthurian tradition and many versions of the Grail story spread through other traditions. There are certain factors in the human mind which are common to all men and, when expressed in symbolism, will be expressed in related symbolism. There are others which have been developed within a specific school of doctrine.

The Grail story concerns the common needs of all mankind; the healing of the Wounded King by a specific method concerns a particular school of doctrine. The one is a primary, the other a secondary legend. In dealing with the mythology of the Mysteries, the scholarship required should afford a background that covers the whole range of cognate thought, so that you can judge of a given story, whether it is a primary legend with its roots in the deepest instinctual level or human need, the level from which dreams arise, or whether it is a creation of the conscious mind to point a moral.

There should be a scholarship adequate to the understanding of the sources of these two types of material. To understand a primary legend, you need knowledge of the human mind at its primitive level, both in the present and in the past. Knowledge of its primitive level in the present is to be sought in analytical psychology; knowledge of its primitive level in the past is to be sought, first, in the records of primitive mankind in ancient days, and secondly, in the customs and beliefs of peoples who retain their primitive level of culture.

The sources of secondary legends are literary, to be sought in the superficial meaning of primary legends interpreted in the light of contemporary influences, religious and cultural.

So therefore, in studying a given story, scholarship is needed to determine the date of its first appearance. Does it go back to the archaic forms of the traditions and the earliest records of them? Does it first appear in primitive form, expressed in terms of primitive thought, and are there analogous stories in other traditions? Or does it appear only at a later date in a sophisticated form and is it peculiar to the Arthurian tradition?

This will enable you to determine and distinguish what is fundamental and valid – the word of true seers – from what is superficial and misleading – the work of the moralising theologian or literary fancy. I want to correct one point: the earlier form is the work of many minds, the racial mind, not the individual seer. There are however many seers at all levels of culture, and true seership may shine through a purely literary work.

Now let us trace the matter historically. The earliest form of all legends is in the work of the story-teller to the tribe gathered around the camp fire; it is childish imagining concerning the nature of things. In the next stage the minds of the priestly caste work over the primitive stories. At a later stage, a new concept of religion may arise and push aside the primitive, or conquest by invaders may bring a new race and their culture into influence, and the old culture will be forgotten except by the story-tellers among the submerged people. So the primitive tradition returns into the custody of the bards once again. Then the new culture may grow effete, and efforts be made to re-illumine the altar fires from primitive sources. So men who constitute themselves the new priesthood of the new age may seek for inspiration in the Bardic tradition once more. So you see the alternating generations of Bard and Priest. It follows from this that accurate scholarship in the historical sense cannot exist in such matters. The basic sources of the Arthurian and Grail stories are pre-Christian, Bardic, to be sought in the primitive Celtic religion. The literary and moralistic influences which worked over the primitive story are to be sought in mediaeval religious thought and the Troubadour viewpoint.

Medieval religious thought confuses the issue by obliterating the traces of the primitive impulses and viewpoint of mankind and moralising the subject-matter. But the Troubadours have the same viewpoint as the Bards, for they developed their culture in the land where the influences of the Old Gods lived on, the Southern part of France, the home of the Albigenses. The Albigenses owed much to the same source. A great Mystery Cult centred around Mont Segur, the background of the Troubadours, the secret cult of Queen Venus; and without understanding that, you will not understand the Arthurian romantic tales.

The Arthurian Tradition falls into two divisions: the Round Table stories and the Grail stories, but they are woven together by later annalists into the concept of the Quest. The knightly quests, which concern adventures with Elemental forces, are elaborated into the spiritual quest of the Grail, and the Grail is restored to its place in the custody of the women.

The Round Table formula concerns Elemental forces, and the Grail formula concerns Spiritual forces, and these form the Lesser and the Greater Mysteries of the Arthurian Tradition. Look for the basic roots of the tradition in Druidical influences; seek its finest flower in mystical Christianity. And remember that in the background is the secret cult of Queen Venus.

So you have these three factors: the Druidical, the Witch-cult, and Christian mysticism. The Druidical is a Nature-cult, sun-worship, the Northern cult. The worship of Queen Venus, the Mediterranean or southern culture, draws its inspiration from the remains of the Roman culture which derived from Greek sources primarily, with secondary tributaries from Mithraic and Persian sources. The Greek tradition owed a very great deal to the Egyptian; and the Egyptian, in a later and debased form, influenced Roman thought.

These are your factors in the Arthurian tradition, and scholarship is needed to determine the varying degrees of their influence in any given form of a legend. The early forms are naturally the most valuable, because they are nearest to Druidical influences, but the Trouvère forms are also valuable because the Trouvères were initiates of the cult of Queen Venus, and as such, they understood the Bardic viewpoint[1].

The Trouvères and Troubadours represented the esoteric and exoteric aspects of that brief flowering of Mediterranean culture that was stamped out in the Albigensian persecution. You will need to be on your guard in dealing with legends which are given a specifically Christian form of the Roman Communion as distinguished from the mystical Christian form of the Celtic tradition, and you can tell these apart quite readily: where the exponent of the Christian viewpoint is a priest, a nun or a monk, you are dealing with the Roman influence; where the exponent is a hermit or anchorite, you are dealing with primitive Celtic influence.

Those are the lines that scholarship should pursue in relation to the Arthurian myth, which refers to the history of the early ages.

The Roman civilisation was a conquering, military civilisation; the Greek was a civilisation of the mind and its influence was intellectual. The Greek culture, which is the basis of European culture, derived from several sources. It was first influenced by its own archaic tradition that lingered on in the islands and highlands of Greece when the cities became sophisticated, and this primitive religion, like all primitive religions, was a fertility cult of crops, herds and human beings. Then came the development of the state religion of the Olympian deities, and the Old Gods were forgotten. A later age outgrew the state religion and turned to Egypt and Persia for the inspiration of their Mysteries. Persia derived her Mysteries from India and Chaldea. Egypt derived from Atlantis, and the influence of Egypt reached even to India. So we trace the root source of all to Atlantis via Egypt and the Far and Near East, and also to those Sacred Islands in the North Sea and north-western coasts of Europe where Atlantean influence penetrated. The Druidical Mysteries derive direct from Atlantis as do the Egyptian; and the Greek Mystery cults drew their inspiration from Egypt and Persia (the priestly influence), and used the ancient material of the traditions lingering in the folk-tales of the highlands and islands of Greece as their symbolic texture (the Bardic influence).

Rome drew her civilisation originally from Greek influences and when she became sophisticated drew on the Mystery cults of Greece, Persia and Egypt. These cults, as well as the State religion, travelled with the legions, and whenever Roman troops settled down in occupation, Mystery Schools were established.

The Roman policy was to assimilate the barbarian, and leading men of the local tribes were encouraged to send their sons to Rome to be educated. Very often they were taken as hostages when they were children, and given a Roman education, and then sent back to their tribes to rule under the tutelage of Rome. So Roman civilisation became naturalised in the conquered provinces.

The Mystery cults, being derived from primitive sources, presented no difficulties to the people of the conquered provinces, who had been nurtured in a similar tradition, and they were readily identified by them as their familiar deities. So the Mystery cults took hold and flourished, and when the Roman legions were rolled back by the barbarian hordes, the Mystery cults lived on, having struck root in the soil. They persisted as a Pagan, or, as later termed, a witch-cult tradition that still persists in the folk-lore of remote parts where the civilising influences of the centres of culture have not penetrated.

It was on these sources that the Trouvères drew. Now the Trouvères and the Troubadours and the Cathari and the Albigenses all developed their thought and systems under an impulse of intellectual activity which defied Catholic Christianity and formed part of the great heretical movements that were stamped out by persecution.

The Trouvères, who represented the pagan mysticism of that movement, developed a cult of Mystery schools based on the ancient traditions of the old Mysteries brought to their land by the Roman legions, who derived them from the Greek and Egyptian Mysteries. This Bardic tradition of the Trouvères, recognising cognate material in the Druidical tradition of the Arthurian stories, made use of that in the same way as the Egyptian-initiated Greek mystics drew on the primitive Greek Nature-cults for the myths which gave the formulae of the Eleusinian mysteries.

The Druidical form of the Arthurian Tradition profoundly influenced the Celtic Christianity that developed in these lands. So we may say then, that the true Arthurian Tradition is to be sought in the Druidical, the Celtic Christian, and the Trouvère sources, which know nothing of priesthood or monasteries or nunneries but are familiar with hermits and holy pilgrims.

The hermit, the pilgrim, the magician and the faery woman – those characterise the true tradition; and the priest, monastic organisation and the witch characterise the sophisticated mediaeval or Renaissance glosses on the primitive tradition, which are to be discarded as misleading. For instance, King Arthur being taken in death by the Faery Women is primitive material and as such psychologically valid; Lancelot and Guinevere repenting them of their sins in their respective religious communities are later glosses, and as such, to be discarded from the Mystery tradition.

You see now how and where to trace your sources.

At the back of the Trouvère recension of the Arthurian myth was the Queen Venus cult which was kept secret and later developed into the witch-cult, which contained features not recorded by the historians; and there was a highly-developed cult of the women which showed itself clearly in Trouvère and Troubadour literature and in the Courts of Love, but which was discreetly ignored by the worthy Malory. Chrétien used Trouvère material and demonstrates more insight[2].

Ashtoreth was the forerunner of Queen Venus, and Guinevere was her successor; the records have been deliberately expunged. So we take their bones, in this valley of dead bones and clothe them with the Mysteries, so that bone cleaves to bone and they become alive again.

[In reply to a question re the Arabian Nights stories)[3].

These stories are valuable because the East does not repress its consciousness. So, when we get a tradition in a fragmentary or distorted form, we look to cognate traditions for similar stories. At the present time in this our work we draw on Bardic tradition for the formulae.

[Questioned as to the difficulty of finding the right books).

That is a service to be performed by accurate scholars. It is not my task. I can show you where and how to look for what you want.[4]

Study the teaching, working systematically on the Tree[5].

Notes[6]

There is a difference between the imagination and fancy; the Bards, working with tribal material worked on a deep level of consciousness, the folk-lore or ballad level. The literary man, working on a superficial level, produces fanciful works. That is the difference between the Bardic and the literary. The Bards were initiates and priests.

The Trouvères were men who partook of the great spiritual revival in Southern France which culminated in the Albigensian movement. The Troubadours were minstrels[7].

It is the difference between a hymn to Pan of the Greek pastoral people, and the affected imitation of the drawing-room poet. The theologians and the moralists overwrote the old traditions in the same was as is done in a palimpsest. There is need to distinguish between the Arthurian tales as mystical folk-lore and drawing-room entertainment; also between the old myths and the moralising of the mediaeval theologian.

In the Celtic church there were no convents or monasteries. Similarly, with regard to Guinevere, she never fell into disgrace, as is shown by the fact that she was buried beside the King.[8] All her married life she held an honoured position at the court.[9]

Albigensian Revival: The Albigensian revival was a premature Renaissance and was stamped out by the Roman Church as the Renaissance could not be. [10]

The Quests: The difference between the Quests is the difference between youth in its strength, and maturity with its spiritual understanding. This is symbolised by the fights with giants, etc., of the earlier myths, and the search for the Grail of the later.

The Round Table tradition of chivalry is earlier and is the cult of the Sword.

The Cup is a Christian concept and was grafted onto the cult of the Sword. Thus, in the Celtic Christianity you have a valuable linking of the two concepts instead of a conflict as in Latin Christianity. Celtic Christianity was at one with Nature, there was no asceticism. By going back we avoid the antinomian heresy.

The Cup: The Cup was restored to its place in the custody of the women, in substitution of the ideas inherent in the stories of Joseph of Arimathea and the Fisher King.

Venus and Keridwen: The same goddess but Keridwen represented fertility, whereas the later cults of Queen Venus represented polarity.

To primitive man with his primitive needs the Cauldron of Plenty represented no more hunger. But to highly civilised man, children are often a liability instead of the asset they are to men in more primitive conditions.

You have the contrast of fertility, which means numbers, and polarity, where quality is the first consideration, if there are children, and the relationship is the more important thing.

There is this to be noted: that the more fecund a woman is, the less magnetic is she. The most magnetic women have no children.

Mithraism: Mithraism did not influence Druidism because it came with the later Roman occupation when Druidism had dispersed.

Cathari: A sect that broke away from Rome and followed an extreme and unbalanced form of asceticism, purging the body. They thought to please God by abusing the body, whereas the Albigenses sought oneness with God by meditating on God's love.[11]

Hermits: The Hermit was the characteristic holy man of early Christian thought. In Celtic Christianity he built himself a hut in the forest. There was no centralised authority. The custom was abolished only some centuries later by the discipline of Rome and did not reappear until after the Reformation.

Pilgrims: The Pilgrim or Palmer, with his scallop shell, went to the Holy Land to get merit and sometimes to escape his creditors! In the Holy Land, the true pilgrim often met old initiates and came back with a certain amount of magical knowledge.

Magician: The Magician was a Druid with knowledge of Elemental magic, who had never accepted Christianity.

Faery Women: The Faery Woman was either an astral being, or an initiated woman on the physical plane. The Lady of the Lake was an astral being; Morgan le Fay was an initiate of the ancient Mysteries.[12]

Celtic Christianity: The great point is that in Celtic Christianity the Nature cult of the Druids and the spiritual cult of the Christians achieve an harmonious synthesis not found in the Roman Church.

Celtic Christianity is joyous, simple, and highly individualised, and blends with Nature. Holy men saw Nature as an environment in which they could develop their holiness. It was a new inspiration breathed into Nature-worship. In this form of Christianity, man loves God because he enjoys His bounty, and the sense of sin is absent. From the Celtic viewpoint there is no sense of sin in natural things.

Celtic Christians were Nature worshippers, who saw a wider vision; they recognised the Sun as the giver of life and the new teaching brought realisation of a great, benign Intelligence who manifested through the Sun.

Seek through the traditions of the Roman colonists and link with the Mediterranean cults.

The Arthurian Tradition is connected with the Druidic through the Sword and with the Celtic through the Cup.

The Mission of Merlin

First comes Merlin's teacher, a Great One from a previous evolution, who was without father and without mother.

Merlin was the son of a virgin nun and a fire spirit of a high order; so he was half human and half elemental. His teacher hands the teaching on to him and he, Merlin, has to find a vehicle for its expression. This has to be a human being because the message is to humanity; but he has to be a specially-bred human being. In Britain there was no clan of Priest-Kings so Merlin has to establish one.

So we have three generations:

1. The non-human Master of Merlin;
2. The half-human Merlin;
3. Arthur, wholly human, the executive.

Arthur's mother, Igraine, Duchess of Tintagel, is reputed to have been an Atlantean princess. She marries and has a child, Morgan le Fay, half British, half Atlantean. Igraine is a suitable mother for a high, dedicated being. So Merlin chooses Pendragon, a British king of royal blood to be Arthur's father. Thus he was specially bred to be the vehicle of Merlin's plans. After his birth he is taken by Merlin to be trained and as soon as he reaches maturity, he is sent to the Lady of the Lake to be initiated into sex. She gives him his sword. He is seduced by Morgan le Fay, his ambitious half-sister, who makes play with the scabbard of his sword. He has intercourse with faery women before and after marriage. Merlin arranges his marriage with Guinevere but their marriage is not consummated; she is his mate on another level. To satisfy Guinevere, Merlin brings Lancelot who is her lover.

Their spiritual son is Galahad (the spiritual son of Arthur and Guinevere) who is brought to birth by the first Elaine to be Arthur's successor. In order to provide a mate for him, Merlin brought the second Elaine, who falls in love with Lancelot. Through the error and the jealousy of Guinevere, this plan fails. Lancelot becomes insane, the second Elaine dies and there is no suitable mate for Galahad; thus the dynasty ends.

Mordred, offspring of Arthur by his half-sister Morgan, brings about Guinevere's ruin and the fall of Arthur's kingdom. After Mordred's death, Arthur is reconciled to Lancelot and Guinevere.

Each character in this drama is two-sided. There is triumph and tragedy. By their tragedy we are warned; by their triumph we are instructed as to the true path.

The formula, placed on the Tree, forms a glyph from which are extracted the formulae of the Aquarian Age. It is a glyph which in the outer is a romance, but on the inner contains the key to the formula of the coming age.

From the heyday of each race one comes over when the decline sets in to teach and record the wisdom of the past. So the Master of Merlin came from the fourth race to the fifth, to the Isle of Britain, the Holy Isle of the fifth root-race. With the sixth sub-race the contacts will go West to America and English teachers will carry it there. These seed-bearers will have no physical bodies, but will manifest in vision and are therefore perceivable only to psychics. Merlin was specially bred to communicate with his Master. In certain sub-races entities enter bodies from which the human being has voluntarily departed, for the purpose of bringing the teaching.

Merlin was born of a virgin and a high Elemental. Arthur was born of royal stock and his mother was not a virgin. Consider the commerce between human and non-human. Exchange of magnetism takes place, but no physical impregnation. When magnetism is sufficiently concentrated, a great spiritual force will come down and a spark of the Unmanifested Light enters the once-born. Think of the Unmanifested Light as utter darkness and inertia, the twice-born as a shadowless light of intense activity. Unmanifest is unrealised. That which is realised becomes manifest.

In the beginning of evolution a shower of Sparks falls from the Unmanifested Light and these are the far-wandering souls of men. When these come to the physical plane they can only incarnate by human and natural means. But if superhuman incarnation is to take place a fresh Spark comes down and enters the mother through the medium of a non-human father.

When a Being proposes to form a body without father or mother, he contacts telepathically a group of suitable persons and draws from their etheric substance for a physical form which is built by visualisation and is only visible to people who have etheric sight. Hence the sudden appearances and disappearances of the Great Ones. Those born without father and without mother are souls of high initiation and are of the highest grade. Those born of a divine father and a human mother are new souls and are of a high grade. The latter bring teaching; the former bring a new ray or influx of power unknown before.

Merlin brought in wisdom of the concrete mind, which is the special development of the fifth root-race.

We are engaged in preparing for the incarnation of the souls of the sixth root-race whose wisdom is of the abstract mind.

The Atlanteans had the wisdom of the instincts. Place humanity's fifth root-race in Malkuth, a descending arc coming in via Netzach, and you have the wisdom of the instincts. Take an ascending arc going up through Hod and you have the Aquarian wisdom of intuition. In Malkuth you have human wisdom of intellect. In the individual these things correspond with souls.

Subconsciousness of Netzach; Consciousness of Malkuth; Superconsciousness of Hod. Arthur was initiated into manhood by the Lady of the Lake. Fairy water-Elemental; pure water.

In the Atlantean Mysteries initiation of youths was always undertaken by mature women of the Temple, who taught how to fecundate or to avoid doing so as the case might be. That was done with all young manhood and was done by women who had passed the change of life.

Another aspect of the work was the science of magnetic mating, and this was taught after they had fulfilled the duties

of the house-holder. This initiation was by women in the glory
of their womanhood; but they would not deflect their love to
one single mate, for they were way-showers.

Temple women were specially gifted maidens.

Parents brought their daughters for various reasons:

1.   Financial difficulties.
2.   Fulfilment of a vow.
3.   They were of a priestly family.
4.   Girls and women who felt they had a vocation.
5.   Destitute women and widows who acted as temple-
     servers and domestic workers. Suitable women were
     chosen from these for higher offices.

Temple servants were not denied sex life. Some were married
legally and were allowed to make a home (though if they had
knowledge of esoteric things, they did not withdraw from the
temple; their offspring were always in the temple and did not
go into the world as they knew too much).

Those of the server class worked a formula of sublimation
and their magnetism was used in ceremonial work; they were
kept virgin. Did they desire to mate, they were advanced to
the priesthood or relegated to the position of temple servants.
They were not forced to remain virgin, as if you enforce
virginity, the unused forces breed incubi and succubi which are
not under higher control but are Elementals tuned to the key
of physical lust, and they function on that level. Such persons
cannot be advanced to the polarity of the priesthood, but are
used as temple servants.

Temple-servers practised sublimation and their force was
used in ritual and group working.

The Priests used polarity-working.

Merlin trained Arthur and had to arrange for his initiation.
Arthur, the twice-born, was initiated by the Lady of the Lake
(Vivienne). She was a Faery woman, one who had no physical
body, only an etheric one. Arthur had connection with her on
the etheric; that is what was taught to the twice-born.

The science of polarity-working lies in the power, and the physical act is used as a vehicle to carry etheric forces.

Mutual satisfaction was taught in the temple, and passion was used for proper mating to breed children. Etheric mating was used for satisfaction elsewhere, for from that is generated an etheric form.

The father who officiated at a virgin birth by astral magic made also an etheric form and produced the same reaction in the ovum as occurs on the physical plane.

When a special vehicle is desired for the incarnation of a high type of soul the father is usually a human being, in whom the overshadowing entity temporarily incarnates at the astral level (as in mediumship). Thus was Arthur born; for the Duke of Tintagel was not of royal blood and not a fit father for Arthur. In this way are the higher souls brought in. A youth who has been initiated into polarity-working so that he practises magnetic mating, will initiate whom he mates with, and so it is passed on and he will have magical children at his next mating. Arthur should have remained virgin save with the Lady of the Lake, until he mated with Guinevere for the carrying on of the race; hence the failure to establish a priestly clan. The Cosmic line returned in full circle to the next sub-race for development when special polarity was coming again.

Morgan was earth of water; the Lady of the Lake was water of water.

Morgan is married to Uriens of Gore, King of the North (the legend of Orion). Blood and urine magical.

Morgan had four sons; earth has four sub-divisions.

King Arthur and Faery Women

Galahad was the spiritual son of Arthur and Guinevere, not of Lancelot and Guinevere. Each figure is two-sided; on the Tree and in the Qlippoth.

Woman gives the sword to the knight and teaches him the right relationship. It is better that a youth should get the teaching from an experienced, cultured woman who will instruct him what should be done and how to arouse; this is done by a woman past her youth. The next to instruct is a woman in the full bloom of her womanhood, who has for him a powerful attraction; she takes him for her page, it is not a meeting of equals, but one of child and lover. From her, he passes to his true mate of his own generation whom he will know how to love.

The sword was given to Arthur by the Lady of the Lake, but these matings are not as the human kind. The sword is graven with strange symbols and runes, and is consecrated with a magic of Nature-forces. No one can escape the symbolism; the power is straight from Earth and Nature.

Man is a virile animal before he is a gentle knight. A gentle knight is no weakling, but a strong man controlling strength. So Arthur receives his first initiation.

A boy's first love is ideal and such an ideal is made an astral form from the substance of his own being by those emissions of force which take place spontaneously in youth. Such outpourings are the "white blood" or "gluten of the Eagle", and give off magnetism and provide Elemental force out of which is built an astral, magical body. The Being so formed is then ensouled and used as a channel by the Goddess, the All-Woman (Isis in Kether) and it is with her that the youth has his first experience of love. She has her priestesses who are the initiators of the young men. I do not say that such a woman should never have sex relations, though it is not generally desirable and rarely necessary, but it may be wise when the body of the youth is inhabited by the soul of a high initiate. But such relationships are a passing phase and should never be legalised marriage, but should take place in secret, behind the veil of Isis.

The Lady of the Lake fulfilled her relationship with Arthur; but with Merlin she was an evil seducer as they were not of equal grade. Morgan-le-Fay made the same mistake with Arthur. She was of human birth and royal through her mother. She was trained as a magician by Merlin in a different manner from Arthur, as she was not of such high lineage. She was mated to Uriens of Gore, King of the North, symbolic darkness. He was an Elemental being of Earth, therefore their four sons were the four doors of the Elements, half human, half faery, Earth of Water, Earth of Air, Earth of Fire, and Earth of Earth. Uriens was King of the Gnomes. The Hebrew Uriel means Son of God; all names represent two poles of the Astral, the breast-plate of the High Priest. (Note: Urim = Light).

Morgan wished for a higher grade, so she seduced Arthur because of his higher magnetism, which was of a cosmic order, aroused by the Lady of the Lake, so that he could arouse the corresponding level in her. When there is a mating with a faery woman, the higher centres in a man's nature are roused so that they become functional when he mates with a human woman. He then arouses corresponding centres in her as they lie face-to-face, Malkuth-to-Malkuth, Yesod-to-Yesod and so on up the Tree as far as they are functional. In most primitive types only the Malkuth centre is aroused, but if his Yesod has been roused by a faery woman it will rouse the Yesodic activity of the woman he mates with. A human woman cannot do this for a man.

The centres must be roused from Malkuth up the Tree and no centre can be missed.

In Malkuth wakes the physical thrill of sex orgasm. When a man's Malkuth is roused in sleep, it is then he unites with a faery woman; this is said, very wrongly, to create incubi and succubi. A woman does not get this as she has to have the stimulus from the physical plane. The man is her initiator.

The faery woman is an ideal image built by a man's emanations and ensouled by the Great Isis in dreams of unmated youth. It is a mistake for a youth to have relations with human maidens till a sufficient period has elapsed for faery meetings to take place. The Western way of letting him live in dreams to develop faery relationships produces a higher flowering of sex then when he enters into relationships with human maidens prematurely. The period of celibacy and dreams leads to the spiritual aspects of the love-life.

The two faeries represent the Kether and Malkuth of magic. Vivienne, the vehicle of the heavenly Isis; Morgan, priestess of the earthly Isis; both have their place and function in the magical scheme.

Merlin took charge of both Igraine's children and used both in his work, Arthur for work for the British race, Morgan for personal and magical work in polarity with him. But he was not able to mate with her as she was not of his generation. So he mated her with Uriens of Gore, even as Guinevere was mated to Lancelot when Arthur could not fulfil her. It was without Merlin's knowledge that Morgan seduced Arthur so that she could become a Mistress of Magic, and so produced the Qliphothic Mordred, son of unbalanced force. Because Arthur and Morgan, being of like blood, were of similar potency, and therefore did not equilibrate each other, Morgan brought out the baser side of Arthur's nature when Guinevere could have stimulated his higher. The Lady of the Lake had given what was necessary to Arthur from the faery side but Morgan-le-Fay reinforced the Elemental factor in Arthur and provided unbalance.

Mordred represents Arthur's baser nature and eventually destroys him, both in the personal and cosmic aspects.

The Lady of the Lake did for Merlin the same thing that Morgan did for Arthur. Merlin's power was broken, and he remained imprisoned in the underworld until the wheel of Cosmic time swings full circle, and these great beings come again, not to earth but to manifest in the soul of the race; they come as the Gods of the new age, and are coming now.

These Qliphotic aspects abide in the past as a warning, barring the roads to the underworld. To Mordred is assigned the black quarter of Malkuth, and he stands as a warning of what not to do. He is the son of the ambition of a priestess of Elemental magic, rising out of her proper sphere, and the weakness of a priest-king lowering himself below his sphere. Morgan exemplifies what happens when a priest-king breaks away from the direction of the initiated adept who is the power behind the throne, and it is he (Mordred), who works up the scandal concerning Lancelot and Guinevere. This breaks up the magical relationship; he organises sedition and rebellion which lead to civil war in which Arthur loses his life, and the kingdom ends.

Thus Morded represents all the evil in the high history of the Round Table and he stands in the black quarter of the gate to the Qliphoth; this is opened by Mordred so that whoever has in him any of the qualities of Mordred can pass through that gate.

Both the faeries were good and right in their proper places, and only evil when they quitted them.

Q: Could you say anything more about the "sword graven with strange symbols and runes, consecrated with a magic of Nature forces?"

A: The sword represents man's virile force. It is consecrated with a ritual of Elemental nature. As I have told you before, spiritual force descends from above, and Elemental force rises from beneath. The "strange runes along the blade" refer to Nature forces, and the jewels in the hilt to Spiritual forces. The life of man is like a web woven between the positive and negative poles of existence, between Kether and Malkuth.

Q: What is the explanation of the statement that "a human woman cannot do this for a man?"

A: A human woman cannot, only a faery woman; but when a human takes the greater grades, she becomes as a faery. When she functions in her higher self, she operates as a faery woman. The faery woman operates magnetically; the priestess functions over the whole range. The reason is that a human man is positive, and a human woman's powers are latent.

Q: But could not a woman operate positively on the higher levels — emotionally or mentally?

A: That raises a problem of far-reaching pathological implications. The unaroused female is neuter magnetically; should she have an active brain it is probable that she will become pathological. It is a very wide topic and really comes under the medical aspect.

Q: Can there be a recurrence of the same tragedy or fulfilment?

A: Life is cyclic; the cycles are of the nature of a whorl. Thus the cycles grow smaller and smaller until they change over and become larger and larger. It depends what phase you are in whether the cycles occur in one life, or in several.

King Arthur and Human Women

We have considered Arthur's relations with faery women, and we must now consider his relations with human women. As you know, Merlin took him to the Lady of the Lake to receive his faery initiation. This was done in due form. When he should have awaited the coming of his bride to bring power down to the physical plane Morgan intervened. We have considered this in detail.

Now we will consider how the development would have proceeded if all had gone well.

As a youth he receives instruction from a faery woman. Being thus taught, he passes as a squire to an older, human woman. Morgan could have fulfilled this role had she been selfless; but she used the youth for her own ends.

In the career of a man there should be first the faery woman; then the mature priestess; then the human woman. The mature priestess teaches him the art of manhood. So he passes on to the human maiden whom he initiates, for, as so many tales tell, her womanhood sleeps until he awakens it.

So then, Arthur should have had the experience of a romantic friendship with a mature woman, who might well have been Morgan-le-Fay, and, outgrowing her, should have received his bride, the maiden.

"Faery" – woman – maiden – three types of women.

He initiates the maiden, making of her woman and priestess. Then they work together, priest and priestess. Had things gone thus, there would have been the son to carry on the dynasty, and a mate for him, the daughter of Arthur's friend. Arthur and Guinevere should have brought in Galahad and Arthur's greatest friend should have been the father of a daughter to be wife for Galahad. But it fell out otherwise.

Now it is the law of human life that the duties of humanity must be fulfilled, and its experiences undergone and lessons learned, before magical work is undertaken with the forces that pass from pole to pole. The ascetic formula in which life force is deflected before it has passed through the nadir, is an averse formula. It involves the destruction of the personality that uses the formula; and its use can be black magic because it involves the use of a person for ends other than his own. His forces, which should be for his own development are taken and used by others.

Inhibition of these forces may cause a person to contact the inner planes, but one can pay too dearly. *After* power has been brought down, it can be diverted with benefit. Even if power has been brought down only once, nevertheless, the circuit has been made, but it is better that it should be stabilised in the lower centre. I do not therefore, mean a single experience, but a single relationship. There is never in a man that peculiar aridity you find in the unfulfilled woman. A man may be unfulfilled, but he does not have the problem of starvation. But woman is the negative, passive factor and she will slumber like the "Sleeping Beauty"; her pathology is starvation; his pathology is congestion.

If he is of the twice-born, he has power to direct his forces to the higher centres, examples of which you have in the great saints and mystics; if of the once-born, the power finds an outlet through the lower centres. In woman, the overplus is confined to the higher centres, chiefly the mind, because it never comes down. It is like a rope waving loosely, it is just as if a violin string, instead of being fixed between two poles, is looped back to the same pole; there is no music.

When a woman is initiated into life, her spiritual forces are brought down plane by plane, and then rise to Kether. In the case of a man, the process is reversed. The faery women draws the forces up until they reach Kether and then the spiritual forces flow down. When the man initiates the maiden, he should address himself first to her spiritual nature, her ideal, and win her heart there; then he should stimulate her mind and show her how her ideals can be given expression; then he should arouse her emotional nature, and finally awaken her instincts and senses and all the powers of her body.

But when the faery women initiates the boy, she starts with the senses, spontaneously awaking the animal instincts, and she links these with the ideal of beauty, so that he associates the satisfaction of his desires with the aesthetic emotions. From there he is led on by the mature woman to understanding and thence, for her sake, to a spiritual ideal, because of his adoration for her.

Remember this always in the Mysteries: *Men and women are quite different and should be treated in a different manner.*

So now you see how Arthur should have initiated Guinevere, and how he failed to do so. When Guinevere was brought to him, he failed to initiate her, for to him she seemed savourless after faery women. But he, being a good man, had for her the compassion of a father, and she, being a good woman, had for him the dutifulness of a daughter; and between them was the love of friends. She nobly fulfilled the function of Queen, and outwardly all was well ordered. Inwardly she was barren, and he withdrawn from reality save when the ecstasy of battle drew down the life forces to the physical plane. In consequence, he was a king who led his people well in war, but could not guide them in the arts of peace; for these are arts that arise from the woman's side. Women developed all the arts of peace. She was the first agriculturalist, the first tender of animals; she wove the first shelter from branches. All the arts of civilisation arise from the woman's side. And because he lacked the right relationship with a woman, Arthur remained the sterile warrior who could destroy and could not build. Hence you see in all the tales of his story, that he dealt with immediate problems and solved them with the sword, and he never dealt with the principles and solved them with the sceptre. And all such knights that were not mated, died violent deaths on the pilgrimage. Only those who found their women built themselves castles, ruled their lands, and died in peace in their beds at a ripe age, leaving their heirs to carry on the work.

A later king, Alfred, united both functions; he led his country in war to victory and laid the foundations of law in peace. For he was a balanced man, which Arthur was not. And another king who has gone down in legend, Richard, Coeur de Lion, was another such as Arthur. And observe, later, Queen Elizabeth, round whom have gathered legends, and her sister Mary. Mary, good, religious woman, obedient to the Will of God, unmated and unbalanced, brought evil to the land. Elizabeth, mating as she would, was balanced and brought good to the land, though to be reckoned among the sinners according to the righteous.

Arthur is chosen as the central figure of the national myth rather than Alfred who was successful, because of Merlin and the Grail. There was a consciously magical factor lacking in

Alfred, who was altogether human. The historical basis of Arthur has become mythologised just like that of Jesus-ben-Joseph.

Q: You expressed disapproval of early celibacy, in that it involves using people to the detriment of their personal development. How does this apply to our own fraternity?

A: Unless a person has known life in its fulness, his experience is necessarily incomplete; an incomplete person is not a perfect specimen. A man, by virtue of his nature, cannot escape experience, but a woman is latent until external stimuli bring down the power into her organism.

A virgin is an undeveloped female. There is no such thing as a male virgin after the age of puberty. In other words, the expression, "virgin parchment", is appropriate to human beings in that a virgin is a blank page waiting to be written on. She is latent until stimulated into activity.

Now with reference to the use of the term "virginity" in magical working, it would be more correctly termed "sublimation", but it is not possible to sublimate a force which has never been brought down into manifestation. A virgin, in the true sense, is one who has never felt the emotion of sexual love, and therefore has nothing to sublimate. Sexual love, as used here, includes the emotion generated through the imagination, even if there be no person concerned. The "virginity" referred to in magical working, means the direction of force through the channels within the nature, from a lower to a higher level. It is not incompatible with a full sexual life, but for a period before the operation is undertaken, continence must be observed. In this manner, the forces which have been dispersed through union, will gradually gather head again. When the point is reached when normally union would again take place, these forces are sublimated to a higher level or centre. They are drawn so completely off the lower level, that no sensation or emotion is felt relating thereto and all sexual

ideas, in consequence, automatically disappear from the mind
– the consciousness is then that of virginity and the person is
ready to perform magical work.

A person should always be in this state in performing
magical work, even when it is the work of the Green Ray.
For though this last is Nature magic and, as such, in certain
aspects, sex magic, it is completely impersonal and there
should be no personal sexual feelings or ideas introduced
into it. Consequently, for the Grail working[13], the technique
of sublimation is part of the knowledge, but the preservation
of virginity is no part of the formula. In other words, the
maidens of the Grail are pure women, that is, women who
have complete control of their nature, so that the force
cannot stray from plane to plane involuntarily, thus becoming
impure by the admixture of alien elements, but they are not
ignorant or inexperienced women. These latter, in fact, are
not necessarily, nor often, suitable as Grail guardians, because
they have frequently undergone a partial and incomplete
stimulation and the forces are astray and out of control. Thus
they are ignorant and inexperienced, not virgin. In the work
of the Grail, you will frequently have to deal with persons of
this type, both male and female. They should be regarded as
sick or deformed persons, and treated as such. In some cases,
it may be possible by careful and prolonged treatment to bring
them to a state of understanding of their own nature, so that,
though inexperienced, they are no longer ignorant and their
sickness is healed. For the adjustment depends not so much on
physical experience as on mental attitude. A person can have
physical experience, even habitual physical experience, and the
mental attitude remain stubbornly unmodified. For example,
he can have an enlightened mental attitude in the absence of
physical experience, but not in the absence of all emotional
experience. But in cases where it proves impossible to modify
the mental attitude, we must assist these cripples, chronically
deformed, and give them such comfort and happiness as they

can receive, making use of such powers as they possess, that they may not be altogether barren but have the satisfaction of some fulfilment at least, even if only a partial and imperfect one. But such cannot go to the higher grades.

Purity depends on control, not on ignorance and the absence of functional experience.

The Servers of the Grail must be pure. That is, they must have perfected their technique of sublimation, so that it is easy and effortless, imposing no strain. This will seldom be achieved in the absence of fulfilment.

For those who need fulfilment to complete their experience of life, the Green Ray work is valuable. Those who are naturally gifted in the arts of the Green Ray need experience of the Grail Vigils in order to ensure that they can keep pure the forces with which they work. Purity consists in the absence of any alien admixture, not in the level of manifestation of a force. A force needs to be pure in Malkuth just as much as in Kether. If the sexual feelings are contaminated with fears and inhibitions, they are impure and it is the alien admixture which constitutes the impurity, not the sexual feeling.

Q: This is not easy of application.

A: I give you the science; only experience gives the art.

Q: Should attention be given to the tides with regard to meetings? And does the frequency of the meetings have any influence?

A: Tides affect us very little. It is well to start any work on a favourable tide, but once started, the tides need not affect it. It is always possible to make a magic circle within the tide. But if you are working with Planetary forces, then you must work on their tides. In such work, generally there is need to meet at regular intervals; if there is too long a pause between meetings, the power will fade and need to be rebuilt.

Q: You have spoken about the mating of a mortal man and a faery woman; could you say something about the mating of a mortal woman and a faery man?

A: That is a wide topic of teaching, and of course you get that with the mating of Morgan-le-Fay, and the King of the North and Merlin.

Queen Guinevere

We will consider briefly the story of Guinevere. She was a virgin bride, unmated and unawakened, for King Arthur had spoiled himself with faery women. So Merlin in his wisdom counselled what was common in that age, that she should take a lover, and the King consenting, gave her to his best friend. Thus Lancelot was the initiator of Guinevere that she might be the High Priestess of the Women's Mysteries in Arthur's court, as a queen should be.

But when a soul is to be brought into incarnation, it comes through the man, who gives it to the woman to nurture in her womb. Lancelot could not give to Guinevere the soul she should have borne, for he had not advanced sufficiently in understanding till she was past child-bearing, so he gave the soul to another and younger woman to bring into incarnation, and thus was Galahad born. Lancelot was destined to be the father of the Queen of Britain, the mate of his best friend's son, according to Merlin's plan but this failed because Guinevere, not having received the supreme initiation (which Lancelot could not give her as Arthur could have done) waxed personal when she should have been cosmic. And Galahad went unmated although she to him was the mature woman, the priestess. But there was no maiden to whom she could give him when the time came.

Thus the kingdom ended. And the Grail, which should have been the Cauldron of Plenty, guarded by the Earth-Mother, became a cup of poison which slew those who drank of it; for all who achieved the Grail quest died, and Britain lost good knights sorely needed.

Thus did the Cauldron of Plenty, the sacramental Cup of Inspiration, become the Cup of Death and Sterility.

Yet each of the men and women, wholly human or half-divine, leaves for us a teaching and a Magical Image, not only by virtue of what they achieved, but also by virtue of their errors and failures, for all died in faith, unembittered and loving each other.

Thus was the evil magic of Mordred brought to naught by nobility, generosity and compassion in the hearts of those who failed.

The Court at Camelot

Here you have the phases of a woman's life, just as we have the formula of a man's life in Arthur. We see her first as a pure virgin in her bower, protected by the armed warriors of her father in his castle. Merlin sets in motion the negotiations for her hand as the bride of Arthur. The negotiations are satisfactorily concluded, and Arthur sends his best friend to bring home the bride. Herein is the first mistake made. It is the tradition for the groom to go to the house of the bride's parents and receive her at the hands of her father. Thus is she truly virgin in imagination, as well as in body. This Arthur did not do. So the bride is brought home by Lancelot, and he and Guinevere look upon each other.

So Guinevere comes to the court of Arthur and is received by her bridegroom for the initiation of the nuptial bed. And he, his mind being on the faery women, fails to initiate her. She is deflowered, but left virgin. Thus, she is unfitted to take her place on the throne at her husband's side and be a Queen, Ruler of the Ladies, Teacher of the Maidens, High Priestess of the Women's Mysteries, Initiatrix of the Youths, Ministrant of the Grail to men.

Let us consider the function of the court in the national life, considered magically – and remember, every centre or focus of social life is a court and governed by the Formula of Camelot. Whether it be the King's court in London or Windsor, or the miniature court of the Lord of the Manor in some remote village, the formula is the same, and if it be lacking, life is impoverished thereby. One of the formulae of the New Age is that of Camelot, and we will consider this next before proceeding further with the study of the formula of Guinevere, because the queen cannot be understood apart from the court, and you will then be ready to understand the formula of Lancelot.

First then, let us contemplate the picture of many-towered Camelot, placed in great beauty among green fields beside a fair river, gay with banners, with all its bells a-chime, its streets filled with sturdy citizens, and the fine habiliments of knights and men-at-arms; with the craftsmen sitting in their open-fronted shops, plying those crafts which in their hands are fine arts; with beauty and gaiety and music and colour and all the pageant of life in rich procession through the streets. And in the centre thereof the King's castle or more strictly speaking the palace, for the whole city is a walled and defended area and in the centre is the palace where the Queen rules supreme.

Now let me indicate the difference between a "castle" and a "palace". Tintagel was a castle, the man's place, wherein the women's quarters were confined to one part – the Bower, which is a miniature palace wherein the man enters and the women come forward and unhelm him and take charge of his armour and weapons and there entertain him with the arts of peace, thus refreshing him. They tend his wounds and minister to him the graces, the tendernesses and the arts of life. Thus is civilisation born and nurtured.

The Bower is a secluded haven of peace in a world of war. It is like the Ark of the Covenant in which the holy vessels are preserved during the sojourn in the wilderness. To each man his home should be a bower whether he returns from his war with the world, which is his formula for rest and comfort of body and refreshment of spirit. This is the formula of Tintagel, the formula of the preservation of sacred things in evil times and amid a hostile environment.

The formula of Camelot is the formula of the cultivation of a high civilisation in times of peace, in an ordered environment, and it is a Queen's formula as Tintagel is a King's formula.

In the palace of Camelot the predominant influence is that of the Queen and it is her task to civilise the fierce warriors, and to mould into gentlemen the rude youths. And as the Queen ruled the court of the land so each maiden is potentially a queen in her own court, as Lady of the Manor in some remote village or the Grande Dame in her salon in some centre of culture; for there is the Queen Formula.

So she must teach her maidens the women's arts which include the management of men. She teaches them beauty, courtesy, the care of the house, the care of the garden, of the home-farm, the care of the sick, the care of young children.

These things the maidens should learn. They should learn them from their mothers in their own court before they come to the great Court and practise these services for the Queen. Thus are the virgins prepared to be queens in their turn.

And Guinevere was well equipped at the hands of her own good mother. But her mother died while she was yet young and she had not completed the training of her young daughter in certain matters of women's wisdom taught only after puberty.

The Queen's ladies are wise in the arts of gallantry. Now the word "gallantry" can teach us a great deal, for it means both feats of arms and feats of love. And it is they who are responsible for maintaining the high tone of the court which should be gallant, though the word "gallant", used thus, does not mean a quarrelsome set of men, nor a promiscuous set of women.

The knights of Arthur's court were encouraged to seek worthy quests, not to compete among themselves as to who should be the greatest. The ladies did not engage in idle amours, but accepted the worship of the true knight if he proved worthy.

Again we can learn from the word "courtesy" – the art of the Court. It is something more than polished manners; it implies the finer grades of feeling and a high code of honour. "Courtship" is another of the arts of the Court and implies a fine culture of the approach between the sexes.

It will thus be seen that the Queen, that High Priestess of the Temple of Life, had no light task to fulfil but one demanding high qualities of character, deep knowledge and wide experience. It will thus be seen that Guinevere, unfulfilled, could not fulfil this office.

Now the manner in which the defects were made good is the formula of Lancelot.

Q: What was the civilisation of Camelot like?

A: It was a civilisation of craftsmen; skilled hands as well as skilled minds are very important arts of life.

Q: Where was Camelot actually situated?

A: Camelot is a valley among the hills; it is the country of the heart. Tradition assigns it to many parts.

Q: Was the court of Arthur on the physical plane?

A: History is not important. Where was the manger of Bethlehem? On the physical plane? We have no concern with history, but with myth. Historic fact is scanty and tells us nothing worth knowing. Myths grow up around a nucleus of some touch of greatness in some human being a little ahead of his time. He dies and returns to dust; but the light that shone upon him illuminates the scene, and it is his vision and not the bare facts of his life which live on and form the nucleus of the myth. That which comes down to us in song and story is the high imagination in the heart of the hero and not its imperfect manifestation in this imperfect world. This you see clearly exemplified in the case of King Richard the First, of whom we have both the history and the legend. He inspired the imagination of his contemporaries because he himself was a man of inspired imagination; but his deeds did not equal his dreams.

The myths are built about the dreamers and their dreams live after them, and their historians are not the annalists, but the bards. For the annalists deal only with the manifest but the bards share the vision. The manifest deeds determine the present; but the vision moulds the future, and it is this that the myth enshrines. The myth is the matrix of the future wherein the seed ideas are held till the time is ripe for their sowing.

After long centuries of barbarism, the dreams of a chivalrous king are bodied forth in acts. How much of his dream do you suppose King Arthur could realise in the crude culture of his day? Very little. But he made of them archetypal ideas with which he inoculated the Group Mind of the Race. Consequently today we draw upon this source for our inspiration.

Sir Lancelot

The story of Lancelot covers a very wide ground. In order to understand the story of Lancelot and Guinevere, you must examine it first from the historical view – and remember that it has an earlier, middle and later form. The earlier form is based on Druidical material wherein Guinevere is the Earth in spring, the fecundity maiden, who has to be fertilised. As you no doubt know, in all mythologies you get the story of Mother Earth; first as a maiden in white or pale green, crowned with flowers, the magical virgin with whom the god or the hero mates, (in this connection it is invariably the hero), thus bringing the earth back to fertility. And in her second aspect she is the all-bountiful matron of the earth in harvest-time. You will remember the two aspects of the goddess or archetypal woman, her fecundity aspect, and her polarity aspect. If we go back to the Druidical basis of the story of Guinevere, we find that it represents the transition from woman as a primitive fecundity symbol, to woman as a sophisticated polarity symbol.

Guinevere then, in her first aspect, presents to men's minds woman as a polariser, as a priestess of the Mysteries. The Druids knew the magical lore of Atlantis, of which this knowledge formed a part, and the revelation of their Mysteries concerns this secret. It was knowledge entirely beyond the capacity of the average man and woman of Arthur's historical epoch, and it constituted a deep secret of the Mysteries of that day. There were women among the Druidesses specially trained for this magical working, the concept being borrowed from the Greek and Egyptian traditions, wherein it was highly developed.

Let me make the last paragraph clearer. The *idea* was derived by the Druids from Atlantis, but knowledge of the *method* of developing the priestesses was derived from Greek and Egyptian influences. For not only did the higher culture spread along the trade routes, but there was much making of pilgrimage for the sake of knowledge from primitive parts to holy centres. Now, is this point clear, that the Guinevere concept was first developed among the Druids as a polarity cult, as an advance on the original Keridwen fertility cult? Before Christianity, you have women as something more than the breeding animal, she is important in relation to a magical polarity. The Druids got the idea from Atlantis, but, making pilgrimage to Greece and Egypt, became initiates of their Mysteries and brought back the *knowledge* to these islands. Cultures spread through the trade routes. The Mysteries were one brotherhood and they influenced one another much more than is realised, because men made pilgrimages and grafted the ideas brought back on to their primitive cults, so that Mystery cults are largely interchangeable. The traditions of Egypt will throw light on all these cults.

The second phase was developed when the mystics of the Middle Ages were using Druidical material in the same way as the Greeks who made the Eleusinian Mysteries drew on the folk-lore of the pre-Hellenic earth-cults.

Now the Troubadours and Trouvères, who were the mystical Bards of the Middle Ages, were men of their times, and it was against the background of the moral concepts of their times that they formulated the Arthurian myth. They lived in an epoch in which women were not merely completely subjugated, but regarded as temptations of the Devil! In the original Arthurian epoch, women were segregated for safety and protection but were venerated as instruments of the gods.

There you have an important difference in the attitude of the two epochs.

The Troubadours and Trouvères wanted to recapture the polarity concepts and methods, and their efforts resulted in the chivalrous, romantic concept of woman. But in so doing, they did not wholly transcend their age. They lived in a period when woman was a chattel owned by some male; her father, or her eldest brother, or her nearest male kinsman owned her till she was sold in marriage; then her husband or, if she was widowed, his kinsmen owned her. She was not a separate entity with rights of her own. Women lived under a religious system in which no divorce was possible, so the emancipated minds of the age, wishing to develop their cult of the secret knowledge, made their own arrangements among themselves. And it was the pride of the initiates of the cult of Queen Venus to be generous in the matter of their wives.

Thus you got the custom of permitting, or even ordering, the wives to receive the attentions of a lover selected by the husband. This is all a matter of history. Originally it was a matter of emancipation and magic among the initiates of the cult of Queen Venus, for whom the Troubadours and Trouvères acted as Bards; but it spread beyond the initiates, and many a minor nobleman made capital out of his beautiful wife if she attracted the attentions of his overlord. A man was proud of the admiration bestowed on the beauty of his wife and, if he were a member of the cult of Queen Venus, would consider himself narrow-minded, old-fashioned, and disloyal to the Goddess, if he did not permit a fellow initiate to have access to her as part of the cult. All this can be verified as historical fact concerning the manners of the Middle Ages, especially in Southern France, but the cult-significance has not been appreciated.

It was against this background that the story or myth of Lancelot and Guinevere was developed as a reconstruction of Druidical material.

In the third phase of the story, the French sources that the worthy Malory translated from, in working over the old tales, (which they did not understand, not being initiates of any cult) felt obliged to give them a moral twist. Thus were Lancelot and Guinevere made to die repentant but this should not obliterate the lines of the original story. Indeed the Glastonbury Abbey tradition of Guinevere being buried with her royal husband under the High Altar is hardly a fitting end for a "harlot". And the fact that Lancelot saw the Grail and remained the king's best friend and chief knight to the end indicates that the original authors of the Arthurian mythology regarded the whole matter from a different point of view from the later convention. This third concept we must eliminate and discard as so much extraneous and misleading matter. We must concentrate on the second, or Trouvère form of the stories, using our knowledge of the Druidical and other Mysteries to interpret them.

So we get the concept of Guinevere as a polarity goddess in her archetypal aspect, and as the priestess of a polarity goddess in her human aspect.

You will remember that I drew your attention to the fact that the Earth Goddess, as the Spring Maiden, mated with the hero, not the gods. So we get Lancelot, as a human man, in his higher aspect as priest matching Guinevere in her lower aspect as priestess. So you get a three-plane working: the Goddess on the higher plane, the archetypal woman in Tiphareth; the priestess-priest working in Yesod; and the human male in Malkuth. And you will see it more clearly when I remind you that Guinevere was of royal blood, i.e. of the priestly clan specially bred, and Lancelot was not; and that Lancelot, though rewarded with a vision of the Grail, could not enter the Chapel of the Grail to receive the Sacrament.

Now let us consider the position of Arthur in the matter. He was a Priest-King; he had magical training, but the real knowledge abode in Merlin. And you will understand the whole myth better if you know it from the point of view of the men who created it in the Middle Ages, using Bardic material and giving a Christian dress to pagan Mysteries. They were dealing with a tradition that was well known, and they could not, therefore, depart from its general outlines, but could only give them a symbolic and mystical interpretation. The story of Arthur was a tragedy ending in failure, so they had to follow the lines laid down for them. And, in consequence, the Mystery story of the Round Table became a mythology in which the two sides of the coin, or double-sided shield, were an integral part of the Mystery. The neophyte was shown what the hero attempted to do and why he failed. You will understand this viewpoint better if I compare it with the Qabalistic. In the Qabalistic glyph the ten Holy Sephiroth are shown as the Tree of Life with the ten averse Sephiroth or Qliphoth, represented as reflected in the waters under the earth beneath them. So you have two separate Trees just as the tree growing by the bank of a river would be seen reflected in the water as a tree with its branches downwards. That is the Rabbinical method, but in the Arthurian method it is as if the two Trees, having been depicted on a single piece of paper, the paper were folded at the point of junction so that the holy and the averse were brought into juxtaposition.

This point is clearly indicated in the story of the two knights who fought over the colour of the shield, one declaring it was black and the other that it was white, only to find that it was black on one side and white on the other. You will see this viewpoint implicit in the concept of all the principal Arthurian characters. And you cannot understand the Arthurian Mysteries unless you first place yourself at the same standpoint and in the same attitude of mind as their creators. These were mediaeval men, emancipated from the tyranny of the Church by the influence of a pagan tradition derived through Rome and Greece from Egypt, and working over a tradition that was primarily Druidical. This is the basis from which we must approach the story of Guinevere and Lancelot.

Each of the major characters in the Arthurian story is an imperfect human being whose tragedy is brought about by their imperfection. Thus the holy and the averse Sephiroth are shown as interacting on the physical plane.

Remember that the physical plane consciousness is the surface of the pool, a point of junction between subjective and objective.

I regret the length of this preamble, but the whole story is very complex, and many sided. I shall have to keep on referring to points previously raised in another connection. It covers a very large section of polarity working, and it forms the glyph for the morality of the New Age.

The implications are not yet explained; you must understand first the basis in myth. That is why I was anxious to have the services of a competent scholar. There needs to be built a coherent body of doctrine from my chaotic communications, backed up by history, and supplied with a psychological commentary.[14] I will give you a great deal of material; you must supply the coherent form and the support of scholarship.

There are different kinds of polarity relationship enshrined in the Arthurian legends and they make an interesting pattern. Look up the literature. Notice:

King Arthur had relations, not necessarily physical, with three women: the Lady of the Lake, Morgan-le-Fay and Guinevere.

Lancelot had relations with three women in the same way: Guinevere, the first Elaine and the second Elaine.

Guinevere had relations with three men: Arthur, Lancelot and Galahad.

You can make a classification of different types of polarity functioning, e.g. Guinevere and Galahad, or Arthur and the Lady of the Lake.

The principle running through all is that of magnetic relationship.

When Arthur received initiation from the Lady of the Lake, he received something of her magnetism and was put in touch with her plane of being. When he polarised with Morgan-le-Fay, Morgan received something of his magnetism, which included that of the Lady of the Lake. Because of Arthur's Lady of the Lake initiation, any woman with whom he subsequently had relations he raised to the astral faery level of consciousness.

Again, although he failed fully to initiate Guinevere, he gave her something of the Lady of the Lake; and when Lancelot had relations with Guinevere, he got something of what she had received from Arthur; hence Lancelot received something of the Lady of the Lake.

Again, take two types of achievement of the Knights of the Round Table. There are the few who achieve the quest of the Grail, and they are virgin and the Grail is in the custody of maidens. But there are also the Knights who become seneschals of castles, who govern districts for the king, and they marry. Knights fall into one or other of the types, and some fall between two stools.

Malory is sufficient for reference purposes.

Galahad, the supreme type of spiritual knight, was produced by a purely physical passion.

So you have Grail Knights and Castle Knights: two different formulae.

Lancelot was of the type who fell between two stools, hence the long years of insanity and his parting from Guinevere. Owing to the belief that the quest of the Grail was the highest, Lancelot erroneously followed it instead of leaving it to Galahad.

The Cup and Sword formula is very important.

These formulae and the Arthurian pageantry are to be used for the younger generation. They will appeal to the older people because they are traditional, and to the younger because they are romantic.

There are three grades:

Grade of Arthur: *Symbol* Excalibur.
                  Work Chivalry, righting of wrongs.

Grade of Merlin: *Symbol* Sceptre.
                  Work Knowledge of the use of the
                  invisible forces for the Group Mind
                  and racial consciousness.

Grade of Guinevere: *Symbol* Cup.
                     Work Knowledge of polarity and its
                     highest aspect which is the key to all
                     occult knowledge, namely, knowledge
                     of the aura.

𝕿𝖍𝖊 𝕯𝖗𝖚𝖎𝖉𝖎𝖈𝖆𝖑 𝕸𝖞𝖘𝖙𝖊𝖗𝖎𝖊𝖘

The clue to the development of priestesses in other Mysteries has already been given. It was said that the Ancient Wisdom must be re-stated for the New Age in psychological terms, and psychological terms must be applied to the methods of the Mysteries.

You can get the methods of cognate Mysteries by study and, reasoning by analogy, conclude what must have been the methods of the Mysteries of Britain, about which less is known. In the course of our talks, I shall have occasion to tell you things that will be useful to you. In order to make you understand the middle recension of the Arthurian stories, I shall have to tell you about the Druidical Mysteries. These statements cannot be verified historically because so little is known of the Druids but they can be counter-checked scholastically by comparing them with better known systems. That is why I was at some pains to indicate sources in our previous interviews. For it is right that you should be placed in a position to counter-check these matters.

In our previous talk, I tried to make you understand the historical background and point of view of the men who used the Arthurian legend to make a Mystery School.

These men, breaking away from the ascetic viewpoint and dead traditionalism of Rome, sought to find a basis for the Good Life in the Eternal Verities. They wished to establish the right relationship between a man and the world, consisting, on the one hand, of his duty to his feudal overlord, and on the other hand, of his duty to his serfs. And again, they wished to establish an ideal of the right relationship between man and woman, in an age when the woman was a chattel and no readjustment of the marital bonds was possible save by death. Both these aspects, which were worked out by the idealists of the Dark Ages, have lessons for us today; for, though conditions change, the Eternal Verities, on which the Good Life is based, remain constant.

The formula of Lancelot contains some very deep teaching and far reaching implications, therefore I must lay the foundations deep and wide.

You will remember that I said that each figure in the Arthurian mythology is a two-sided coin, and that the lesson they teach is taught in the form of a tragedy, brought about by their errors and weaknesses, so that you may see what it is possible to do and why erring human beings failed to accomplish it.

Let us review briefly the position of King Arthur; the details of the different points can be elaborated later.

He is initiated into the methods of astral polarity working by the Lady of the Lake; he is seduced by Morgan-le-Fay into the unconsecrated use of this knowledge. If the sacred knowledge is used for unconsecrated ends, it is never possible to use it again for its higher purposes.[15]

Consequently, Arthur, having degraded his powers with Morgan-le-Fay, could not use them when the time came for him to mate with the specially-chosen Guinevere. Therefore another man had to fulfil this office, and the Cosmic forces worked themselves out according to the pattern of the age.

King Arthur does not go out himself to court his virgin bride, but sends his best knight, Lancelot, to bring her home, and she is taken from the seclusion of her bower and placed in the care of a man acknowledged by his contemporaries to be the best knight of his age. She looks upon him before she sees the King, and although both are loyal to their duty, his image is imprinted on her imagination. The King fails to initiate her and she, being unpolarised, cannot fulfil her office as High Priestess of the Principle of Polarity. Her husband then sets an example to his knights by rising above instincts of jealousy and possessiveness reinforced by the chattel concept with regard to women of the age. And, judging the matter in realistic and not conventional terms, retains her whom he cannot put away as Queen, she being suitable for that office, and he ordains her initiation and polarisation by a man fitted to perform that function.

In this story, we have a formula that is both profound and practical. The value of marriage as an institution upon which the stability of the racial life is based, is balanced against its value in relation to the principles of polarisation.

We might express this formula by the symbol of the equal-armed cross, in which the vertical line represents the continuity through time of the relationship of generation to generation, and the horizontal line represents functional polarity in the ever-passing present. Viewed in this manner, the Christian cross is an unbalanced symbol. The equal-armed cross, which is the Cross of Nature or Cross of the Elements, is a symbol of Power in Equilibrium and indicates the solution of the problem by referring the two conflicting factors to different dimensions. Thus, the stability in continuity of the race is a different factor from the polarisation of individuals. And these two lines intersect at one point only, and their extended length is free in space.

So then, we have the vertical factor of Guinevere's function as Queen and the horizontal factor of her personal evolution as woman.

How are these to be properly assessed in relationship to each other? How are they to be kept separate and yet combined?

Putting aside all preconceived concepts, let us seek reality in terms of function.

Let us consider what would have happened if King Arthur and Queen Guinevere had mated magically as priest and priestess, and if they had brought into manifestation the divinely begotten child to carry on the dynasty.

First, experience shows that, though theoretically possible, such a consummation is, in practice, impossible, because the life-force, being utilised magically on the astral plane, is not available for the building of the physical form of the child on the earth plane. Magical women are nearly always sterile. Consequently Guinevere could not be the magical priestess of womanhood and also the breeding woman, for the latter is a different kind of magic. Supposing, on the other hand, she had been the fecund mother, bringing forth a dynasty, her polarisation would have been with the Group Soul of the Race, not with the individual man. For a woman can never be mother and mate with equal single-heartedness.

The formula of Husband, Wife and Child is the formula of the Pairs of Opposites expressed in a Functional Third;

the formula of polarity working is a formula of functional development of the factors concerned; and for their expression creatively each turns outward from the polarisation and extends into space, being productive separately, not jointly.

To understand this matter, we need to bear in mind the fact that individuals go through phases in their evolution, and that the whole of life-experience, in all its aspects, is not worked out in a single incarnation. These phases in evolution may be likened to the cycle of the moon, of which the four phases, the dark, the full, the waxing, and the waning, each have their function and are presided over by a different goddess. But there is also a rhythm within the cycle. In each incarnation the phases are recapitulated, and the phases of incarnation resemble the Sun rhythm, with its alternating day and night, midnight and noon, dawn and dark, all within the twenty-four hours, as distinguished from the twenty-eight days of the moon-cycle. Woman is a creature of the moon and man a creature of the sun. The nature of the relationship which is proper between a man and a woman is determined by the phase of the woman in her moon-cycle of 28 incarnations, but, as the sex of the body alternates[16], a soul in the course of its moon-cycle has fourteen feminine incarnations, or the double seven.

In the phases of the moon there are two extremes, the dark and the full, and between these, transition periods of waxing and waning. At the dark of the moon she is introvert, the underworld goddess, the astral moon, Mistress of Magic, the Dark, Sterile Mother. At her full she is extrovert, the Bright, Fertile Mother; among the Egyptians, these phases were distinguished under the two aspects of Isis, the Bright Isis and the Black Isis. The Bright Isis was the goddess of fertility, manifest on the physical plane, seen of all men, shining in mid-heaven. The Black Isis was the goddess of polarity seen only by initiates, the Moon-behind-the-moon, whose shadow is faintly seen at the dawn of the first quarter, and the dusk of the last quarter. She is the Moon-behind-the-moon, the

Moon of Magic. In the earlier phases of evolution, the soul passes slowly round the circle of necessity and several lives may be spent in passing through a single moon-mansion or lunar day. In the later phases, many mansions may be passed through in a single life; so that a woman may be both Bright Isis and Dark Isis in different periods of her life but never both simultaneously.

With a man it is different, for he is of the Sun, and his rhythm is more rapid, and in the course of 24 hours he passes through his phases, going out into the world of men during the hours of sunlight, and returning into the woman's sphere when the sun sets.

Let us consider the practical implications of these matters. A given woman, at a given time, may be passing through any phase of the moon. Thus, in the course of her life, she may be virgin, waxing toward fecundity, or, having fulfilled her function of fecundity, withdrawing from extrovert function towards the astral plane. Or again, she may be in incarnation when one phase is predominant. She may be simply the Mother, requiring nothing of the man save fecundation and protection; or she may be in her sterile, astral phase, a giver of polarisation. But each of these phases, in its pure form, lasts but three lunar days of the Moon cycle, and all the other Mansions represent a dual functioning in ever-varying proportions.

In determining the standards of morality of the Aquarian Age, the phases of this spiral within the cycle have to be taken into consideration. What is right at one phase is wrong at another, and it is the phase of the woman which is the determinant; for the man, with his rapidly recurring rhythm, can pass through both factors in a cycle of 24 hours. The morality of a woman depends upon the moon phase through which her life is moving. The same considerations do not apply to a man, for a night's sleep will change his phase.

Thus it would have been immoral for Guinevere, as queen, to have been promiscuous; it would have been immoral for her, as priestess, to have rejected Lancelot. Yet Lancelot's function in relation to Guinevere was unaffected by his relationships with the two Elaines, save inasmuch as Guinevere's jealousy destroyed the magical plan of the second Elaine; whereas his relationship with the first Elaine, of which Guinevere was ignorant, in no way affected the relationship. Equally, Arthur's relationship with the faery women did not affect his function of kingship. Morgan-le-Fay's extra-marital adventures did not affect her magical value to Merlin. And the Lady of the Lake, symbolised by pure water, would have sinned if she had refused to fulfil her function of initiating priestess to the youths sent to her to be initiated.

So there are women who polarise with the Group Soul as mothers, but can polarise with no man; and there are women who are polarising priestesses and fulfil no function towards the race directly; and there are women who partake of both these natures in the course of their lives. Whereas the type of the male is not fixed, but freely alternating.

The Dynastic Tragedy

Merlin's original plan was to breed a race of Priest-Kings but the plan went astray. The whole story is a tragedy. If the original scheme had gone through, Guinevere would have borne one child, and one only, and would have known the full cycle of womanhood.

In dealing with the Arthurian myth we deal with tragedy, but in dealing with the Merlin myth, we deal with archetypal ideas. When I talk about Merlin, I will show you the scheme as planned. When we talk about Arthur we talk of the imperfect reflection in the waters of Earth, and you learn from the story of the failures the method of the remedies attempted in the persons of the two Elaines, and that knowledge is valuable, just as valuable as the knowledge of the archetypal scheme. But I wish to deal first with the primary myth, before dealing with the archetypal scheme.

In dealing with the story of the relationship of Lancelot and Guinevere, we must bear in mind the viewpoint of the men who used this myth to make a Mystery-cult.

When the great, new life-impulse poured into Provence, there were two aspects to this premature Renaissance. There was a mystical, ascetic aspect, and an intellectual, pagan one, and those were combined in the Mystery-cult in an attempt at an ethical synthesis. Breaking free of the trammels of superstition, men's minds, for the first time since the decline of Greece, looked Nature in the face and sought to found their philosophy of life on natural fact, instead of coercing men's minds to conform with an abstract ideal.

In dealing with the material of the Arthurian myths, men were indeed brought face to face with Nature, for the Druidical sun-worship was a Nature-cult and the lines laid down for them in the traditional stories. Confronted with the eternal triangle of Arthur, Guinevere and Lancelot, they considered the solution therein propounded and applied it to the problems of their own times and lives. And we can do the same. Let us examine the problem.

Here was a man, King Arthur, holding an important office, in which the co-operation of a woman was needed. The woman chosen to co-operate could not play her part because he was unable to give her what was needful to enable her to do so. What then did he do? Did he accept frustration for himself and for her? Not so! Counselled by the wise Merlin, he sought a remedy. It was not possible that he should break up the structure of the social life of his age by putting away his Queen; and indeed, had he done so, there is nothing in the records to indicate that he would have fared any better with any other woman.

So he caused her to be initiated into her royal office by a suitable man, who, though not himself a king, fulfilled the necessary human function and made of the maiden a woman. The ceremonial marriage of Arthur and Guinevere made the princess a queen, and the functional mating of Guinevere and Lancelot made the maiden a woman.

It needed these two factors to make of Guinevere a priestess; the Initiation of Consecration that brings down the spiritual power and the Initiation of Experience that calls up the personal magnetism.

These three persons, co-operating in perfect selflessness, served Britain and made of King Arthur's court a true shrine of chivalry. This relationship continued to the end between Arthur and Lancelot, and Arthur and Guinevere, but there was a breach in the continuity of the relationship between Guinevere and Lancelot because of Guinevere's failure to be utterly impersonal.

Now, what do we learn from these things in relation to the problems of our day and in relation to the life of the New Age?

We learn that mating is both sacramental and functional, and that these two aspects need to be fulfilled. The sacramental nature of the relationship has reference to the Race, which rests upon the foundation of family life which alone gives the conditions under which the proper nurture of children is possible. The sacramental aspect demands absolute loyalty and brings through the power to enable its conditions to be fulfilled; that is to say those who undertake to found a family must abide by their pledges to the Racial Life.

The functional aspect likewise demands its own kind of loyalty, but that loyalty is to Nature, and its ethic is efficiency.

This doctrine we see clearly exemplified in the relationship of Arthur, Lancelot and Guinevere. Arthur, unable to give efficient natural mating to his Queen, availed himself of the efficiency of Lancelot for that purpose; the King, Queen and Lover remained faithful to the sacramental pledge given to the Race.

The same principle was again exemplified in the relationship of Guinevere, Lancelot and Galahad. Guinevere, proving sterile even as Arthur had proved impotent, the dynastic successor was bred by Lancelot by another woman, and Guinevere loved him – Galahad – as if he had been her own son.

In the relationship between Lancelot and the second Elaine, we see the blighting influence of a conventional concept of relationships which spread ruin and devastation around it and benefited nobody.

Thus, we see the difference between a code of conduct based on reality and a code based on ideals which are formulated without regard to reality. The one gives life, the other destroys life-values and even life itself.

We shall find that, if we examine the experience of life impartially, women divide into two types: the maternal type and the magnetic type – and that each individual woman inclines in varying degree, to one or other of these extremes. If she is of the purely maternal type, she will ask nothing of her mate save to fecundate her year by year, and protect and provide for her offspring. He, consequently, will have a large portion of his nature left unused. If she be of the extreme magnetic type, she will be sterile, or, if she should bear a child, will be indifferent to it and will be without desire for children or understanding of them. Should she enter into marriage with a man, she would leave his instinct to found a family without expression. Consequently such women should not marry, nor be expected to marry, but should have their place as priestesses of the Great Goddess.

Equally, on the other hand, the woman of the purely maternal type should rest content with the man's services to the home and make no claims on a personal loyalty, which for him is little better than celibacy. Such a woman, if she is true to her own instinct and nature, would deny all access to herself until her youngest child is weaned, and then only permit access until she knows herself again to be pregnant. Thus the husband of such a woman would be mated to her for but two months in two years. He would thus be denied normal functioning but, on the other hand, would know pride of citizenship in its finest flowering.

The woman of the magnetic type, if true to the law of her own nature, would deny herself to no man who called upon her in his name of the Goddess. That is to say, who called up by the magnetism the powers of womanhood within her. She is therefore rootless and solitary and free-moving, and if true to herself, will not bind herself even from one hour to another.

Between these two extremes are women in whom the temperaments are blended in all degrees of variety. Putting aside the deforming effects of the pressure of convention, let us consider how these women would act if true to the law of their own nature. This is a law which is neither one thing nor the other but passes through alternating phases. And if such a woman were true to her own nature, she would react to these phases. She would be free-moving till she found a man who appealed to her nature and then she would become maternal. She would desire home and a child and she would be true to the maternal type and its law until the child was sufficiently grown no longer to absorb her energies. Then she would again revert to the magnetic type, and when fulfilled in mating, enter the maternal phase of her cycle again. When she had passed the age of breeding she would still continue her cyclic rhythm, requiring alternately, the companionship and security of a settled home, and the free-foot wandering of magnetic adventure. In proportion as a woman inclines to one type or the other, will be the proportion of the alternating phases in her life cycle.

Now let us consider the man's point of view. He, equally with the woman, is a two-sided creature, but as I told you before, his rhythm is based on the sun and no more than a night's sleep may mark the division between his phases. Thus he can give all that the maternal woman, or a woman of mixed type in her maternal phase, may require of him, deriving deep satisfaction therefrom for one side of his nature, while, after no more than a night's sleep, he may find fulfilment of his magnetic needs and function with a woman of the magnetic type or one in the magnetic phase of her life cycle.

Thus it will be seen that a man can minister to many women and a woman minister magnetically to many men, but neither a man nor a woman can fulfil the duties of more than one home at a time, for children need more from a father than the provision for their material needs.

A problem therefore arises concerning women in the minor phase of their life-cycle; the woman, for example, who inclines to the maternal, and is passing through her relatively brief phase of free-moving, magnetic activity. The solution in her case, consists in the recognition of her nature, and the prevention of conception until she finds a man who is prepared to make a home with her.

The problem of the magnetic type of woman, during her brief phase of maternal desire, is solved by the adoption of her child into the home of a maternal woman. For, unless deformed by false concepts, the maternal woman loves children, whether they are flesh of her flesh or not. And the magnetic woman has no feeling for the young of the race, even if it be the child of the man she loves, born of her own body. Not only will she have no love for it but, if she is of the more extreme type, she will tend to hate it. Custom may coerce such women – that makes no difference to their inner feelings and the result for the child is no different either. Equally, no doctrine of duty is needed to coerce the maternal type of woman into caring for the child because she will love it spontaneously.

For human beings to reach the full stature of their development and to make the utmost evolutionary advance possible in a given incarnation, they should at all times be true to their own nature and society should be so designed as to permit of this being done.

The key to the problem lies in the recognition of the two distinct factors in   womanhood: first, of the existence of some 25% of each type in a relatively pure form, and of some 50% of mixed types with a cyclic life; and, secondly, of the recognition of the fact that men have so rapidly an alternating cycle that they are capable of both relationships practically simultaneously.

Let us now deal with the position of children in the circumstances I have outlined. They will come to life in the home of the maternal woman, or the woman in her maternal phase, or will speedily, within a few hours of birth, be transferred thereto. Therefore they will be reared in an harmonious atmosphere, and not in an atmosphere of repressed resentment of their demands. They will therefore be objects, in the first three years of their lives, of unremitting solicitude on the part of their mother; for it will make no difference to her whether she bore them or not; the maternal woman loves best the youngest, who is in his turn pushed aside in her esteem when the new-born child arrives.

But Nature has ordained a rhythm of between two and three years of human breeding, allowing for the time of gestation and nursing, and the resting of the mother between pregnancies.

Thus, each child in turn has her unremitting care and undivided attention while it needs it, and is pushed out of the cradle to play with the other children while it is still too young to know any emotional loss.

The woman of the magnetic type, as soon as she knows she is pregnant, would make arrangements for the adoption of her child by a woman of the maternal type who has failed to breed that year, and whose youngest child has found its feet and run off to play, leaving her with an empty cradle. And on the average, Nature would maintain a just balance.

Among men similar proportions will prevail. There will be the man whose metier it is to found a family; and the man who should never be aught but a bachelor; and the men of mixed type who, too, will fulfil their needs according to their phases. The paternal type will derive extreme pride and satisfaction from the children in his house and his tendency will be to plan for their place in the world, their successful launching in life. Thus the withdrawal of the mother's attention as they grow older is supplemented by the father's growing interest, which gives the child self-confidence, and fosters its individuality.

In a household where one or more children are there by adoption and not birth, there may be more than one father interested in the security and well-being of that home.

Replace the desire of exclusive possession with the desire for efficient function, and you solve the problem of jealousy. That is the clue to the morality of the New Age.

It will have to be realised that children are among the assets of the nation. The fertility of the soil, the flocks and herds, the mineral treasures of the rocks and the fisheries of the rivers and around the coasts, the integrity, intelligence and industry of the people and their fertility, are the assets of the race, and the government should control all these basic products in the national interest.

But is must be realised that no law, no subsidy, no planning can provide a substitute for the personal factor, and all planning should take the recognition of that as its basis. For there is no such thing as mass-production of living matter. For, in dealing with living humans, two qualities are required which can neither be coerced nor bought, and these are love and judgement. Therefore the legislators must legislate and the planners must plan in such a manner that love and judgement are mobilised, each after its kind, and true to its own nature, for its nature cannot be altered. We love what we love because we find it loveable; and we judge soundly what we understand because we understand it; and neither "the King, nor all his horses nor all his men" can argue the matter.

But there is another important factor in national life whose price is beyond rubies, and that is the creative imagination, and the nation should pay whatever it requires to give it scope. For it is worth an equal share with the other factors.

One third of a nation's wealth consists of its material resources; one third in the character and quality of its people; and one third in the individuals of creative imagination that appear sporadically in its midst.

Aspects of the Grail

There are three aspects to the Grail – that of the Sword, the Sceptre and the Cup.

The Grail sought by the knights as an ideal.
The Grail of the Round Table.
The Cup.
The Grade of Arthur – the Warrior King.
The Grade of Merlin – the Wisdom behind the King.
The Grade of Guinevere – of the Cup – the symbol of Woman.

We know a good deal of the first Grade; we know something of the second; there is a great deal more to be learnt about the third.

In the Grade of Arthur, the people will learn to "live the life" and follow the Ideals – live the life wherever they might find themselves. It corresponds to the Path of the Mystic, and the people are those "who are directed".

In the Grade of Merlin, specially selected people would be taught how to handle the Group Mind of the Race, and they are the people "who are directed how to direct". It corresponds to the Hermetic Path.

In the Grade of Guinevere, a few are taught how to work with Power, and they are those "who direct". It corresponds to the Green Ray.

In each of the three Grades, the chosen people are as channels for the Work of the Masters.

I will go on to give you certain teaching concerning polarity and its application. The old Piscean Age was very fixed and rigid. The New Age will be marked for its fluidity – the people will move about because transport renders it easier, and fluidity will show itself in all things, and in personal relationships.

There are many different kinds of polarity. There is the polarity between teacher and pupil, where the teacher supplies the stimulus, being positive, and awakens the latent within the pupil.

It is not fully understood that the Magus is negative in function. He himself stimulates the Lodge, and the Lodge returns the stimulus to him. He then changes his polarity and becomes negative, and power is brought through from the inner planes. This is the Law of Alternating Polarity.[17]

You can polarise with one person, but not with two people at once; but you can get a group of people together and polarise with them, as the Magus polarises with his Lodge. In the case of the Triangle, where it takes three to bring through the Power, the two at the basal angles polarise with each other, and the third at the apex acts on a higher plane, and is in polarity with the inner planes.

There is, too, Vertical Polarisation, which is the polarity between the Higher and the Lower Self. Every soul has to learn to stand foursquare upon its own feet, and there will come times when he will find he is polarised with no one except his own Higher Self. This is a very valuable lesson, and is the period of depolarisation, which is detachment as opposed to attachment. No one should feel a sense of loss when a soul "goes away", and stands quite alone and then returns again refreshed and strengthened for further work.

So these are the principles concerning the Grade of Guinevere in the Aquarian Age. You should learn how to form these magnetic relationships when work is required to be done, and learn also how to break them at will. The Path will not be easy, it never is easy and there is much to be learnt. I can give you the principles, the application you must discover for yourselves through test and experiment. You will need wisdom and discernment, and you will need courage in this pursuit of Truth. You may make mistakes, you may fall into error, but we learn through mistakes, and the Way is made easier for those who follow after. Yet if you work with ever the spirit of Dedication, the mistakes you may make will not be irreparable, and if you find one door closes, another will immediately open up, if you are ready yourselves for the knowledge that you seek.

The Guinevere teaching formed part of the Arthurian Mysteries; you will remember that those divided into Grades of which the Guinevere was the highest and most secret. I cannot tonight embark upon that; for the teaching of those higher grades there has to be certain preparation made on the inner planes and that I have not made, but we can transact much other work tonight and at a future date continue that work already begun.

Notes

[1] The terms Trouvère and Troubadour are used somewhat loosely throughout this passage. Troubadours flourished in the south of France from the earlier part of the 12th century and wrote in the Occitan language and their culture was largely suppressed in the Albigensian crusade of 1214. The Trouvères were of the north of France, somewhat later in time, (the latter part of the 12th century), and wrote in Old French. It was they who introduced Arthurian and related themes into the literature, through Celtic stories adapted from Breton bards, whereas the Troubadours largely confined themselves to shorter lyric poetry and song.

[2] It should be pointed out that Sir Thomas Malory was writing some 300 years later than Chrétien de Troyes, and translating the best French texts that were available to him, written some 50 years after Chrétien, who flourished between c.1160 and 1180. It is generally conceded nowadays that both Chrétien and the composers of the

parallel Welsh stories of *The Mabinogion* drew from older written manuscripts, now lost, or direct from oral lore.

[3] It is possible that the questioner may have had in mind *The Fisherman and the Jinnee* which has certain resonance with Grail and wisdom symbolism.

[4] Since *The Arthurian Formula* was written there have been a plethora of scholarly works supporting Celtic origins for the Arthurian tradition, principally by Professor R.S.Loomis in America and Professor Jean Frappier in France. More importantly for the esoteric student however have been works by practicising esotericists who have displayed excellent scholarship allied to practical inner experience, including the works of R.J.Stewart, Caitlín and John Matthews, Mike Harris and Wendy Berg. Refer to Gareth Knight's introduction for further detail.

[5] The reference is of course to the Qabalistic Tree of Life, and most directly to Dion Fortune's own work on the subject *The Mystical Qabalah*.

[6] The provenance of these notes is unclear, and some of the statements made open to question.

[7] This short paragraph is somewhat wide of the mark factually. It was the Troubadours who were more closely involved with various intellectual and social movements in the South of France, spiritual or otherwise, and there was far from any concerted programme of events in this melting pot of heretical ideas and movements in 12th century Languedoc. Troubadours were of various ranks of society and many would not have liked to have been regarded as minstrels, which included popular entertainers, also known as jongleurs, who performed rather than composed lyrics, and who supplemented their acts with anything from tumbling to juggling.

[8] This refers to the claim of the monks of Glastonbury Abbey to have discovered the tomb of Arthur and Guinevere in the grounds in 1191. Generally considered with some scepticism these days, whatever help it may gave given the Abbey and Plantagenet pretensions it was somewhat at odds with the tradition of the King having been spirited away to Avalon – unless of course Glastonbury be physically associated with that otherworld island.

[9] There are of course varying traditions, and Malory's sources see her disgrace as part of the break up of the Round Table fellowship.

[10] 12th century France undoubtedly saw a premature Renaissance in many ways, but not necessarily confined to or even associated with the Albigensian movement.

[11] This is a very simplistic and somewhat subjective analysis of a very complex and little understood subject owing to the destruction of original records, as is the fate of many subjugated heresies. It is plain, however, where the communicator's sympathies lie, under whatever historical name.

[12] This is an interesting differentiation and valid as far as it goes, although there are other, equally valid, and not necessarily contradictory alternative theories and differentiations possible with regard to various characters in the legends.

[13] These remarks on Grail working relate to The Church of the Grail which was a mystical side to the Hermetic work of the Fraternity that developed out of the Guild of the Master Jesus after 1936 under the aegis of C.T.Loveday, Dion Fortune's close collaborator since 1922.

[14] It is arguable that this desideratum had to wait until the 1980s and 90s for a body of esoterically informed and experienced writers to explore some of these issues – i.e. Stewart, Matthews, Harris, Berg and others – often following alternative lines of interpretation but overall opening up a wide vista of interior knowledge that is not necessarily self-contradictory. The line of interpretation encapsulated here is in keeping with Dion Fortune's concerns over contemporary sexual and moral attitudes of the 1930s which she treated also in her later novels as also in her semi-publicly performed Rites of Pan and of Isis. Most of these concerns became things of the past in the social and moral revolution of the 1960s, the seeds of which she may well have helped to sow in her day.

[15] Presumably it is not possible for the *same man* notes the original compiler of the script, probably Arthur Chichester, Warden of the Society 1946-79.

[16] This does not appear to be a universal rule notes the original compiler.

[17] For further detail on this line of thought reference can be made to *The Cosmic Doctrine* channelled by Dion Fortune from another contact in 1922/4, currently published by Red Wheel/Weiser. On a less abstract level *The Circuit of Force*, a series of articles written by

her in 1938-40 is also relevant, published in volume form by Thoth Publications with commentary by Gareth Knight in 1998.

The Arthurian Formula
Part Two
Margaret Lumley Brown

The Archetypes

The Arthurian formula came from Atlantis; the story of the Grail and the legends connected with types of the soul of man fulfilling various initiatory experiences; and all the types in some way or another are in each initiated person, although an especial Archetype will work behind one especial person. The names and grades in the legends are derivations of ancient symbols, and were originally in a different concept of language because words and language as we know them now, had scarcely evolved at all in Atlantis, being very simple arrangements of sounds. These sounds were, however, of extraordinary effect and power when used by the priesthood. The familiar places in the legends, and the familiar characters, were all Atlantean as was the particular symbol of the Round Table as it grew to be called and the Grail as it also grew to be called; the former a symbol of the great Universe and the other Universes behind it; the Grail, the symbol of the development possible in the soul of man during the completion of evolutionary experience, the evolutionary experience not only of the phase of Atlantis, but of the succeeding phases.

The Round Table was the sphere of the stars and of planetary space; the Grail was in itself what was then thought of as the heart of man, but really the crucible of all his experience during his evolution, or rather, of those experiences possible to him if he chose to take the means of following them out. And this has always been known as the Quest of the Grail; made by one who is willing to take the means of the soul's full experience in order to develop it to its highest point in many successive phases. Then came the Pagan religions of the early days of this evolution, and lastly the great Christian phase. And all those phases have used the Grail and imprinted various symbols of their own upon it, symbols of inestimable value, for they come from very much more ancient knowledge than some particular religious revelation gives.

There are too, the characters, the Archetypes; the great Magicians who teach the Royal House and who also, as was done in Atlantis, experiment in carefully chosen methods of birth to bring about certain influences, for mating and the intricate laws governing it were known to their last degree in Atlantis, but by the over-elaboration of the symbols and the absence of principle in the priesthood when using their knowledge, in later days the tremendous evil crept into the Lost Continent. Such mating and such birth, I need scarcely remind you, were brought about with the utmost impersonality. It was thought out and planned by the chief Priests of the Temple with important people in the land belonging to the race of the Scribes and Warriors, which was the Royal clan, and applied according to the esoteric need.

Merlin, the great Priest of Atlantean power and tradition, brought this knowledge to Britain. The way he used it by bringing about the birth of Arthur, in what from the Christian point of view was a very immoral fashion, was just the way in which the Atlantean priesthood would use it. He selected a certain father and mother and brought them together; to him the end justified the means. Also the ideas of sex morality were entirely different; in some ways they were much harder and sterner. He got the father and mother and brought them together in order to produce a certain type of offspring which would be fitted to rule the Dominion of what we now call Britain, which he and the group of priests and Atlanteans with him had taken under their charge for the purpose of development, and for the purpose of continuing their ancient Mysteries after the well-known Fall of Atlantis had taken place.

Now we come to a person somewhat forgotten in the legend – the mother of Arthur. She was an Atlantean princess mated to two Britons in turn, to Gorlois and to Uther the father of Arthur. It is said she also had an Atlantean husband to whom she returned in the end, and that this husband was the father of at least one, but probably all, of her daughters. That is only in the inner tradition. And the other questions that arise somewhat concern this because her daughters were brought up in her own Atlantean tradition as far as she could manage it, even when they came to Britain and lived there. This, of course, was translated into the tale of the nunnery in which Morgan-le-Fay was instructed.

Then you have Guinevere the Queen. In her was meant to be the tradition of the Atlantean Priestess-Queen who could rule in the royal sense in the palace and yet had a strong connection with the highest grade of the priesthood, even as was carried later on into certain other traditions such as in ancient Egypt and ancient Mexico and Peru. The Royal House was in its inmost sphere, to start with, part of the High Priesthood, though in the world and not able to live the life as it was lived, for example, in the withdrawn Temple of Naradek. Nevertheless the greatest of those kings and queens had always "a trial run", if one may use that expression, in the secret Temple for a time if other indications showed them to be worthy of it. This particular being, Guinevere, in the Arthurian tradition should have exemplified all this; she should have shown the contact with the ancient goddess-powers of Atlantis and brought them through into the life of the Court. We all know that she failed and why. But that was Merlin's whole plan which he was never able completely to bring about.

Then there was the other side of the Merlin tradition. He also failed for a time, and like Arthur, had to sleep and wake again, and then make up for the time he had lost. Merlin of course, in the end, cut off from sunken Atlantis, with superhuman power and knowledge, became an instrument of mere sensation for a time, and you know the result. He lost the deep impersonality that was the greatest part, if rightly understood, of the religious side of the Atlantean priesthood. Each of these beings, Arthur, Merlin, Guinevere, you will recall, goes to rest, disappears for long ages with the tradition built up around them that they will come back again. That was how the tradition began.

Then you have the other types of character, the knights and ladies, the astral beings, the Lady of the Lake and others. All these have their place. It would take too long to go into the various characters and traditions which made all the knights and all the ladies into the various legends appertaining, but if you think them over you will see the myriad workings of the human character under certain given conditions, and how they overcome those situations or fail.

We have, too, the places connected with the legends; the great castles which are also places in the "geography of the soul", one may say. They can be, and should be, astrally built and realised. There were the various castles of the knights and ladies which have definite relationship to certain inner plane spheres. There is the castle or fortress of Caerleon, and the palace of Camelot, and these are real places of the soul in our own British tradition, and should be held and realised astrally. The more the Arthurian formula develops the more shall we have need of these places and to work within them on occasion.

There is the tradition, too, of the shields of the knights and the quarterings of their shields. Those, too, will yield a great deal to meditation even as does the great heraldic bearing of Arthur himself, the dragon which was the crest of his helmet. That dragon has passed into our Island tradition for it was borne by Celtic princes and by the earliest Saxon monarchs, and now is connected, only, I think, with Wales. The dragon was a monster fabricated largely by the fear of a forgotten and misunderstood religion. It refers to Atlantis; it was a monster, in short, risen from the flames or from the sea, composed of many parts and not understood of men. Then it passed into a form of devil, like many old symbols.

The tradition of the intercourse with faery women that you find in Arthurian legend, and which also exists in other British legends too, is of great value if properly understood for it ensouls the teaching behind the form of magical fantasy and work connected and brought through from that; but it is an especial teaching of great secrecy and intricacy. I do not wish to dwell upon it now. I would, however, suggest that you find the various cognisances and shields of the knights and ladies in the tradition that you have, and let each who bears an Archetypal Name have some symbol in his private apartments or in ritual robes or dress connected with Arthurian rites which bring in that traditional symbolism; have this shield or crest in so far as you can find it.

There is another tradition that I would touch upon and that is that Merlin is often referred to in some legends as a Druid. We know that he taught the earliest Druids and much of his teaching passed into the teaching of the Druids of whom many were themselves priests who came over with the tin merchants and others to colonise from Atlantis. There is so very much to dwell upon in this great racial power that I myself am at a loss to wield the power enough to bring it into some kind of whole which can easily be handled. At present we can only take certain parts, developing these bit by bit.

The Patterns

During the ages of evolution when the Great Lodge of the Masters has contacted certain groups within the world, there have been certain patterns connected with the particular idea upon which it was necessary to build during a particular phase. These patterns of living (for so it is better to denote them) are summed up into several major symbols. Do not confuse such symbols, which I shall explain, with the symbol systems of cosmogony and types of human force such as are the Tree and Tarot; we are concerned here with patterns, main patterns, to which the Group must grow through initiation, finally becoming amalgamated with the patterns. Of these patterns I am going to dwell first on three major ones; there have been others, but they do not now concern us. These major ones derive from Atlantis and Chaldea and the European reconstruction of the Mysteries during the Middle Ages.

Of these three, the first is the symbol of the Sun and seven Planes or phases of force that was the pattern of the great Sun Temple of Ruta. We will call it a solar pattern. The other two are, in different ways, stellar patterns.

The second is that great symbol made known to you as the Table Round. It was another form of Rays and Circles, this time brought through from a great stellar group of influence then strongly contacting the Fourth Root Race. This stellar group is formed of the seven stars of the constellation of the Great Bear, and from this influence was born the pattern, based on very remote cosmic origin approximate to the Rays and the Circles in *The Cosmic Doctrine*, and also approximating to the Zodiac and the Sun. That is the basic origin of the Table Round.

The third of these patterns also concerns Rays and Circles in yet another arrangement. It is the pattern of the Rose-Cross, and it is in a special sense connected with the stars, and also with the planet Venus, for the Rose is composed of three sets of leaves, three in the centre, seven around, and twelve on the outer circumference. Around this form of a circle made of a rose there go out once again the Rays, but the Rays and Circle this time are impaled upon a Cross; they are impaled upon the Cross of Matter and Time. They represent a later development of initiation more in conformity with the further evolution of man's mind in ours, the succeeding Root Race, the Fifth. Now two great Manus are concerned with this pattern directly and indirectly: the first of them is the great Manu of the Atlantean early days, Narada, who founded and conceived the plan of the great Sun Temple of Atlantis with its cosmological buildings and ideas, and communicated them to that relatively small group, the Sacred Clan, and mostly, of course, only to the Priesthood of the Sacred Clan. The Round Table, however, which also came from Atlantis, was brought through by a Great One sent by Narada; you know his name for he is the Arch-Mage of our own Islands, but his mandate was from Narada. Now this second pattern of the Round Table represented the subtler and somewhat more complex form of the initiation plan; it included not only the Priesthood, but the Warrior caste as well, making a certain type of priest in each of them. The first teachings of the Table were given to Narada, and when Atlantis finally sunk in the last cataclysm, Merlin was allowed to bring that great pattern in the form then known to the other land.

Now we must dwell on our third pattern which is that of the Rose-Cross. To the Fifth Root Race, which is our own, there came another great Manu who had also been in Atlantis. He brought the knowledge of the teaching of certain planetary ideals belonging to what you call the planet Venus, and he transposed them to those of earth in its earliest days. He was the first great Manu of this Race and, indirectly as it may seem, developed out of his teaching and the sphere from which that teaching came, the great conception patterned again in a Circle and Rays and bearing the emblem we associate with the planet Venus, the rose, save that it is the Rose of the Universe and has very many deeper meanings. The Cross concerns, as I have said, the deeper and more continued development of man.

These three patterns directed to the world by three great Teachers of different kinds, whom we call Narada, Merlin and Melchizedek, are enclosed symbolism for the guidance of the initiate – the origin and the end of man and his development in between. From these three great symbols all esoteric schools in some way or other have some type of direction; they have worked them out differently, but they appertain to one of the three, perhaps to all of the three. When the higher initiation of the Promethean type is fully developed, then we may work on all three; at present our work in this particular Group is concerned more largely with our own type of development of the Table Round and of the Rose-Cross.

There were in Lemuria, and even before, certain other patterns, but they do not now concern us, for the Lemurian race was in so much earlier a stage of development that its patterns, though interesting, are not of the same essential value as those born in Atlantis when the concrete mind and the emotional mind were beginning to develop in man, and he was becoming to all intents and purposes what we now know him to be.

I am not now going to dwell upon the other matters concerning the Table Round, the great archetypal forces of the Knights and so on, because they would take many addresses in themselves, but I am giving one address in as short a space as I can on the subject. Today I prefer to think upon the Table. We have lately had a very remarkable Ceremony in which the Table was brought through again by one who bears the Archetype of him who brought it first to us. [1]

Connected with this Table naturally and inseparably is a second symbol, that which you call the Grail; and the Grail really implies the various powers by which the initiate shall develop himself to the great pattern of the Table – the pattern, and the power to enable the initiate to achieve the pattern. That is as concisely put as it can be; there are endless elaborations of course. And connected with the Grail and the Table, we have the three symbols, minor ones in a sense, which connect with three types of development – the Cup, the Wand or Sceptre, and the Sword. The Sceptre or Wand is the symbol of Merlin, the Sword is the symbol of Arthur and the Knights, and the Cup is the symbol of Guinevere and the Ladies. The Sceptre, the Sword and the Cup – these three symbols you have all studied to a large extent, and I do not propose to dwell upon them at the moment, but they do imply three grades, so to speak, the three lines of definite development; and you will notice, if you really think it out, that in Merlin himself all the symbols are assembled, for it was he who first found Arthur and gave him his take, who found an instructed Guinevere, and in whom the knowledge and power of these things were known and achieved; the real Merlin.

However, I do not wish to dwell upon the Archetypes who surround the Table at this time; I would have you think of the Table itself, the Table that came from the stars, the Table that brought through the far-off knowledge, from the remote centres of the cosmic spheres, focussed within those mystical stars in Ursa Major: that power was shed upon the earth, the pattern sent through, the symbols built, and is the origin of the Table Round within our midst. It was also in this beginning an Order, an Order of an early type to which the Hierarchy of Masters gave its power and its blessing. To the higher grades the Masters themselves belonged at the time.

Around these three patterns I have described, many stories and legends are formed. You can use such stories and legends as magical formulae if you wish, but reflect also upon the pattern itself – what it came from, where it came from, who sent it, and all it means, for it refers really to each man in the world when he shall have reached a certain part of his development. If you remember, the old tradition of the Table tells us that it was sent to Christian and heathen and all men in the world when they should have achieved certain things. This is pictorial language which you can easily translate. It is indeed sent to all in the world regardless of race or creed or colour. It concerns the passage of man through his evolution from God and back to God again till he himself is as God.

"The Table Round remains with men,
brought back by Merlin to the dawning age."

The Knights

It is now time to reassess this work and to bring into it, so far as we can, further streams of knowledge and further reconstruction, for the great Arthurian concepts constitute, as you know, the especial Formula for our own race. I am, therefore, proposing to give three summaries of certain essential factors and realisations of this Arthurian work. One lecture I have already given upon the details of the Table Round itself; the other two I propose shall deal with the Knights and the Ladies of the Legend, respectively. I shall not enter particularly into the Grail teaching as such, for it involves so many issues and there has already been a fair amount of discussion and instruction upon it, but I shall deal especially in these three addresses with the Table Round and the people involved in the Legend.

Today we will take the Knights, but as it is not possible to go into the particular history and symbolism connected with each Knight, although such exists, we will take some of the principal Knights and their connection with the Legend.

You must first of all remember the essential symbolism connected with the Legend of the Grail and the Round Table, namely that of the Lance, the Sword, the Cup and the Stone, and in the Grail Legend especially we hear more of three of these symbols, the Cup, the Sceptre and the Sword. The Grail itself involves, of course, the Cup symbolism in particular; the Table in itself is built around the Sword symbolism, and the Sword symbolism in its relationship with the Tree is the

Lightning Flash that comes down all the planes from side to side.

The essential thing to remember about the Table Round in its relation to mankind is that, as Merlin said when he instituted it as an Order, it was for all types of men, all creeds, all sorts. It was, in fact, a Centre of Mystery-training delivered to the Race. There were all kinds of Knights there - and here we must consider a little the foolish falsification and corruption which, in the course of history, have crept into the Legend in attempts to align it with the preconceived ideas of medieval churchmen. It is much older than the Church in any case, but like all Mystery teaching it can be used in any way and for any race and any form of doctrine, even as on the Tree you can align with Tiphareth many others besides the Crucified One.

Let us now take some of the Knights, and let us consider how Merlin acted about this Table. In the Norman French dialect mixed with the Middle English, in which this work has largely come to us in England, you find the seats of the Knights around the Table referred to as "sieges", or "sièges" from the French, and it is of these that I shall first speak, for Merlin with especial care arranged these various "sieges" round the Table, and constructed them in special patterns to suit the type of force which should sit therein when that type of force was perfected. And that brings in again the question of the Tree alignment with the Table. It is not until Chesed that every man can become truly king of himself and fitted to sit down among the Knights at the Table Round. His Knighthood is not confirmed in him until he can achieve Chesed. That is by no means the end of his achievement, of course, but it is not until then that he may be counted confirmed in his "siege" or seat.

Let us think now of the Knights themselves. They were, indeed, of strange types and psychological mixtures. Each of them was intended to achieve according to the height of the force he brought through, to become perfected in that force, and that means to run through the whole gamut and range of that force and bring each side of it to perfection.

There was, for example, a Saracen Knight, Sir Palomedes. It is said devoutly by the medieval writers that he was converted to Christianity, but that, I think, was not precisely Merlin's meaning. That Knight would be beyond an especial creed, but he would have started his development in one creed, in his case Mohammedanism. He would have brought that Mohammedanism into alignment with other creeds and have been able, therefore, to have understood Christianity not less well but better. He was a great Knight, in no way less spiritually aspiring or good in intention than the other Knights.

He is involved in the Legend with two very great Knights, Lancelot and Tristram, of whom I will speak together because they are somewhat like each other. They represent two aspects of a certain condition, and you will recall – those of you who know the Legends well – that Merlin himself called attention to those two Knights as outstanding ones and great beyond most. They are each made especially memorable by one particular thing, the great tragedy of ill-advised love – or so the ordinary legend writer has described it – and, indeed, all things till well understood must be ill-advised. They are much alike but the difference between them is that Tristram died without being able to see beyond his own particular tragedy, while Lancelot died being able to see beyond his. Of course you must take with very many grains of salt the constant asseverations of medieval writers of the retiring into convents and monasteries in sign of repentance. Those things were simply added to conform with the preconceived ideas of the times, but the fact is that you see in the adventures of the Knights tremendous struggles of various kinds but especially against the deeper forces of nature. They all had to fight and overcome their enemies and they all had to learn that thing very hard to learn until the initiate is much progressed, the deep truth of vertical polarity; and for that they went through this tragedy and terror, day in and day out, till they were able to see beyond it, not because it was wicked or not to be understood

but because it was something that was to be developed into
yet another thing, and something that must aid growth and
not stop it – a very great truth to learn, my brethren, for all
of us human beings, and the deeper and the stronger the
human being probably the more difficult to learn, but also,
the greater victory.

Then, among other types, I will take two outstanding
examples, one of them not human at all. We have talked of
the faery women, but there are also the faery men belonging
to the Legend who have, indeed, their place and who should
be very carefully studied and considered. This particular faery
man of whom I will now speak was King Arthur's brother-in-
law, the faery husband of Morgan le Fay, Uriens of Gore, who
was indeed a very good Knight of the Round Table and one
of the first to be admitted. Some say that he was the King of
the Gnomes. You may think of him so, but he was in fact an
Elemental Being, an Elemental Being mated with an Atlantean
Priestess, who, it may be said, behaved exceedingly badly and
wickedly towards him. He indeed had the virtues of the almost
redeemed Elemental within him, behaving, though not a man
in the ordinary sense, as a true Knight, true to his own ideas
and his own type of Elemental conditions, and developing
from these into human conditions more and more as he made
perfect the "siege" provided for him by Merlin and took his
seat therein. He was a very good type and a true Knight,
dependable when he lent his help and a type that all people
who have in them a great deal of the Elemental power and
much of the non-human irresponsibility, might very well study
and follow.

Now we come to another type, more remarkable really than
any because all the basis of the rest was developed within
him so that he was able, entirely and early, to put away the
conditions of Earth from him and enter into the higher life of
the Mysteries, and this is Galahad. The mystery of Galahad is
a very deep one and a long one to explain, and it, too, is flawed

with the flowery sentimentality of ladies' pretty talk and with the medieval Church's interpretation so that he has become to certain eyes a rather pale, washed-out figure that might just as well have been a monk, whereas, indeed, he was much more than that. The purity for which he was so famous must be considered in the same light as that, for instance, of Pallas Athene; it means the undivided will, the wholeness of purpose which looks neither to the right hand nor to the left hand but continues through life and death into achievement. That is the true purity; as to the other merely physical kind of which so much is made, there are references which suggest that it was not exactly as was said: he was a true priest whose spiritual ability and whose vertical polarity were absolutely balanced with the horizontal kind of polarity, and neither did the other damage as is the case with the less pure or the impure, and that is the true meaning of Galahad. You will recall that Merlin especially contrived for this Knight the Siege Perilous, the special chair at the Round Table where none other could sit but him who was both perfect Knight and perfect Priest, fit to go on and to become a Master in the end, fit to join the Company of Merlin and of Merlin's Master in the end, and quicker than many of the other Knights. That, my brethren, if you will forget the "pretty-prettiness" about the Legend, is the true meaning of Galahad, a Knight that was indeed a soul of flashing steel. There was nothing effeminate or over-gentle about him, or he could not have gained to where he did gain.

You may also remember how this Siege Perilous being constructed, gave great fear to many of the Knights, for only Galahad could sit there. Now why was it perilous? The other Seats were not said to be perilous, though each had great symbology and teaching connected with it. I will tell you why it was perilous and why Merlin gave such special instructions about it. It was the Seat of a type and condition rather than of a man – as indeed were all – and it was a perilous seat because it was meant for one who had reached a certain condition of height of character and understanding, and who would, therefore, have a very terrible fall did he fall. Galahad, as you know, did not fall, but Merlin's warning is kept for us in the title which the Arch-Mage gave to Galahad's Chair at the Table Round.

As to the appearance, in the legends, of the Lord Jesus, they may very well be true, but remember that the whole Legend is founded on what is much older than Christianity and references to the great superhuman beings, such as the Lord Jesus, may also refer to yet others of the Great Ones who have gone on before. Do not let us forget that, for when we have developed to a certain point we must remember all of the Masters and not be able to think only of one; that is for the exoteric religion.

I have not spoken of the chief Knight, Arthur himself, for he has already been very much studied, but he counts as one of the Knights, of course, as well as their head, and you know how his varying conditions were brought about; how his fall came, as with other men, through his own fault; how Merlin gave him his strange birth and watched over his destiny; how he had the strange experiences with the faery women, the teaching of the etheric and astral planes, before he was truly fitted to have that teaching and that this etheric and astral condition, wrongly used, to some extent, took his power as a man away as it will do if injudiciously handled.

With one of these adventures a son was born, Mordred, the son who eventually slew him; and in Mordred as a symbol there is also much teaching – Mordred, the son of Arthur and Morgan, the usurper of the Kingdom, the one who made the great trouble among Lancelot and Guinevere and Arthur, the one who disturbed that great triad and finally brought it to ruin, Mordred the Qliphothic figure, for so he was. The legend is that he was born on May Day, that great Celtic season of witchcraft and Elemental force which can be so great and so high and can be also so positively evil when mishandled.

So, briefly, you have these tremendous symbols borne in our Island Mysteries but brought over from Atlantis and used again here in guise of a story, a story which has spread over the whole of Europe, for all the Knights came from different places and with Arthur's death they dispersed to their homes again, having learnt the lesson of the Table Round, giving themselves finally to their utmost achievement before leaving the physical plane. They took back to the countries of their origin the great Seed Atom of the Legend of the Table and it grew and fostered in other places; above all, in Spain, Italy and France and parts of Germany; while all over Britain you have various places where the germ has sprung into seed in local legends also.

I would have all of you think well of this great teaching, this Table Round which was drawn from all ranks, all races, all creeds, all evolutions, to bring each to the summit of its evolutionary power. And remember that the Forces which brought this Legend especially to our own race are about us all again, and we renew again the story in each one of us, holding within each one of us all the Archetypes, Archetypes of our own supreme development, which is, indeed, the development of the Spirit itself and the using of the Personality as an instrument for that development and thus being warned not to make the mistake of using the Personality only and living in it and forgetting the rest.

So, indeed, was the great Table also another symbol, for it was a perfect circle, the complete circle of the evolution of Man, the complete circle of his whole being, Personality, spiritual development, Seed Atom, and all, one complete round of the individual and of the evolution. So you should consider it, and grateful indeed should you be to him who, under the name of Merlin brought in ancient days this great symbol from beyond the stars to us. Let us be worthy of that teaching, my brethren, we do not wait all the time to be told the thing; we ourselves spell it out, spell out with tears of blood each message for ourselves. Then, when we have set out to do that, One from beyond will come bearing Bread and Wine of a fuller teaching and the development of knowledge, and so shall it be with all of you who endeavour to learn the teaching of the Table Round.

The Ladies

The legends of the Grail are very intricate and somewhat entangled but if they are followed out and the pattern can be discerned, you find notable analogies and similarities among all the types of women. These types are great keynotes with which we have again to deal in the Aquarian Mysteries, and in all these tales you fill find they follow in forms, as it were, of three or of four.

There are four women with whom the legend of Arthur himself opens. He is married to Guinevere and he has three half-sisters, and these three half-sisters in another guise, and two with different names, take him to his rest in the end. They are archetypal figures.

Let us first consider his mother and then his wife, and remember that in going over this story you must put from you all the foolish apologetics of medieval would-be "Christian" comentators, and you must also put from you as far as you can the confusion resulting from the mingling in one, by various writers on these figures, of the many tales which rose from one great source. Arthur's mother was an Atlantean Princess who had three daughters by another husband, or other husbands, than the father of Arthur. Then she was used, with what may seem to many as the old Atlantean ruthlessness, to bear a child at the dictates of Merlin and in a manner especially chosen by him to ensure the right king for the race. She, as a Princess of Atlantis, was one of the Sacred Clan, brought up therefore with full knowledge of the old Atlantean teaching of the priests and of the kingly race. She knew all the Temple formulae and the habits of the courts of Atlantis but she had had to put these to some extent to one side while she lived the ordinary life of the great lady of that time in Britain, yet in her children, partly British and partly Atlantean, are all these ancient symbols expressed.

There is Arthur specially bred and born and chosen to become even as was a Priest-King of Atlantis, and there are the three daughters, strange symbolic types of mystical women. One of these is the Queen of Orkney, Morgawse – so famous for her beauty that she sought to rival Guinevere but failed: she is the type of the woman of the world, successful in the sphere of Malkuth but not able to contact the spheres beyond. Then there is Arthur's second sister, the Queen of Garlot whose name is Elaine: she is the rather undeveloped, ordinary type of which there are many hundreds. And there is the third, Morgan, who was sent to a school of magic and initiation, very respectably called a nunnery in the medieval story – but not at all like what you call a nunnery – and who became proficient in the ancient arts of Atlantis: she is the type of "magician".

As you see, all these women had it in them to develop perfectly, but they did not do so; they were all failures in various ways and had to come back on another arc to do their work again.

Then you have Guinevere herself, the Queen. She should really have been the Queen-Priestess of Atlantean conception but she, too, failed, partly through her own fault, partly through Arthur's fault. It was Merlin who brought her to Arthur's notice and who specially recommended her for his mate as one who had within her all the potentialities of the great Atlantean system, and, according to some writers, the Table Round was Guinevere's dowry and finally decided Arthur in choosing this particular bride, for in the first instance Merlin had given the Table to Guinevere's father. There is much teaching in that. Were there ever such tremendous, almost alarming potentialities involved within a marriage – a marriage made with the Table Round so to speak.

Then we have yet another form of woman, the "faery woman" of whom there are several examples in the legend. There is the Lady of the Lake, several lesser Ladies of the Lake, earth-spirits and faeries, and also Morgan le Fay, who though strictly speaking not herself an Elemental, had learned to use the Elemental power and had married a non-human therefore ranking in a sense among the "faery women". Here we come to Arthur's great fall in the matter of matrimony, because owing to his relationship with these two faery women in particular, the Lady of the Lake and his half-sister Morgan, he was unable to fulfil his duties as a husband to his Queen, and the whole relationship became split, for she was mated to Lancelot but Queen to Arthur.

What exactly does this relationship with the faery women mean? It means a very special and, to modern ears, unusual type of polarity working with the forces of magnetism upon the inner planes, a type of working which was used in Atlantis and was one of the Temple secrets. This magnetic force, contacted on the inner planes and on the Elemental sub-planes with non-human beings, had a very great effect upon the human being on the Earth plane for it was liable to close down his normal potency as a man on that plane unless worked, as in Atlantis, with the greatest dedication and care. Had Merlin watched over Arthur in those ways certain difficulties might not have arisen, but, also, Arthur no doubt bore a certain karmic liability which had to be worked out.

At the end of Arthur's career you find once more those three strange women coming in the barge to meet him, with great wailing and great sorrow. These women were still his sisters but two of them bore other names indicating that they had redeemed themselves and passed to another level whence they were able to come and bring Arthur away. The first of the three mourning Queens is Morgan le Fay – but now gone to her right place as Queen of the Land of Rest and Queen of the Healing Power; and the second is she who was the worldly woman

Margawse, but who now is called the Queen of Northgalis, and she has become a seer; the third is the ordinary woman, Elaine, Arthur's second sister, now called the Queen of the Wasteland having become a recluse, which is to say an initiate. So here you have all three Queens again, in themselves one person but developed in three different aspects of initiation and, therefore, fitted to initiate Arthur in the spiritual sense of the inner planes which was what he lacked.

And with these archetypal figures you see associated the two great feminine symbols of the Grail – the Stone and the Cup, the Stone relating more to the magical powers of ancient days, and the Grail to the initiated powers of spiritual development. Thus there are priestesses of the Stone and priestesses of the Cup, but each should be a priestess of both these symbols.

The Stone had a great deal of significance in ancient days for it was a definitely magical weapon; it was said to speak and to move and to foretell the future. It was the instrument of destiny.

The Cup was the symbol of inspiration.

The knowledge of destiny and the ability to inspire are two great powers of woman. The knowledge of destiny is much more than sorcery; it is the innate knowledge of type and it includes the ability to educate and guide a type according to the sort of power that type is meant to have. The Cup of Inspiration is the way by which the soul is meant to go and to show forth its power upon every level. In this way in Atlantis were the priestesses taught to be ministrants of the Grail and of the powers of the Stone.

This is a brief summary of the Atlantean ideal of women which was grafted on to the Arthurian Legend. This ideal, as you know, like the ideal of the Knights, largely failed since there are always two sides to each figure, and it is only by the welding of these two sides in correct proportion that the true development of the human being is carried through rightly.

There was one case where it was never carried through, nor ever could be, the case of Mordred, who represents the Qliphothic power only, born, as he was, from the unbalanced force of two souls who could have been and should have been at a higher level of development, namely Arthur and Morgan – yet Mordred too is a part of each man and woman.

You must put from your minds the ecclesiastical over-refinements of the legend which would make nuns and monks of Lancelot and Guinevere and the rest; that indeed was not so. It was Lancelot who buried Guinevere by Arthur after being instructed from the inner planes to do so.

These great archetypal figures which are in all of us, far more than ecclesiastical fancy would make them, represent the stages of the soul from the ancient initiations of Atlantis to what should have been a newer and higher grade of initiation in the new land of Britain. This failed and the cycle had to return again on a new arc for its fulfilment; therefore the Aquarian Grail and the Aquarian Round Table are now working in our midst; the root of Atlantis is working to its full blossoming, and all these types repeated as they are frequently in confusion are in each one of you. It is more especially of the feminine Pillar of which I now speak. Realise, my daughters, that each of these queens and faery women and recluses from the world, is in each of you. Yours it is to be ministrants of the Stone and Cup according to your several abilities and levels – and in so being can all complete the Table Round.

The Table Round is more especially connected with the knights but in a sense the Grail is more especially connected with the women, and in the largest sense of all one represents the masculine Pillar and the other the feminine. It is a never-ending cycle, a never-ending unfolding of truth, and the more you dwell on these ancient tales the more will the great archetypes behind them bring down their force to you. The great forces of Atlantis have never been surpassed as prototypes of the Mysteries – the Priest-King, the Queen-Priestess, the great

Magician, the Wise Woman, the Faery Woman, the initiated Woman – the cycle does indeed contain them all in proportion of grade.

Morgan le Fay
[Directed Reverie]

"...and the third sister (i.e. of King Arthur) Morgan le Fay was put to school in a nunnery: and then she learned so much that she was a great clerk of nigromancy". Malory.

The Education of Morgan le Fay

Morgan was the youngest daughter of Igraine and Gorlois Duke of Cornwall, her first husband. Igraine was an Atlantean princess of the sacred Clan whose ancestors had escaped to Britain on the fall of Ruta.

Different forms of Atlantean magical mating were used by Merlin to bring about the births of Arthur and of his half-sisters Margawse and Morgan. In the latter case, an over-shadowing was caused by non-human Adepts on the inner planes.

One of the Atlantean Colonies which had settled in Britain founded a College of Women for the education of girls of royal and noble parentage. Its curriculum derived to some extent from the Temple-education of Ruta but had developed certain differences. The teachers were Druidesses and not Christian "nuns". The Head of this College was an Arch-Druidess of great magical power and knowledge who had been a High Priestess of the goddess Brigantia in the Hibernian Mysteries. She it was who first made Beckary a "little Ireland" long before the time of the Christian nunnery of St. Bride; in far later days the forces of St. Bride in Glastonbury fell heir to much of the great Hibernian Tradition, and periods, people and circumstances have become intermingled in the popular legend.

As in the case of the male Druid System, the girls of the Druidesses' College were divided into three grades of which Arthur's three step-sisters were respective members. These grades were somewhat like the three Lesser Mystery Degrees of a Fraternity.

The First Degree was named "The Spinners" and its members were taught to concentrate on the arts and crafts practised by great ladies of the time. It was an initiation of Malkuth, and these girls were not expected to be especially proficient in occultism. Attention and reverence, however, was especially paid to the exoteric worship of the gods. Elaine, Arthur's step-sister was in this Degree. She is variously named and aspected as wife of King Nentres of Garlot and Queen of the Wastelands.

The Second Degree was that of "The Wise Maidens". The girls of this grade were taught the occult principles behind women's life and work, and were instructed in herbal and medical skill. They were also tuaght the "Seven Secret Songs" synthesising the message of the Seven Atlantean Races. They were also instructed in the art of relating tales to entertain company. Such tales were expected to "come alive" and to be magically "built". Of this Degree Arthur's step-sister Margawse was a member. She was the mother of Gawain and his brothers and was Queen of Orkney. Most legends also describe her as the mother of Arthur's son and enemy, Mordred.

The Third and highest Degree in the College of Women was that of "The Fays", i.e. fairy women – not denizens of Elfland but women who were entirely or partly human. These were mistresses of magical art and wisdom. It was to this grade that Arthur's youngest step-sister Morgan belonged. The maidens in this Degree were initiated into the ancient secrets of Atlantis which included the principles behind magical mating and shape-shifting. Morgan outstripped her companions in magical attainment and fell into the temptation of using her proficiency for her own ends.

She was Merlin's pupil in the higher magic but also studied under another non-human Master. The latter Being appears to have been the one who overshadowed her birth and by whom she was withdrawn at the end to the inner Avalon to which she really belonged. It was intended that she should bring healing and growth on this Avalonian plane to those souls whom she had harmed on earth. The Water-Temple of Hod is connected with the Barge of Avalon in which Arthur was taken at death, and Morgan is the Psychopompos of this sphere, at a certain level of the Celtic Initiation system – the Devachanic plane of the Eastern tradition – to which King Arthur, Ogier the Dane, Thomas the Rhymer and others were withdrawn when summoned by its Queen.

The Legend of Morgan and the Scabbard of Excalibur which she stole for her own ends from Arthur.

This side of Morgan was strongly Atlantean showing her power as a shape-shifter and one versed in magical mating. She would transform herself and others into large stones and change back afterwards when the danger of recognition was past. The Scabbard related to the direction of magical mating and the sheath of Excalibur stolen from its owner and the Sword intended for it is significant of this. Morgan, surrounded by the murmur of the Forest, held the Scabbard on her knee and the "King of the Wood" and other elfin entities tried to grab it. The Scabbard, taken from its right surroundings, could thus be used as an instrument of "Confusion" – the evil side of the Ring Chaos.

Like Excalibur, the Scabbard was personalised and meant to be polarised only with its rightful sword. The sheath was black and silver damascened with strange symbols and studded with pearls and other jewels; it was also winged at the top like the Caduceus to which it bore a faint analogy for it was the wisdom of the power of polarity. According to Merlin, the Scabbard was the most important part of the Sword and therefore was Arthur especially charged never to lose it.

The Barge of Avalon

This is the ancient Barge of Death and/or some forms of initiation. As Miss Weston says, there is a link between the Barge and the three mourning Queens with the "Wailing Women" in the Mysteries of Tammuz. There is also a link with the Egyptian Boat of a Million Years which bore the Pharoahs down the Nile to burial while the goddesses Isis and Nephthys stood guard over the corpse on its last journey.

The Barge of Avalon was moored in a secret and remote water waiting till it was wanted. It seems that the Barge comes from across the Atlantic coasting southern Ireland before entering the Bristol Channel and the Severn marshes. Intimately connected with its mooring-place is a whirlpool which does not exist on earth.

When the time comes for the Barge to sail it is loosed by unseen hands and starts off alone and empty, stopping at certain stages of its course; and these stages are processes of the human spirit. Morgan le Fay enters the Barge first at one of these stopping-places. Further on, at another stage, her two sisters greet and join her and begin their wailing chant, for they are "Assessors". In this case they weep because they realise what is entailed by the judgement they have delivered and it is delivered in sorrowful love and not in revenge or delight in chastisement. Morgan herself, however, is not an "Assessor" for, like Ishtar in the Mysteries of Tammuz, she redeems the wrong she has done to the dead man in life by taking the same journey to the Land-of-no-Return that she may be a Wayshower to his soul.

The last halt of the Barge, before it reaches the shore of Avalon, is to take on board the Lady of the Lake who sits motionless till the Sword is thrown into the Lake and then gives the signal to approach the shore. The Lady of the Lake is concerned with the life on Malkuth and the three Queens with life after death and with Karmic debt. The Barge is painted black and the inner plane figures within it are shadowy. The Lady of the Lake and Morgan le Fay are robed respectively in white and dark opalescence like aspects of strange water.

When at last the sword Excalibur is thrown into the Lake by Bedivere at Arthur's command, it is the signal for the Barge to approach the shore and put the dying King on board. For that signal Arthur impatiently and anxiously waited and the failure of the Knight to give the signal to the inner planes must have caused the King acute agony.

Elaine of Carbonek

Grades of initiation are shown in the life of Elaine. Her experience in the burning bath can be connected with karma and the separation of the emotions from the instincts. After the birth of Galahad (Tiphareth) the various experiences of bringing up the child, nursing the mentally sick Lancelot etc., are symbolic of the Paths leading from Tiphareth. There is a Daath contact in the devotion and detachment of Elaine towards the Elemental life and the needs of the Work. She helped Lancelot's Higher Self to fulfil its destiny and she served the Racial Spirit by giving birth to a Grail Custodian, using her Personality as a vehicle for the Great Work. She was born of a "priest" and trained from childhood – signifying the initiate of very early contacts. The "Carbonek state" represents the Grail conditions secretly existing in the Wastelands.

Note

[1] A rite based upon the Holy Grail written by the then Warden, Arthur Chichester, and regularly performed.

The Arthurian Formula
Part Three
Margaret Lumley Brown

The Threads of the Labyrinth

The Legend

Disabuse your minds of "historicity". The Tradition is that the Legend is a Mystery Tale brought over from Atlantis – a tale which exists in many forms and many lands but which has such a strongly developed British form that we are justified in counting it among the esoteric Mysteries of these Islands.

Like all esoteric Mysteries, the Legend develops with the souls it trains and is not intended to be static either in psychology or geography. Its "countries" and "events" are those of the soul itself; all places and people can have their share.

However, since certain spots have been hallowed by an especial connection with the Legend, those spots (though by no means forming essential contacts) may well be easier, by reason of one's imagination and sentiment, to build strong associations in the mind.

"We build this Temple anew each time the Lodge is set up" – we make the contact first in the heart and mind whether that contact be Chaldea, Jerusalem or Avalon. History, archaeology and geography are little connected with the data of occultism which is based on oral tradition, meditative reverie and symbolism.

The Places

The places are, in fact, the centres and surroundings in which certain forces work. These places built in the imagination are equivalent to "Lodges" or "Shrines". Their description may be based on that of the same places in the Legend, or they may be created by the Magus even as he creates descriptions in a path-working. It is interesting to note that, in regard to many Arthurian traditions, Cornwall seems important. Arthur was born there; his mother, his wife and the Round Table all came from there. Moreover it is the site of the drowned land of Lyonesse, that last piece of the drowned Continent of Atlantis.

One may say there are four principal centres of force – Carbonek, Camelot, Caerleon and the Lake. The Lake is the force of the karma of Atlantis which lies drowned beneath it and it is the Sword of the Lords of the Shining Face which rises in it and is, in the end, returned to it.

As the Legend is a legend of life, all Sephiroth of the Tree can contain it in some aspect – the three Castles, I think, align well with the Pillars. Caerleon is the force of Endurance whence comes vertical polarity; Camelot the force of Energy and the earlier stages of horizontal polarity. (These are suggestions and you must work them out for yourself). Carbonek is as the Middle Pillar of consciousness which contains all aspects of the Grail. Naturally Caerleon links up also with Geburah, Camelot with Netzach and Carbonek with Tiphareth and Daath. The Lake could be on Yesod for it corresponds with the designing of the representations which rise up from the "framework" of Atlantis.

There are of course many other castles and other centres but these are the more important ones.

I count the Arthurian Legend of such importance because the inner circle of the Fraternity may be counted as founded on its implications. Although of course the broad outlines of the Western Tradition come from the Qabalah, we have based our own Fraternity teachings (in their individual sense) especially on *The Cosmic Doctrine* and on the Arthurian Cycle as well as on the Qabalistic doctrines.

There are two main motifs which run through the Arthurian Cycle – the Grail and the Table Round. The twain are inextricably linked and form a Vesica Piscis. The Grail refers to the development of the individual; the Table Round to that of the Group. Actually the Table, like the Chalice, works out (but in the Group sense) upon the levels of the Middle Pillar. It begins with the control and use of its environment for the good of the Group it represents; then it works (like the Earthen Cup) for the good of others; then it sacrifices itself for other groups or for one special group; then it becomes a ritual group; then an illuminated group; finally the Table Round perfects its own type and becomes the full spiritual group for which it was designed at which all Grail-Finders sit.

The group has to break up so that its members can develop individually before rejoining each other in the end, when the Grail is placed on the Table, since all have attained it and therefore it can appear equally to all. The Table Round holds the Force which was meant to be especially demonstrated by the West – the concrete mind so developed that it realises Truth and passes into the realm of spirit.

The Threads of the Labyrinth

This is not a misnomer. There are so many subtle stresses within the Legend which have been yet further tangled by pious tales, that we have inevitably to unravel a vast skein in which a story far older than Christianity has been Christianised into forms acceptable to the Middle Ages.

Thus the Sacred Clan becomes a kind of Table of Arthur's kin and that of his friends. Hermits and nuns and Kings, Queens and Knights are the Priests and Warriors and their womenfolk.

The lands and buildings with their strange evocative names are not necessarily etymological but sound-powers inherited from an ancient secret language.

Such "history" as can be found is esoteric tradition and not documented facts. It is a Stellar Legend based on the working out of Earth's development according to the Plan shown in the Great Bear. This constellation is also appropriately known as Arthur's Wain. The crest and standard and surname of the King are drawn from the great Dragon constellation of ancient cosmogony which held the former Pole Star. Thus the House of Pendragon brings through the old truths into the Aquarian Age. I would say also that the great "working out" of God in three Aspects is repeated again and again. There is a threefold significance in the stages of the principal characters, i.e. Arthur's three sisters who can be aligned with the Mourning Queens of the Barge of Avalon; the three goddess-forms met by Euain; the three Guineveres; the three stages of child, active adult and sage shown by Merlin and many of the Knights. This is a brief summary of the environment of the Legend and we may now move on to the characters.

I would also point out here that the whole gist of the Grail Ceremony of this Fraternity came through from the inner planes and for those who hear with the inner ear contains not merely a fine ritual but a definite form of teaching.

We will now begin to work on the various characters of the Legend.

Merlin

Just as the Compassion Aspect came through the Christ Force into the various teachers who brought that Force into contact with humanity, so does the Divine Wisdom also operate through teaching channels in the same way. Thus it was said there were several forms of Hermes and Thoth. One of these forms came, according to esoteric tradition, to Britain in very early ages. This being – "Merlin" – came from Atlantis to Ireland and founded there the great Hibernian Mysteries. Then he crossed to the other Islands of Britain at a different date and continued the same teaching but from another angle. In parentage and method of birth, Merlin was only semi-human. A vehicle of manifestation was built through a great Atlantean High Priestess and a Lord of Flame. As with many of the great teachers, Merlin manifested himself both as child and as adult. His mandate was to bring to the Fifth Root Race the plan of the ultimate group-development which should become a "Council of the Gods". This mandate involved the coming of a new Pole Star (in the Little Bear) and the influence of the Earth's great prototype in the Great Bear. He implanted what we might call blueprints both of monarchy and of the social group which have always worked out in a special way in these Islands, and it was Merlin who gave us a sidereal Magna Carta and Habeas Corpus. The fact that these great esoteric messages were given to the West through the British Isles is of great significance and cannot be quite forgotten despite our many national and racial failings.

Somewhat like Our Lord, many thousands of years later, Merlin ended his teachings to humanity by descent into the Underworld where the Elementals were given a version of the training given previously to men. From all this of course has been built up the legend of Vivienne etc., and the imprisonment of the Arch-Mage in the tree or the cave.

Even in the legends Merlin appeared in several forms, suggesting that he built an etheric shape at will, as the Inner Plane Adepti have so often done. Apart from this, shape-shifting and esoteric mating were definite forms of Atlantean magic, and we know that Merlin arranged an esoteric means for the conception of Arthur. The Table Round was brought to Cornwall probably from Ireland but under another name, for the Dial of Evolutionary Phases was in Atlantis and doubtless entered into the Hibernian Mysteries. On this Dial was a certain point which indicated what we now call "crossing the Abyss". This point was symbolised by the Siege Perilous.

The teaching given by Merlin was not so much of profound Cosmic facts but of the nature of Man and of the development of a certain national type as we have said before and herein lies the deeper secret of the British Isles.

Asked if the actual Merlin could be still contacted, the communicator answered: "even as Hermes can still be contacted".

Arthur

Arthur was meant to be the Priest-King of these Islands and thus to carry on the tradition of Atlantis. In the Lost Continent the chief ruler was chosen before birth which was carefully planned by esoteric means. After birth, special training both as warrior and priest-magician were given to the future ruler. Hence the legends of Arthur's prowess, for actually he was set to perform esoteric tests and, to put it briefly, he achieved as a warrior but failed as a priest. Hence also, all the legends woven round Excalibur. "Take me up" was written on one side of the magic weapon and "Cast me away" on the other. Arthur indeed could take up the Sword but only cast it away by proxy until the time at length should come of his return.

(At this time a tremendous "Arthur" force swept into the room. It was a mass of iron and strength, of blood and slime, but inchoate. Something in it suggested the Isle of Man for some reason. It was realised that it represented the marvellous potentiality of Man – still incomplete and largely unformed.)

We have to consider Arthur's kin if we are to understand his life. His mother Igraine was an Atlantean princess probably

descended from the Sacred Clan. Uther, his father through
Merlin's strategy, was of the ancient royal blood of Britain
– that blood had been established on the throne in a previous
Atlantean migration and not only that but held in its stream
Hibernian and Lemurian strains symbolised by the Dragon
constellation. This family and its kin had in very remote
days already established a brotherhood of esoteric warriors
– "the Pendragonship". To re-establish this as well as to
make its hereditary leader the father of a future race of kings
was Merlin's object, Thus the old "Pendragonship" became
merged in the Knighthood of the Table Round with Uther's
son both as Pendragon and leader of the Knights of Merlin's
newer Order of chivalry. Lyonesse and the Scilly Isles were
outposts of the Lost Continent, and from Camelaird, one of
these districts, first came the Table Round as dowry of the
daughter of the King of Camelaird – Guinevere. Merlin on
one of his previous visits to these Islands had left the teaching
and institution of the Table Round in Camelaird and now
requisitioned it for the whole of Arthur's Kingdom.

Now we have to come to a long and intricate discourse
on Arthur's relationship with women: the Faery Women and
Guinevere.

The Faery Women

These "Faery Women" are names given by monkish medieval
tradition to great Atlantean female "Chiefs" and/or High
Priestesses of certain ancient cults. When Merlin had
established the Atlantean laws and teachings on a large scale
and the Colony from the Lost Continent increased and spread
all over Britain, the "Faery Women" also sought to establish
their influence.

The Lady of the Lake

The Lady of the Lake was one of the feminine hierarchy
of matriarchal powers which remained in Atlantis from yet

remoter days. When differentiation of the sexes took place, such powers were of the utmost help in teaching the new adjustments to humanity. Moreover, in Atlantis, the training and development of the astral life and of emotion first took place. The Water Element is connected with the female sex and a lake has always been a sacred Temple symbol and the astral lake contained the palace and dominion of the Chief "Lady" of the Lake who lived there with her attendant "ladies" to whom she taught her arts and whom she trained as types of polarity priestesses who were, in their turn, to instruct others. Like many other Arthurian characters she (the Lady of the Lake) had a child-form (Nimué or Vivienne, in which she "beguiled" Merlin) and an adult-form in which she instructed and helped humans. Merlin sent Arthur to her for sex initiation and Lancelot was in childhood drawn by her into the Lake and brought up and taught by her till he was fitted to express his manhood in the world of men. Thus the Sword given by and returned to the Great Water was a male symbol implying the fighting and sexual aspects of manhood. (All this has been already set down in the first edition of the Arthurian Formula and with certain additions and amendments, I still endorse the first edition).

We must remember that Cornwall has an especial Arthurian connection linking up the Duchy with both Ireland and Atlantis and no doubt weaving together legends deriving from the Irish and Cornish Atlantean settlements. We will continue with the study of the Lady of the Lake. This being was an aspect of the Goddess and as are sea and lake "female" beings – also connected with Lunar power. She worked potently on both astral and physical planes and, in those primeval days, there was very little demarcation between inner and outer levels of consciousness, but she was non-human. With her I align the first initiation into sex and training of boys in sex which was practised by the older women of experience in the Temple on earth.

With the Queen of the Lake and her Ladies this initiation was on the astral plane. She also trained women in this way and as a Goddess of Atlantis was invoked upon these secret teachings in the Priesthood. Debased memories of these matters passed into the European Witch cult. These inner plane experiences are, however, Temple workings and require purity of motive and dedication every bit as much as if taking place in the earth sphere. It was here that Arthur failed. He could not or would not "earth" the results of his training with a human being like Guinevere, whose training was, as a maiden, his responsibility to carry out. In short, he found a woman savourless after a Goddess. Lancelot was the Lady of the Lake's better pupil. She not only trained his youth but reared his childhood but though he, unlike Arthur, could "earth" his inner plane teachings, he could not restrain the forces of glamour which surrounded his earthly experiences. Hence his tragedy and his "madness". Through him, however, as well as through her husband, Guinevere received the auric contacts of the Goddess, for magnetism is in fact transmitted far more profoundly than physiological actions which of themselves only affect the animal conditions. In her own sphere the Lady of the Lake was a Queen and a magician but she aspired to higher contacts than she could reach alone. This entailed training and tests which would take much time. Thus, she persuaded Merlin through her own specialised knowledge into passing on to her some of his special knowledge before she was fitted to receive it.

The Lady of the Lake correlates with that Lunar aspect of the Goddess which instructs and guides and the astral force she used – which works in dreams – is of the nature of Lilith. Had she not sought after power and been content to gain her place at the right time under Merlin's tuition, she would have coalesced with the rest of the great Isiac Archetype.

Now we must hasten on with the other sides of this script.

N.B. My findings do not always correspond with Malory, for

they are drawn not only from another source but are designed to be of special use in this Fraternity. The Lady of the Lake was not meant to mate with Merlin because she was not of his grade.

Morgan le Fay

The two Faery Women of the Legend are the Lady of the Lake who was an astral being and Morgan le Fay who was a pupil of Merlin and a priestess of the ancient Mysteries. Morgan's mother was Igraine, a princess of the Sacred Clan of Atlantis; (thus she was Arthur's half-sister) but her father was Igraine's first husband Gorlais who was not royal but an overlord of the ancient Cornish stock i.e. a line descended from the giants of pre-human race. We shall better understand the mission of the Faery Women if we take the Legend backward. In the Barge of Fate which fetches Arthur to Avalon are Nimué and three "mourning Queens" – the last three can all be aligned with Arthur's half-sisters and their chief is Morgan le Fay who is also the Queen of Avalon. Thus the Faery Women who so influenced Arthur's life meet him again in the hour of his death for all four mystical women are seen to be Archetypes of Fate and the water bearing them across (whether lake or sea or the River Styx) is the boundary between two worlds. Although the Fates are usually three, Venus Urania is in certain tales reckoned as one of them and this may account for the last visit of the Lady of the Lake for she belongs to the White Isis aspect.

Morgan is sent to an Atlantean women's Order to be taught the ancient magic. This is termed a "nunnery" and she became proficient enough in magic to become Merlin's pupil. She is not, like the Lady of the Lake, a priestess of the White Isis but of the Dark. Neither does she (Morgan) belong to Water and Moon but to the sunset and the inner side of Malkuth and to the First Moon and the Underworld and the Well of Memory wherein are mirrored Tir-nan-Og and the Hesperides. She is

Earth of Water which represents the primeval slime from which man and Earth arose. She is that part of the Venus Cult which had centres in the hills and underworld where her followers are spirited away for set periods as in the case of Thomas the Rhymer, Ogier, Tannhauser, etc. In the Arthurian Formula Morgan is aligned with the Temple Priestess who taught the science of magnetic polarity – (not always dependent on sexual mating though the latter necessarily included the former). The Lady of the Lake initiated the youth and Morgan, the Priestess or woman initiate, initiated the Squire into the romantic friendships, so that when he reached full knighthood he could himself initiate a human maiden. The Lady of the Lake was old in evolutionary status and Morgan was an initiated woman at the height of her beauty. Thus was the Arthurian Formula founded on the Atlantean Temple-working. We revived this teaching to serve the needs of the Aquarian Age and to make a traditional basis for the "new" morality. The Arthurian Tradition could thus be revived again on another level and in tune with the Mysteries. The true laws of polarity have rarely been properly understood, when they are you have a valuable key to mythology and also to psychology. This does not by any means exclude vertical polarity – rather is it a road to the perfected formation of the spiritual Androgyne. Dedication and impersonality are emphatically needed for the Arthurian Formula – in every case the failures in the Legend arose from this lack. There are many forms of polarity; there is both physical and etheric mating and strange systems of Cosmic union, the truth of which the medieval world admitted though it counted such things "of the Devil".

Morgan was mated by Merlin to Uriens of Gore (Uriens has reference to the legend of Orion – blood and urine i.e. Elemental and human). Uriens was King of the Gnomes – that, of course, is not the same as Ghob who is King of the Element of Earth. Morgan desired to contact the higher polarity forces and stole the scabbard of Excalibur from

Arthur. In plain language she mated with her brother to fulfil her ambition of gaining the higher polarity powers which the intermingling with the Lady of the Lake's aura had bestowed on him and which he was thus able to pass on to other women. From this unbalanced force Mordred was born. Had Morgan waited till she was of a higher grade, she would have earned the right to experiment in the higher magnetism with a suitable partner. Morgan disappeared and was never seen again till she comes, in quite a different aspect, to fetch Arthur in the Barge. She has by then realised her misdeeds and repented and passed on to the higher initiation – the "perfection of place and return to origins" known as the Island of the Blest. Thus, as good magicians should, this mistress of magic enters the sphere of Wisdom for she is a Hod figure – the Hod of Malkuth and the Earth of Water. She is an aspect of Medea on one side and of Persephone on the other. She is the type of human woman trained as a priestess and magician till she achieved adepthood.

The Lady of the Lake is a non-human being and an aspect of Luna or Artemis. Both the Lady of the Lake and Morgan le Fay represent respectively the wisdom of the instincts and the wisdom of the intuition which should work behind the complete esoteric development of the human woman.

Guinevere

It is more difficult to assess Guinevere than any of the characters. She has in the legends three forms or aspects and these can be aligned with the Moon phases and with tri-formed Diana. She was shown kindness by the Lady of the Lake but enmity by Morgan. She should have been the ideal Chief Woman just as Arthur should have been the ideal Chief Man, but, on that round of development, both failed. They will return again as one. This is why I have said that Guinevere represents the highest grade of the three grades formed respectively by Merlin, Arthur and the Queen. The two last taken together

form the Androgyne. But before the Androgyne arrives, the
levels of consciousness of the two sexes must be cleared as
well as developed till they achieve headship of the Kingdom
of Earth. Guinevere should have been Priestess-Queen to
Arthur's Priest-King. But in both cases these faculties were
split and did not work together. For Arthur could not be priest
in Malkuth and Guinevere could not be queen in Yesod.

The system of the Arthurian Legend is that of the working
out of polarity principles and of the realisations behind
magnetic mating on the inner as well as on the outer planes.
The various levels of relationship coalesce till the final
androgynous completion is reached and All is One and One is
All – that final achievement being, of course, concerned with
the two sides of one spirit and not with two separate spirits.
The Redemption of the Archetypes (which concerns the Inner
Greater Mysteries) has however to be carried out by stages
first, and these stages are borne by separate individuals.

The Round Table is Guinevere's dowry, Arthur's heritage
and Merlin's gift. Into these three grades, the whole Company
of the Table Round is divided according to their level of
development. There are those who have received the gift
and use it or not; there are those who realise it is their great
heritage and fight for it; there are those who bring it with them
into manifestation.

These three characters – Arthur, Merlin, Guinevere – are
the main triad of the Legend for it is through them that the
tale unfolds and they represent respectively, the Sun, the Star
and the Moon of our racial forces. The two Faery Women are
the shadows behind the throne, the Mert Goddesses or, if you
will, aspects of the Pillars of this Racial Temple.

We will divide the rest of the Company of the Table Round
into:

1.   Arthur's kin,
2.   Lancelot's kin,
3.   The other Knights,

4.   The Ladies,
5.   Other beings.

I have long wanted to have a synopsis of the full company of characters in the legend, but it was not possible to complete this during the compilation of the first Arthurian script.

Arthur's kin.

Mordred.

Arthur's child is Mordred, born of incest with his half-sister Morgan. (Some say Mordred's mother was Arthur's other sister Margawse, but this statement is not in keeping with the metaphysic of the legend). Mordred is the great unbalanced force let loose on the Kingdom by his father's fault. The father and son meet in mortal combat but finally the father gives the death blow to the son and the son wounds the father to death. Thus some of the karma is paid back there and then.

Mordred is the traitor that destroys his chief and his companions – a form of Set and of Judas in the legend. Yet the likeness to these does not only imply betrayal for Mordred is there to bring to birth a cycle of destruction which is meant to end in rebirth after disaster, though rebirth to another level. Mordred is Arthur's averse side and his Dweller on the Threshold and we know that the Dweller on the Threshold in esoteric teaching has to be transformed from a monster into an angelic figure. He (Mordred) was born at Beltane, that ancient festival when the creative fires if unbalanced become forces of destruction. Through his maternal grandfather Gorlois, he is united to the demonic giants of the Lemurian Sin. Through one side of his father and one side of his mother he descends from the Sacred Clan of Atlantis. For those of you who consider the Arthurian Archetypes, Mordred should be the great force of realisation, rather than of hate and his ultimate achievement cannot take place till Arthur himself returns and the next level (which is spiritual) of the legend takes precedence over the former failure. Morgan's sons are aligned with the sub-spheres of Malkuth and Mordred stands at the opposite end of the pole from Euain. The latter represents man's door to Kether and Mordred is Earth of Earth standing at the door of the Qliphoth for he is the instrument of destruction which is but another aspect of the instrument of redemption. He was conceived (if born at Beltane) in a season of the dark moon of the Sothic Tide in August and this could well have produced the currents of a great Hecate power working around his mother.

His three Brothers-in-Law,
(also Knights of the Table Round).

Uriens of Gore

This was the husband of Arthur's sister Morgan, married to her by Merlin. Uriens is the prototype of the Elemental force turned human — slow but sincere in development. Morgan tries to kill him but is stopped by their son Euain. Uriens is an aspect of Oberon — a King descended from the pre-human races and from the Celtic Underworld but advanced in evolution sufficiently to be the father of the spiritually developed Fifth Race man whose type is Euain. Uriens is King of Gore or Gower.

Lot of Orkney

This was the husband of Arthur's sister Margawse. He was Arthur's enemy and is King of Lothian and Orkney but these geographical names are of little value. He represents the brutal, dark side of the Norse power and is united to Margawse, Guinevere's rival in beauty and her enemy. (Margawse is an evil aspect of Freya). From this berserk valour and Venusian force issue four sons — Gawain, Gaheris, Gareth and Agravaine who also swell the Company of the Table Round.

Nentres of Garlot

This is the husband of Arthur's third sister. He is one of Arthur's Knights and King of Garlot which appears to be another name for Gower. I would say that Garlot represents another level of Gower from Uriens' and Morgan's Kingdom.

The King and Queen of Garlot had no children, but the Queen may be aligned with one of the three mourning Queens who come to fetch the dying Arthur in their barge. Very little otherwise is known of the King and Queen of Garlot.

His Nephews

The Sons of King Lot and Queen Margawse of Orkney

There were four of these Princes of Orkney. They were all famous among their uncle's Knights and their names are Gawain, Gaheris, Gareth and Agravaine.

Gawain

This, one of the greatest of the Company of Knights, seems to have been an "equaliser" or linker of the forces of sun, nature and pagan and Christian powers. As "the Hawk of May" he represents an aspect of Horus and the higher force of Beltane just as Mordred represents the lower. Gawain is strongly marked as a solar hero – his power waxing and waning with the sun and his encounter with the Green Knight at the Winter Solstice suggests a deep cosmic contact with an aspect of the Planetary Being – but this is only my interpretation. He (Gawain) finds the "Healing Herb" which is an aspect of the Grail in Nature. As a character he is fiery but dependable and essential like the sun. He is loyal to Arthur but a champion, though not a lover, of Guinevere; a friend to Lancelot till the later accidentally slays his beloved younger brother Gareth, when Gawain becomes Lancelot's implacable enemy till death brings forgiveness. The Nature magic of the Table Round works in him.

Gaheris

This is the type of the old soul in the young body. He is always thoughtful, controlled, gentle and loyal as well as brave. He is always the one who induces others to think a second time. He tries to make harmony and to induce the spirit of mercy as a part of Knighthood. He is killed in the fight arising when Lancelot carries off Guinevere who is condemned to be burnt. Lancelot is his friend and hero and also his slayer. Gaheris is an older edition of his brother Gareth and more upon the outer planes. They are really two characters of which one (Gareth) shows the deeper development of the other.

Gareth

This is the youngest of the House of Orkney. He is a fuller development of his elder brother Gaheris but his knowledge is deeper and his inner plane forces more those of an initiate in the world. Though of royal blood, he elects to work his way up from scullion to Knight, realising that all experience is valuable and that it is the spirit and not the hands that give dignity to the work. He teaches us that the least knightly tasks are some of the best preparation for Knighthood. His will is extremely single-pointed, unmoved by jeers, insolence and unkindness. He chooses Lancelot as his friend and hero and it is by Lancelot's hand that he dies, though by misadventure. Like his cousin Euain, he is associated with "fair hands" – Beaumains – in this case the fair hands are put to menial tasks by choice.

Agravaine

Agravaine is the shadow of Mordred and is the evil aspect of the four Orkney princes. He is always a sower of dissension and his strongest friendship is with Mordred whom he resembles in a lesser degree. He is always quarrelling with his brothers and is the means of discovering Lancelot with the Queen. In the ensuing fight he is killed by Lancelot. Agravaine appears to have had a certain friendliness towards Arthur himself, but is in most ways a villain.

Thus were the princes of the House of Orkney and Arthur's nephews. It is noteworthy that Lancelot is the keystone of their fate and that Lancelot slays them all but is the friend of three though the enemy of one.

The Son of King Uriens and Queen Morgan

This is Arthur's fifth nephew, Euain, the Prince of Gore.

He has a devotion to Knighthood that is somewhat like Gareth's. He saves King Uriens his father from death at the hands of Morgan. Euain is surnamed "Blanchmains" for he is as was also his cousin Gareth, clean-handed in character. By his choice of the "damsel of sixty winters" and his desire to learn from her, we may gather that Euain had been probably instructed in the Atlantean Temple Mysteries by his mother Morgan. Euain dies a victim of Gawain who slays him in a joust. This joust takes place almost directly after Gawain's vision of the Grail-Quest, which vision is received in evil faith.

Euain is the type of spiritually developed Fifth Race man who has emerged well from the semi-human traditions of the preceding races but yet knows how to adapt and use the earlier teachings. He belongs to the Air of Earth quarter of Malkuth – that quarter which gets a direct influence from Kether and which represents the higher mind of man.

Lancelot and Lancelot's kin

Lancelot has suffered greatly from popular ideas of sin and romance, but actually he is one of the great Archetypes of vertical (yes, "vertical" not "horizontal") polarity and, like Tristram, he is in a passionate search for his own soul through pursuing the souls of others. This is a hard saying and I shall explain it later.

Lancelot is the son of King Ban and Queen Elaine of Benwick, a part of France. He is snatched from his mother's arms by the Lady of the Lake who brings him up in her secret, hidden kingdom and later also takes as his companions his two cousins Bors and Lionel. Lancelot is trained by the Lady of the Lake in the arts of love and chivalry till he is proficient enough to be presented at Arthur's court. There he becomes the leader of Knighthood, the best friend of the King, the example and hero of the younger Knights and the lover of the Queen.

The formula of these Arthurian love affairs must not be sought in conventional Christian morality but in the cult of Queen Venus and in the Atlantean Mysteries. This has been already explained in the first Arthurian Script. Lancelot loves the King as well as the Queen and is obviously deeply loved by both of them. Here we come to the great spiritual factor for which Lancelot stands.

Lancelot and Tristram represent stages in that deep polarity love which is rarely found in marriage – even in a happy marriage. Such a love, when heterosexual, adds all the force of the instincts to the spiritual drive behind a strong and recapitulated karmic relationship. This dual power is necessarily exceptionally hard to control and leads to tragedy. This particular type of tragedy, however, is one of the hewers of the way to the integration of Spirit and Personality and one of the strongest and cruellest hewers of that way. The true contacting of the "Negative" Aspect of God – which is what Love is – brings retribution when used for personal ends but when these have been worked out and assimilated, the attitude of impersonal love to all can be at last realised and the human being has unified the "male" and "female" factors in his own spirit. Some people in going through this tragic way consummate the vertical unity in the end as did Lancelot after the Queen's death when he enters the life of awareness and contemplation. Tristram, on the other hand, does not complete the work but falls during that phase which succumbs to the

Destroyer. Before the spirit enters into its own, as a Logoidal unit of completed power, not only must the Kings of Edom be slain, but their Overlord who is the Queen of Love. Of him to whom much is given, much is required and the ways of the two great Knights Lancelot and Tristram are neither easy nor happy; it is, however, a way to the One Life as much as is the way of the hearth-fire or the Way of the Cross.

Lancelot's son, Galahad

We know that Galahad – the Prince Initiate – should really have been the son of Arthur and Guinevere. As it was he was so only in a spiritual sense and, physically speaking, he was the son of Lancelot and of Elaine of Carbonek. He should have been born of the Priest-King and the Priestess-Queen but instead, he is born of the great warrior and the Priestess of the Grail. He is the great spiritual Knight, one-pointed in adventure and intention. He is contacted from the beginning to the Christ-force and cannot turn aside. It is a pity that the medieval and ecclesiastical descriptions of Galahad suggest a certain priggishness. This is because they were only able to judge the Grail-winner from one standpoint. Merlin has designed the Siege Perilous for Galahad long before the latter's birth for Galahad represents the "One who is to come" among the Knights, the one who achieved perfection yet who was born in what is accounted parental sin and scandal.

Galahad is one of those who disappear, being withdrawn mysteriously from the mundane plane. We have to distinguish between types of disappearance which occur in tradition. There are those who "walk with God and are not" as Enoch, Elijah, Galahad and Percival. There are those who are withdrawn to the Land of Beginnings like Merlin, Arthur, Ogier and Thomas the Rhymer. The first examples return not again in the same guise to the world of men. The second examples come back after long absence to help once more the world of men. The first examples are met upon the planes of Daath; the second examples may be met on the secret side of Malkuth. The first are mystics – the second occultists. Galahad, like Guinevere, cannot be fully expressed in the present age and he will return in another guise for he is a representative of the Cosmic Force of Christ. The Grail Knights have been misrepresented by medieval and ecclesiastical descriptions, for, in reality, they are archetypes of Adepti.

Lancelot's cousins, Bors and Lionel

Bors

This is the great example of the man who is able to keep his feet in both worlds largely because of his fidelity both to his friends and his principles. Though he is a Grail-winner he returns to the world of men to take up his responsibilities again. Arthur, Guinevere, Percival and Lancelot all depend on him and he never betrays that confidence. Though trained by the Lady of the Lake, he is able to be stable on the mundane plane. The glamour of the Green Ray does not dim his spiritual vision and the spiritual vision does not end his friendship with men. His strife is with his brother Lionel but even there he shows detachment and control. He has both detachment and benevolence, being a man among men who saw the Crystal Vessel within the Grail of Earth.

Lionel

Lionel is also seized with his brother Bors by the Lady of the Lake, and both are brought up by her as companions to their cousin Lancelot. Lionel is brave and fiery but less praiseworthy than Bors with whom he often quarrels violently. He takes, however, a loyal part in Lancelot's affairs and is finally killed by Mordred's sons at the fall of the kingdom. He is a lesser Green Ray initiate.

Lancelot's half-brother, Sir Ector de Maris

(Two people apparently bear the name Sir Ector but the communicator considers them as one i.e. the guardian of the infant Arthur and the friend, follower and illegitimate half-brother of Lancelot.)

Ector was one of great understanding and acceptance of responsibility. It is he who watches over Arthur when the latter is handed to him as an infant by Merlin at Tintagel and he also who cares for Sir Lancelot at the end and delivers the funeral oration. He is a great spiritual character who is remarkably selfless in his fidelity and sympathy.

Sir Tristram's Circle

This brings us to the great Cornish forces. Tristram and Iseult represent the deep ritual pain and beauty of horizontal polarity which is not actually so expressed in the case of Lancelot and Guinevere. Tristram is the great figure of the sadness of Netzach – for there are deep extremes in that Sephirah. He is a lover and a fighter but also a harper, and those who make music are able to be in touch with cosmic vibrations. He dies in disachievement, unable to dissociate the Goddess from the priestess. Thus the beauty and tragedy of his story – and he was one of the greatest Knights – find no other level but death. Lancelot on the other hand, realises truth at the end and so passes onward to wholeness.

In Tristram are links both with Atlantis and Ireland for he belongs to Lyonesse and the famous love potion drunk by himself and Iseult was the contact with the Black Pillar of the Irish Mysteries used in a personal instead of an esoteric sense.

His father was Meliodas, King of Lyonesse, and his mother, who was King Mark's sister, died in giving him birth in the forest, giving him the name of Tristram to signify the sorrowful manner of his birth.

Meliodas was a knightly character but Mark, the King of Cornwall, Tristram's uncle, was the reverse – a wily, traitorous and less potent Mordred. Meliodas is a subsidiary character and he and Mark represent two of the numerous petty Kings who were subject to the suzerainty of Arthur.

It must be realised that the definitions I give to these Arthurian characters are not necessarily such as are shown by the popular legends. My definitions are meant to be set to esoteric standards. It would be useless to give details of all the Knights and I am taking but a handful of the more important ones for examples.

The best Knights of Tristram's circle are Dinadan, Marhaus and Palomedes.

Dinadan is one who jests often and his courage and faithfulness are leavened with humour.

Marhaus is the uncle of Iseult and the great link between the Table Round and Ireland. He has great nobility and valour but is slain by Tristram in the end.

Palomedes – the brave Saracen Knight has for us a special significance for he represents the force and wisdom of the East which aligns itself finally with the Western Tradition and also he represents those of another race who become adopted brethren of the Group. There is much esoteric significance in the following of the Path under the symbol of the Questing Beast and in the Christian (i.e. Western) initiation in the form of baptism and also there is a detachment and dedication of a more abstract type than is found in most of the Western Knights.

N.B. The communicator decided that it was unsatisfactory to make an alphabetical list of the other Knights, as at first had been planned. He decided to continue with the more important characters not already included in the preceding lists of circles and kindred.

Percival

Percival like Galahad and Guinevere is unsuitable to be used as a Mystery Name. These three characters are to be assessed as powers to be used on single occasions as in ritual. Each of these characters refers to Paths rather than to individual grades or types. Percival is "The Fool" of the Mysteries, that is to say that he brings down the knowledge gained between rebirth and death added to the wisdom of the Essential Self but cannot at first adapt these powers to that of earth. When he does so he becomes the Grail King.

The Communicator added that Percival was of the Grail lineage on his mother's side and his character works through the intricacies of the feminine side of the Grail. His mother, his aunt, his wife, his sister are all Grail types who touch upon the Second Logoidal Aspect in the microcosm and whose forces work through sacrifice.

Lamorak

This Knight acknowledged by Lancelot and Tristram as one of the noblest of their company was fated to be the victim of treachery on more than one occasion and he died by it also, the actual murder coming from the hand of Mordred but the indirect actions towards it coming from all the Orkney brothers save Gareth. Lamorak was also Margawse's lover and the slayer of her husband.

Aglovale

(The communicator was asked about this Knight and seemed unaware of the story built around by him Clemence Housman which is not borne out in Malory (though it may be elsewhere?). The communicator, however, thinks that all such great archetypes of the West such as Christian personalities, myths of gods and Round Table people may quite rightly be used according to individual need and imagination.

Tor

This was the half-brother of Percival and illegitimate son of King Pellinore. Tor has much to give by study of his brave and resourceful character. He was brought up as a cowherd and became a Knight of real leadership as well as of real courage and his qualities were evidently recognised by Merlin.

Pellinore

Pellinore was the King of Wales (or Galis) and father of Percival, Lamorak, Tor and Aglovale as well as of a daughter (Dindrane). Pellinore was the first to follow the Questing Beast, that strange vision preceding the coming of the Grail to the land. When Pellinore died Palomedes continued in this chase of the Questing Beast.

The Questing Beast may be taken as a symbol of the realisation of Karma and of the Dweller on the Threshold.

Percival and his brothers Lamorak, Aglovale and Tor as well as his father Pellinore may be taken as the chief Welsh circle of the Legend. Percival and Lamorak are great Welsh contacts of Knighthood.

All these preceding Kings and Knights form the four chief "families" or "circles" of the Legend – i.e. Arthur's, Lancelot's, Tristram's and Percival's.

Kay

Before going on, we must not forget that Sir Kay the Seneschal, the grim, discourteous but faithful Knight is Arthur's foster brother, the son of Sir Ector, and should have been mentioned earlier.

The following Knights are important but it is impossible to give more than a few as other work presses.

Bedivere and Lucan

Bedivere's significance is that he was the last to speak to Arthur and the last to hold Excalibur and finally to return the great Sword to its source. He it was also who brought the world the news of the King's passage across the Lake in company of the Mourning Queens. Like so many people he desired to hold on to what was meant to end.

Lucan was also with Arthur at the end but dies before the King. Though grievously wounded he carries out faithfully all the King's last behests. It is he who hands the King the great spear (the name of which is Ron) with which Arthur slays Mordred.

There is much significance in the connection of these two Knights with Arthur's weapons – weapons which are personalised into a definite life of their own.

Balin and Balan

These brothers and their weapons are used by Merlin as great symbols. They represent phases of the initiate's life on the Path. The Higher and the Lower Selves are implicit in their story.

Geraint

This is the sun in polarising aspect. He is a great Knight in strength, love and valour, but does not express the complete sun rhythms as does Gawain.

Urre

I include this brave and good but lesser known Knight for esoteric reasons. He was Hungarian and his name implies the ancient primeval contacts. He could prove a Round Table contact with the Master Rakoczi.

You will perceive that I have left out many names in this list but we are principally dealing with the characters which yield the best esoteric material. There are many Kings we have not mentioned. Kings and Queens represent rulers of both inner and outer plane territory. We can now pass on to:

The Ladies

You recall that these negative forces may be aligned with vertical polarity and are thus included in each completed knightly force. The ladies, however, are in the legend assumed to be forces of horizontal polarity and we must also be able, if necessary, to align them to this aspect as well. To some extent this side has been touched upon in the first Arthurian Script. Many of the ladies are Queens and recluses. This means that they represent priestesses and, some of them, non-human powers.

The best known of these Faery Women – Morgan and the Lady of the Lake – have already been spoken of but there are many others. In general the Faery Women represent aspects of the lunar polarities of the Knights.

Vivienne is the chief Lady of the Lake and an aspect of the Goddess as instructor in the arts of love and war – tutor of the Knights in chivalry where it concerns sex. She was not required to teach Galahad and she misused the power wrongly wheedled from Merlin, but she tries human marriage with Sir Pelleas. Apart from her bad behaviour to Merlin, she is benevolent. Her name is Vivienne and also Nimué. She receives Excalibur back when it is flung into the lake by Bedivere and is also on the barge which takes Arthur to Avalon.

Saraide

Is one of the lesser Ladies of the Lake, the attendant and messenger of Nimué.

Hellawes

This is a sorceress who loved and tried to seduce Lancelot. She was a priestess of one of the ancient pre-Celtic cults and the Lady of Castle Nigramous. She is not highly important.

Blodwenn

Is also not so important. She is a Celtic Elemental formed out of flowers – a creature of delicacy and beauty.

Dame Ragnell

This is the hideous hag wedded to Gawain. She becomes beautiful in the secret hours of each night, provided she is loved and trusted or, in other words, realised for the great crude force of the Black Isis which, as occultists know, turns into the dark, shining beauty when accepted by her worshippers.

The Three Mourning Queens

These come to fetch the dying Arthur in their barge. They may be aligned with his three sisters or, apart from that, realised for the mystical guardians of the "dead" (whether "dead" in body or through initiation) and they belong to the pre-Christian Avalon which is connected with remote human origins. The legend calls them the Queen of Avalon who is Morgan le Fay, the Queen of Norgalis her friend and boon companion in magic, the Queen of the Wasteland who was Percival's aunt and therefore is of the Grail family. These three Queens are working in their own true forces once more i.e. in their own original powers before the world contaminated them. Therefore they are fitted to bring back other souls, equally contaminated, to the place of Origin which is the state before Lemurian sin.

We now come to the more important of the ladies who are not counted among the "Faery Women". (Faery Women in the Arthurian Legend are the women of magical power – whether aspects of the Goddess like the Lady of the Lake or human women of the Atlantean priesthood like Morgan le Fay).

Alice, La Belle Pilgrim

She may be taken as the type of the seeker who despite all the troubles and interests of life and love, yet remains loyal to her spirit's main concern, which is the Quest.

Bragwaine (or Brangwen)

Iseult's faithful attendant, charged with the care of the fatal potion – through good report and ill, ever loyal to her mistress who had been placed in her care. In effect, she is a priestess of the Irish Black Pillar.

Colombe

One of the polarity victims. Her lover is killed by Balin and she then kills herself upon his corpse.

Dindrane

Percival's sister. The holy maid of the Grail in that legend's Christian aspect. She, however, is a mixture of forces for she weaves the sword-belt of Galahad and girded him with the spiritual sword. She is a female bearer of the Christ-Force, killing herself in order to heal another and, as a corpse, she lies on the ship which bears the Grail Knights on their journey to Sarras. She is a variety of the archetypal Psychopompos, but on Christian lines.

Elaine of Astolat (or Elaine Le Blanc)

The maid who dies for love of Lancelot. She is a priestess – for only one of the priesthood could use the barge of initiation as she did. She concentrates on a man the force belonging to the Goddess and thus she herself is the sacrifice.

Elaine of Carbonek

She is priestess and princess of the Grail whose feminine powers are used under dedication. Thus she is an aspect of the Virgin Mother and, as such, gives birth to Galahad. (The term virgin, used here, has of course no reference to physical virginity as usually understood).

Enid

The earth wife of the solar man in polarity. The hearth-fire priestess.

Evaine

The helper of those in distress and the mother of Bors and Lionel.

Felelolie

Sir Urre's sister and finally wife of Sir Lavaine. She has the female contact with Hungary (and the Master Rakoczi). The type of dedicated traveller who ends up in Britain and becomes one of ourselves.

Iseult (or Isoud)

There are two forms of this name.

1. The Qliphothic traitress who is called Iseult Blanchmains and belongs to Brittany.

2. The tragic Queen of Cornwall who is called La Belle Iseult. La Belle Iseult is an aspect of the Black Pillar of Ireland from whence she came as a princess. She has thus an especial contact with the arts for that Pillar stood for creative imagination.

Igraine

Arthur's mother who was an Atlantean princess and was the chief outer means of introducing the blood of the Sacred Clan into the British Royal House. Herself being one who showed integrity but had no especial personal influence, she is an example of an innocent cause used by destiny to blaze a trail of tremendous significance for the whole country.

Linet and her sister the Lady Liones

Who marry respectively Gaheris and Gareth. They involve much adventure and Liones is a type of Elemental beauty and healing. These ladies are types of polarity in romance but Liones is the more interesting sister – an earth priestess of the nature type.

Margawse

Arthur's sister, the Queen of Orkney who rivalled Guinevere in beauty. Hers is the evil, soulless beauty that only seeks for power. She is a form of the evil side of Venus.

This is by no means an exhaustive list, but it may give some insight of the redemptive forces needed in working on the vertical aspect of the legend.

Appendices

Appendix One
The Glastonbury Script Violet
M. Firth (Dion Fortune)

Transcript of a Communication received in Trance through the mediumship of Miss F[irth] at Glastonbury 9.30 p.m. on the night of the Autumnal Equinox September 25th 1921.
Present: Mrs F…, Miss F… and F.B.Bond. The trance was preceded by a few minutes meditation on the subject of the Watchers as Merchant-mariners of the old time and bringers of the New Philosophy to Glastonbury with the symbolism of the Temple.

Joseph of Arimathea was a name – not a person – but a function, or office. There was much coming and going, not one single mission only, and the work was established in connection with the Druidical Orders; and was largely Druidical in its nature. It had a Druidical side.

Question by F.B.B. Is it a fact as stated that the Druidical worship was very similar to the Norse?

The inner side of all religions is similar. This coming and going had been from time immemorial, and both in and out of the body on the part of the illumined. Travel was not so difficult in those days as we are apt to think, for the early voyagers had not the fears of the later. The Phoenicians held the secrets of the Tyrian Mysteries, and the Jewish were closely allied to the Tyrian.

There was a College of Illuminati here at Glaston, which was a great centre of the earlier faith. Members of the College used to return with the tin ships in order to take their higher degrees at the Isle of the Holy Thorn. The thorn was known here before the Christian era.

There were many holy centres about Europe and Asia, and each one specialised in one kind of Mystery, and men would journey from one to another of these centres in order to seek the special wisdom of each. The grades and ranks of the Initiates were known in each one. Thus it was that when the New Wisdom gained ground in Syria, messengers were sent there from the Isle of the Holy Thorn to investigate and to bring back word of what they found. These messengers induced to return with them a small band whose views were not in entire sympathy with the orthodoxy of the East. Hence it was that Glastonbury's first Initiation was due to a schism, and these messengers brought away the Grail, which, truly interpeted, never was a Cup. It was the Brethren of the Minority who, as always, brought the Grail, leaving the Cross, the Spear, and the Sponge, to the Brethren of the Majority; for few can drink from the Cup, although all must bear the Cross. Hence it is that the symbols of the Passion are much seen in the sculptures of the Church – the Cup but seldom. Where the Cup is seen it means that there, illumination to a higher degree has been attained.

Here, in the Isle of the Holy Thorn, all that was best of the Sun Worship, and Serpent Worship of the Northern Tribes, Gaul, and the coasts of Spain, came together, protected by the marshes, for the purpose of prayer and meditation, working entirely upon the mental level; and concerning themselves not with priestcraft, nor statecraft, nor any other craft save the craft of souls. These men lived here, studied here, and healed here, until such time as the orthodoxy of the Church and the State gained power to stamp them out. Then the organisation superseded the vision. Those were appointed who did not see, and those who saw were ill thought of.

Then the great stones were broken, the moulds were levelled, and to this day you may find, among the Abbey stones, stones of a different sort, harder, greyer, and of another formation, hewn from what had once been a Druidical circle.

Those stones that were cast down but not assimilated, returned whence they had come, and the Powers with them. The true power lay in the wattle Church, which was circular. This form was not customary in Christendom, but the Power that was built here remained, and it surged uncontrolled throughout the New Order. Hence there was always trouble in regard to discipline. Glastonbury was essentially unstable; but a centre had been made; Power had been called down and focussed.

Now it was usual, when an altar, shrine, or Temple was to be abandoned, that the seal should be broken, the four walls of the Spirit cast down and the Powers dispersed, whilst those spirits that had been held in prison were bidden to depart. This however was never done at Glastonbury. That which was noble in the Pagan was carried on into the Christian in the time of its original impulse. That original Christian impulse likewise, long gathered up that which was noble into the Paganism from whence it came, being much coloured by the Sun worship of its own land. Hence the Son Worship of the East met the Sun Worship of the North; the male principle met the female, and these conjoined, gave stability.

Here they were conjoined, and when the hour came for the dispersal of the College – the primitive College – and the Church which was built with knowledge before the incoming Tribes backed with orthodoxy, (for there is no iconoclast like a convert) a meeting was held, and it was debated whether the Lodge should be unsealed and the Powers dispersed, or whether a Centre should be maintained for future uses. And one who was Greater came among them and bade that the ground should remain and be kept Holy Ground, and the channels kept open. Therefore the Mystic work was not reversed, and never had been. The enemy was peaceably admitted and as a consequence many who were high became low in the service of the newcomer, that the channels might be kept open. And the newcomer, who was orthodox, finding traditions deeply rooted, took it over and worked it into the Calendar of the Church.

Hence there is here an unbroken line of descent of the Mystic Power and aspiration of the races of the northern Island connecting directly with the elemental powers of the soil; for the soul of the race strikes its root in the soil.

Now the first worship was the worship of the Elemental Powers, whereby man, considering the qualities these powers possessed, planted in his soul the consciousness of them, thus becoming partly self-conscious.

These powers of the Elements, being planted in man's soul, gave him a community of "being" with them, and so, the elemental forces, "being affected", surged up and threatened disaster to Creation. There being thus a danger of a complete loss of balance, He who had previously taught the race returned again and curbed the Elements, thus making the Cross of Nature into the Crucifix by which man sacrifices the Natural to attain the human state.

We are now in the era of the Human – that which you all call the middle kingdom. Now each year penetrates the year behind it, and the year beyond it, just as the colours of the spectrum shade one into the other. Below the human there is the place of the non-human, and above it is the place of the super-human. We are now in the shaded or the overlapping portion in which the human and the Divine interpenetrate, just as at the beginning of the era the human and the Demoniac interpenetrated.

Now in regard to St. Joseph and his brethren – Apostles who were reputed to be twelve in number, there was another Joseph who also had twelve brethren. Likewise there was a Jesus who had twelve brethren. These twelve were degrees, not men; twelve grades of Initiateship ruled by a Thirteenth which was not of this plane but of the Executive Order of the plane above. Therefore there has never ceased here to be open Lodge. The succession has never failed; there has never been darkness here. The Tor has never lacked its Hermit, and there has always been an Upper Chamber within the bounds of the circle of the marshes where one soul in solitude has meditated upon the Mysteries. And thus was maintained even a focus in the flesh whereby the necessary contact could be made on the other side. Those who had functioned here always kept the Channels open by their concentrated thought, leaving merely the thinnest film, like a psychic parchment, lest the Power behind should break through into a world all unprepared and lead to martyrdom, not magic.

Consider well the symbol of the parchment and its osmotic action. Thus the contact has never been broken.

Now the true Church was, as we have said, the Wattle Church and it is symbolic that you should, this summer, have digged down to its foundations. The stone Church was built when the Powers had passed men's minds, and the symbolism alone remained. The Builders knew the measurements; they knew the meaning of pillar, arch, and triforium; they knew how to orientate, and where to place the symbols, but, in Jerusalem, the secrets were lost.

Now the structure of stone represents the interplay of force. The concept in the mind of the architect is based upon the actual interplay and is thus nearer to the truth concerning it than is the representative structure in stone. The Church, Temple, or other symbolic building is an attempt at Microcosm. The architect, conceiving the Macrocosm, attempts to reproduce it in stone. The principles of Cosmic architecture are the same as the principles of ecclesiastical architecture, and great truths are conveyed, though blindly, in the proportions of the structure. But the greatest truths and the profoundest teachings and the truest morality are contained in the architect's failures for when he grasps beyond the scope of stone to express his ideas he is reaching toward the Absolute, and, passing beyond the sphere of translation, he touches That which he cannot bring back in his hand. Hence the dome which falls is often built by the aid of a greater mathematics than the dome which stands, and it will be observed that, as the greater concept has imbued the minds of men, so have materials become known which could do that which could not be done before.

Upon all these points much could be said, but it passes beyond the scope of a single communication.

Here the trance communication ended.

Appendix Two
Atlantean Scripts

Neither Dion Fortune nor Margaret Lumley Brown were averse to making their own clairvoyant investigations into Atlantean realms. It is not possible to identify exactly who recovered what but following notes are extracted from records over the years that reflect upon the subject, and which, right or wrong, will have materially affected assumptions contained in The Arthurian Formula. *G.K.*

The City of the Golden Gates

The City of the Golden Gates was west south west of where Florida now is, (in the Gulf of Mexico) west of Jamaica; the sea is very deep there now. There are even now strange and sinister things over the old site, for all that was good was withdrawn on account of the spread of black magic. There is more of the old Atlantean life left than people suspect – an old form of life with palaces under the sea made of something like glass – not material but practically material.

The City was built on a cone-shaped hill two or three thousand feet high of solid rock with a large piece cut out of one side; there was a sheer drop to the sea on two sides. The River Naradek ran out at the back of the town. Big open boats were to be seen with covered prows and sails painted all over with stencil patterns.

In the later days of Lemuria and the early days of Atlantis the cream of the Lemurians became Atlanteans but, generally, the Lemurians became decadent and intermingled with the lower types; most of them perished in cataclysms. Life was very simple in these earliest times and the average intelligence was not equal to that of a dog of the present day. There were no initiates until the third sub-race of the Atlanteans. Then some were trained from the inner planes and a priestly caste was established which was able to take a little of the mind. They were specially selected but in those days the prime requisite was a clean wholesome stock.

In Atlantis there was rain but the specific gravity was different and there was not much condensation. Men were about seven feet tall and their physical bodies were more porous than now; in Lemuria they were much taller.

On the topmost tier of the hill were great buildings erected by experts. Great squares of marble were laid in bitumen and there were good roads with large marble flags perfectly laid. Down below the houses were very ramshackle and they often collapsed. There were very frequent earthquakes followed by tidal waves – and indeed this was the only method of cleansing.

The air was thick and heavy and for that reason was the Temple built at such a high level for the air was better there and the rays of the sun penetrated more easily.

Between the tiers were waterways supplied by water carried in wooden pipes from the mountains for the Atlanteans knew that water seeks its own level. The pipes were made from trees, softer than those of nowadays, hollowed out and treated with bitumen. There was a great quantity of bitumen available, lakes of it, and the lower town was impregnated with it there being a large morass on one side, which smelt very strongly of this bitumen.

The inhabitants of the lower town were hardly what would now be termed "human". They had hardly any mentality, were black in colour and four to five feet in height with wrinkled ape-like faces and long arms reaching down nearly to their knees. They had no knowledge of building and lived anywhere they chose in the vilest slums, where they bred like animals. During earthquakes and tidal waves some survived by climbing into trees. They lived some thirty to forty years and came to maturity when nine years old.

The inhabitants of the second tier were more of the present Mongolian type – rather yellow in colour – strong with broad features and snub noses. They had large families and practised polygamy, one man having as many as eight wives. Living conditions were better and there was more social life. They had plenty of passion but no conception of tender affection. From the best of these selections were made for promotion to the topmost tier.

The inhabitants of the topmost tier – the priests and warriors – were very particular and exclusive and did not associate with any on the lower tiers. They were what we should nowadays call "civilised human beings" – a whiter type with straight noses and high foreheads. The warriors might have a few wives each, very carefully selected and kept in seclusion; but the priests were either celibate or limited to one wife each and then only during the time he was from thirty to forty years old – after which he had to leave her. The men lived to as much as eighty years and a man aged thirty was as mature as a modern man of fifty. Great care was taken over selection as they were responsible for building the higher type of humanity, and it might take three generations to build a vehicle that could be used for the higher powers.

At mating there was a ritual in an inner chamber of the Temple, the walls there were eight feet thick and a light burned perpetually fed from an oil spring – which was why the Temple was built on that site. The oil bubbled up in the chamber and the "Spirit of the Fire" with the assistance of the Lords of the Flame, would be invoked by the priests to co-operate with them and thus gradually build up a vehicle from spirit-matter to physical for the occupation of an incoming soul. (Some of these souls came from Venus; none came from the Moon).

Virgins were very carefully selected and trained: special rituals were used when they were seven, fourteen and twenty-one years old at which many priests were present. The Temple was open to the sun – an open courtyard of very beautiful white marble. The people from the lower tier were not admitted by the priests who were very strict in this matter, possibly too strict. The Priest of the Sun and the Priest of the Moon officiated at the High Altar.

The arrangements at the Temple were very beautiful. At the Vernal Equinox the young girls, robed in white, were taken to a special ceremony by their mothers. If they were chosen for the Temple they would then be separated from their mothers but the latter could visit them till they were fourteen years old after which, if they were to be mated to a priest, no more visits were allowed. Those who were not so mated were used in group-ritual which included sacred dancing. These girls were chosen by the priest clairvoyantly and at twenty-one years of age those who were to be mated were handed over to the priests and mated to a priest of double their age – forty-two years. This ritual mating differed from the marriage permitted to the priesthood from the ages of thirty to forty years.

During the birth of a royal child a ceremony was held at each stage to ensure the right conditions in spite of astrological influences.

The Royal Clan, who were very numerous, all lived in a large palace rather like the British Museum in appearance. There were big steps leading up to it; it had a large hall, and was built about a central courtyard, square in shape. On each side of this courtyard were double cloisters which held self-contained residences for members of the royal family. The strictest order was kept.

The Priestly and Warrior castes on the topmost level were allowed to intermarry, but they were not very prolific, indeed four children would have been considered a large family. Records were kept and great attention was paid to pedigree.

A man in high position on the topmost level – for example, the head of a clan – would have his own house, built, probably, on the same lines as the royal palace. His official position would entitle him to certain concessions such as a country estate, all the marble he wished from the royal quarries (which he might sell if he chose) and five or six thousand slaves. These last were either the remnants of the previous sub-Race (who could not be left unattached) or captives taken in war.

The Crown held all the land, and all the national resources were exploited by the Crown with slave labour. The King was not the highest in the land, being responsible to the Priest of the Sun. The land was either given to the soldiers in return for military service or used for the endowment of temples and colleges. As a result those on the topmost tier led a markedly communal life and there was a strong sense of union among them. Coinage was not used but purchases were made by barter. All who lived here by right had a "caste-mark" on their foreheads made by rubbing into a small wound a mixture of blood taken from a priest of a certain Degree of Initiation mixed with the juice of a vine-like plant – a sort of passion-flower – which caused the wound to fester and form a small round pitted surface. Writing was in use, a phonetic alphabet which is the basis of the present alphabet. At the date of which we are speaking a great name to remember is Asuramaya who lived in the previous generation and in historic times reincarnated as Euclid. The Priests were vegetarians, the Warriors ate meat, and the lay-priests or "Scribes" (who were of the Lesser Mysteries only) could do as they pleased in the matter. In one way it was a primitive civilisation but very highly evolved esoterically. When a child was born an official came to inspect it and if it was malformed it was smothered. Mothers knew of this and if their child was thus defective they borrowed a baby and reared their own surreptitiously or else sent it to the second tier. In this way inherited "knowledge" and powerful occult blood filtered down to the lower tier. They were very strict on the upper tier as they had trouble in breeding sufficient for the army.

Sometimes people were born on the lower tier who did not really belong there and it was necessary to promote them to the upper tier.

If a man showed signs of capacity he was initiated into the priesthood or given a post in the army. When a boy was just reaching the age of puberty – in those days eight to eleven years of age – he would be brought to the Temple regularly every three months, and inspected regularly every seven years at the equinoxes. The priests sorted them out clairvoyantly. On the upper tier there were three possibilities – priest, warrior, scribe. The scribes received the same training as the priests up to a point; then they stopped and the priests went on. The warriors received special physical training. Every child was inspected and allotted to the Temple or the Camp. Girls were usually left in their own homes except for the few who were picked to be the mothers of priests; they were put in special quarters known as "The House of the Virgins", and given special instruction by the Chief Priest working in conjunction with the Inner Planes. Usually there would be some special design being worked out, such as the bringing in of a new characteristic. The Chief Priest would comb the whole of the upper tier to find those with the specifications he needed for this special breeding: he would find a lad who was developing well along the required lines and have him mated with a girl of the same type to intensify the characteristics of anything of special social value. In these days they were trying to bring in the third plane.

The courtesans on the second tier were a recognised class following an acknowledged profession; they had their allotted Temple day. All crafts belonged to the second tier and outside it no-one was allowed to learn the craft-secrets; they were very carefully kept. The upper tier would have been quite helpless without them – being unable even to mend a broken weapon. The second tier alone had tools and these were considered sacred in a way. Each craft took its tools to the Temple once a year to be blessed. The tools were not very elaborate but were adequate: there was, for example, a sort of trip-hammer consisting of a large piece of stone worked by a lever operated by four slaves, used rather as a pile-driver. The slaves were worked to their limit then thrown aside and replaced: they were cheap.

Generally speaking the inhabitants of the second tier were craftsmen or merchants – they worked with their hands. They were quite different from those on the upper tier and were really a mixed population – the result of cross-breeding between slaves. There were captives with very mixed blood who added to the variety. A man of the upper tier might take some of his slave-girls as concubines, and the off-spring – being of mixed blood – could not remain on the upper tier, nor could they be relegated to the lowest tier, so they were sent to the second tier in due course. There were, too, slaves who had been given their freedom, immigrants, and some exceptionally gifted people from the lowest tier who bought their way in. None on the second tier could own land because they could not bear arms.

On the third tier all were slaves or those who owing to laziness, disease, or criminal character were expelled from the second tier – hardly to be compared with a modern ape. All manual labour was performed by those of this tier; none of the upper tier would carry anything save a weapon or a scroll, and on the second tier were the craftsmen and merchants. Purchase of a slave was a simple matter. The new owner would put a hook on his collar and lead him off to a magistrate to have his own name cut on the collar in addition to that of the previous owner which was then cancelled by the affixing of the government stamp – the Broad Arrow. All slaves were branded on the chest with a hot iron; their skin was like leather and they made no fuss. They ate their dead, and in their little wattle hovels their pickled joints could be seen hanging about. These slaves were cannibals and would kill and eat any one they could get hold of; this accounts for the legends of Ogres that are found in every race.

There was no drainage system. Garbage was thrown over the side of the mountain and the lower population lived on it: similarly with the second tier. Much was left uncleared but in those days the sense of smell was not much developed.

There was not a great deal of warfare at this time; but force was needed to keep the lower population in order. The main external effort was on colonising what is now South America. But there was a constant struggle to keep animals down. There was organised hunting for, though the old antediluvian beasts were dying out there were numerous "cave tigers" (sabre-toothed tigers) in the hills, and along the coast and in the marshes and water-ways there was a lot of savage wild life, creatures like huge turtles and walruses that were man-eaters: they would crawl three or four miles inland and eat the slaves in their huts. A company of the army would be detailed to hunt them. They were very awkward to deal with and the only weapons available were javelins, slings, or swords – not even bows and arrows.

There was a continuous struggle against nature in one form or other – the animals, the earth which was always giving way, the sea with several tidal waves each year. Dykes had to be built and maintained. Rivers shifted their beds overwhelming the surrounding territory. All the water came from conduits in the mountains.

There was an extensive shipping trade with the colonies and along the coasts for in those days a chain of islands stretched nearly across the Atlantic so that it was possible to go across to North Africa in a sailing galley somewhat like in the South Seas today. There was a kind of ridge around the earth – possibly an old chain of mountains including the Caucasus, Alps and Himalayas.

The Three Emigrations

There were three big emigations under the control of the priesthood – one before each of the main cataclysms. The first set off towards the East travelling very slowly and stopping every year to grow their crops. Before moving on again they set up altars – the Stones of Stennes are an example. Such stones were moved by the germination of grain. This emigration settled in China which was reached by travelling across the north of Scotland and Northern Europe. The disposition of the land-surface of the earth was different from now – almost continuous. In China to this day there is great knowledge as a result of this emigration, and all their present Mysteries come from the Sun Temple of Atlantis.

The second emigration went across southern England, France, Spain, and Macedonia into India: there was no Black Sea then and the Mediterranean was a series of lakes. Stonehenge was made by this swarm and from it, too, originated the Lodge in the Himalayas.

The third of the great emigrations went further south, across America to Africa and Egypt.

The Origins of Initiation

There are three main lines of initiation, represented by the three emigrations from Atlantis and their Heads are those who represent the three Aspects of the Cosmic Christ – Wisdom, Power, and Love. Wisdom is of the first emigration (in China), Power is of the second (in the Himalayas), Love is of the third (in the West, the "Nazarene"). These are not three "incarnations" but three "emanations" – the Cosmic Christ is One. Each emigration took with it the achievements of its predecessor. He who has once been initiated always returns to the same Order or to the allied tradition that carries on the succession of that Order. In very truth there are unbroken lines of "apostolic succession" from hierophant to neophyte stretching back to the foundation of the Temple of the Sun in Atlantis and the first Manu who lived amongst men. Thence derive all initiations.

There was a system of testing for intitiation which required the candidates of each Degree to discover for themselves in meditation some of the secrets of the Degree, and the Passwords. If they were successful, they went to the Chief Priest to report them and then received initiation on the physical plane.

The Hall of Mirrors

The Atlantean Hall of Mirrors was a round building, a small circular Temple, containing many mirrors of different shapes and sizes made of metal and highly polished – glass being still undiscovered. These mirrors were probably not set into the walls but were fixed on pivots which allowed them to be adjusted at varying angles as required for the work being undertaken.

Many types of power could be brought through, and also knowledge of karmic conditions and how they were likely to work out in the future could be gained by skilled use of mirror-working in which the Atlanteans were highly proficient. The manipulation of the mirrors was done by priestesses. It was possible deliberately to manipulate a mirror in such a way as to show an inaccurate and misleading result.

The Withdrawn Temple of Naradek

The Temple of Naradek was situated a short distance from the City of the Golden Gates. The great Sun Temple, which was in the city itself, was used for the general worship but outside the city was a Temple of the mystical withdrawn priesthood who took no part in the daily political life. This Temple was on the banks of the River Naradek. It was the great Temple of the "Sun-behind-the-sun"; its priesthood were all mystic and illuminati withdrawn from the political area in contradistinction to the priesthood of the Sun Temple on the topmost plateau of the Sacred Mountain who were closely connected with the government. Such was the Temple of the River Naradek.

Behind the City of the Golden Gates was a mountainous hinterland; the mountain range ran parallel to the coast and an alluvial plain had been formed between the mountains and the sea. It was not much above sea-level, and was frequently inundated. It had originally been a salt marsh.

The River Naradek came from a sacred lake on a plateau of the mountain range in the background, through great gorges and across the plain in a very serpentine course. As it drew near to the coast it ran parallel to it for some distance with a narrow strip of land between it and the sea. Then it flowed into a broad estuary with sandbanks through wich ran the central channel. Thus the river was tidal for part of its course, and near the coast was dangerous on account of the wild life lurking there.

The City of the Golden Gates stood on either side of the estuary. It was in fact about the only piece of high and stable land in the plain where there was an old volcano well clear of the main range of mountains. This volcano had blown its cone off in ancient times and the whole of the upper plateau had weathered flat in the course of time. Some two-thirds of the way down a ledge ran around the mountain. On the slopes lived the merchants and artificers and the lowest caste lived on the level where they were much subject to inundations.

The Sun Temple was on the topmost plateau; but there was another Temple – of a more mystic and esoteric cult; this was on the banks of the Naradek on a bend where the river turned inland in an isolated place three or four miles from the city. This was the Temple of the River Naradek, the great mystical Temple behind the Sun Temple. Its priests were mystoe and illuminati withdrawn from the political arena in contrast to the other priesthoods who were closely connected with the government. A stairway cut out of rock led spirally down the mountain to the path which led to the Temple of Naradek; and there was also an underground passage to it which only certain people might use.

The days were to come when the Sun-Temple fell on evil days, but the Withdrawn Temple of Naradek never fell into decay.

The Hinterland

The Continent of Atlantis underwent a series of cataclysms. Behind the coastal belt the range of mountains shielded a plateau (behind which were level lands). Up there on that plateau were the remains of the very earliest Atlantean beginnings and it was a sacred place. Tradition said that there had been a Temple there and that the remains of the ancient Atlantean civilisation were below the surface of a lake. This lake was formed by the drainage from the central plateau which was shaped like a shallow saucer and since rainfall exceeded evaporation it gradually extended its bounds. From the point of view of history it is doubtful that there ever was a civilisation there as the mountain range was actively volcanic but the people of Atlantis looked to this high uninhabited plateau as the source and root of their Mystery Tradition.

Hermits used to retire to this high plateau and build themselves huts or cells since it was considered a great Power-centre. In a later age, when Atlantis was in its decline an organised group of hermits on monastic lines with its own Temple grew up there consisting of the more spiritually-minded men. But the organised worship continued to take place in the great Sun-Temple of the City of the Golden Gates, whilst the mystical priesthood lived in the Naradek Temple away towards the coast. The solitaries on the plateau were more or less schismatics who withdrew from a civilisation they could not mend.

Atlantean Religion

The important aspect in Atlantis was not so much great knowledge as a very intensive training: the highly-trained priesthood obeyed instructions coming to them from a higher plane. The knowledge was on the Inner Planes, not in the Atlantean priesthood.

The work of the Seers was done in the Temple outside the city, the Temple of Naradek, which was also called "the Sea Temple". Rituals were performed in the city but the political atmosphere was not suitable for the mystical priesthood and the ritual priesthood looked to the "Sea Temple". The Atlanteans called themselves "The Sea People" and this Temple was reputed to mark the place where they first landed.

The ruling caste of Atlantis originally came from Lemuria, the priestly clan of the "Sacred Blood". They were of a different breed and of a different stamp from the common people, and the Sea-cult was to the Sun-cult what the Mysteries now are to exoteric religion.

The Sun-worship was the outer aspect; it was a national religion, a magical religious cult though it is to be remembered there were deep esoteric aspects concealed from the general view. But there was also a sea-worship which was for the seers and mystics and into which the monarch and immediate members of the royal family were initiated. There was an inner group in the hierarchy who were initiated into the Sea Mysteries and who formed the inner nucleus of the Atlantean Sun-religion. They were the "seers" as distinguished from the "magicians" of the Sun-cult. The scribes and warriors – the inhabitants of the topmost plateau of the Mountain were initiates of the Sun-cult in various grades: the merchants and artificers – the dwellers on the second tier – were not initiates into the Sun-cult but worshipped thereat. There was also an aboriginal breed of much lower type who formed a slave population in the town and a gipsy population in the country: these worshipped the Earth-gods and did not share in the Sun-cult.

The priests of the Sun-cult were magicians and psychics up to a point but the higher spiritual seership was found only in the initiates of the Sea-cult and it was they who were the real directing influence in Atlantean affairs but they never dealt in politics but only in the broad spiritual principles of national life. They never furnished priests for the ritual work in the Temples but they supplied the priestesses to be used as seeresses and pythonesses and they had small groups of priestesses trained in the "Sea-Temple" in all the Temples and the ritual priests depended on them for the higher seership. Such priestesses were under the general direction of the High Priest of the Sun-cult, being appointed to serve him, but they were only on loan as it were from the Sea-Temple and always remained under its protection. If the priesthood of the Sun-cult did not follow the guidance of the seeress at one of their Temples she would wrap herself in her hooded cloak and go back to the Sea-Temple and none dared stop her. It was considered a terrible stigma on a Temple if this happened. Also the priesthood of the Sea-Temple might recall the seeress from a racalcitrant Temple and such an action broke that Temple's "contacts".

The Priest-Kings

The monarch received instruction on spiritual principles from the High-priest of the Sun-Temple who in his turn got his material from the Inner Planes through the seeresses. The functions of the priesthood and the head of the executive were thus quite distinct during the continuance of this practice. There came a day, however, when the clairvoyance of the priests in allocating the youth of the Sacred Clan to the category of "Warrior" or "Scribe" failed or was ignored and one who was destined to the priesthood was allocated to the military branch instead. This man received the full military training but also he frequented the company of the priesthood and learnt much of their knowledge thus combining in himself the developed qualities of both priest and warrior. At the same time there were on the scene a woman of strong character and high vision as seeress of the Sun-temple, a monarch who was weak and degenerate and a High Priest of the Sun-Temple unfitted for his office who had just been appointed thereto by the corrupt machinations of the ruler in succession to a very fine old High Priest: further, Atlantis was threatened with invasion by hostile forces with which the ruler was incompetent to cope. The warrior who should have been a priest was given command and repelled the invasion. On his return he killed the corrupt High-Priest – either with his own hand or by his orders – dispossessed the ruler and usurped the throne.

He had not, however, received the initiation into the Sea-cult and its secrets and thus was not fitted to rule, but the Seeress, taking the law into her own hands, gave him the knowledge and the contacts, thus enabling him to establish himself on the throne and combine in his own person the functions of Ruler and High-Priest – the Priest-King – and to curb the powers of the Priesthood of the Sun.

In his hands the arrangement was a source of strength as he was a man of great energy and power but in the hands of his successors it became a source of weakness since it gave power to the rulers and laid responsibilities on them which most of them could not support. The rulers hitherto had been administrators under the priesthood of the Sun who were themselves under the direction of illuminati; now the appointment of priests was placed in the hands of the politicians and the independence of the priesthood was destroyed.

Atlantis had already begun to decay when this Warrior seized the throne and arrested the decline for a period but the seeds of decay were already germinating (as was demonstrated by the failure of the priesthood to recognise the right of the one whom they wrongfully appointed to the Warrior class). The Sea-Temple, however, never fell into decay.

The Sacred Mountain and the Sacred Flame

Approaching the Sacred Mountain the traveller finds only one great gateway or pylon which gives entrance: then there are the three levels or tiers and a simple path winding up towards the summit. On that summit are the great gates of the City with the Sun-Temple set in its centre. The Temple is entered by the great West door which faces the colonnade or avenue of pylons. From the avenue can be seen the vista of the Temple through which gleams the Perpetual Light which is never let out day or night and burns up from the underground tunnel feeding a Flame before the main entrance which is visible for many miles. An initiate is appointed to watch and tend the Flame, either its light in the upper part of the Temple or its secret shrine through which may pass none but the priesthood or the initiate appointed to tend the Flame in its innermost recess.

The office of Guardian of the Flame was not specifically sacerdotal but called for unimpeachable trustworthiness. It was by observation of this Flame that the approaching disasters were foreseen.

The Flame in the tunnel was associated with the great Inner Plane Being who first led Atlantis to the knowledge of the "concrete mind" and the pursuit of science based on electricity and solar magic as well as knowledge of the heavenly bodies. This great Manu is again at work in the Age of Aquarius and the Atlantean contacts are of great value for Aquarians since the Age of Aquarius is the Age of Atlantis on a higher arc of the spiral of evolution. The great Manu may be invoked as the Guide and Builder of the New Atlantis and even now those who shall carry on after the New Age is started are being assembled.

Magical Workings in Atlantis

In the Sun-Temple all the rays of force that played upon the Earth met, and on account of the physical structure of the world at that date, the earth, the waters, and the moon were much more closely interrelated than now, and the volcanic Flame, the solar fire and the stellar rays were a great deal more perceptible in their action on the physical plane. Sun, Wind, Sea, and Earth made the fourfold base of Atlantean mysticism – the two former being considered as positive, the two latter as negative. Similarly the plane of the concrete mind of which the use was beginning then to be developed was still linked up with the astral plane, as earth and sea were interlinked. Humanity were in constant communication with the "inner" planes for these were still fused with the "outer" planes.

The most powerful of the Atlantean magic was worked through magical mating which term covered a far wider range than is generally understood and with which "mating" as understood today bears only small comparison. The Atlantean magical mating included not only that of the planes of form to provide a suitable vehicle for the incarnation of a Force but also strange relationships on the inner planes which resulted in the "birth" of entities for ensoulment by certain Forces. As long as these powers were used for holy purposes all went well, but it is not difficult to imagine the disorder and disasters that would ensue from their abuse – as, in fact, later occurred.

Stellar Forces

The Stellar Work was done in a side-chapel, as it were, of the Sun-Temple which was along a passage and down some steps from the great Image of the Sun in the Temple. This chapel held a very strange type of force swift, strong and deadly or beneficial according to its use – the force had, in fact, many analogies with the present-day radium. During special magical operations the rays from the star or planet selected would be focussed on a priest and priestess working together.

The science of the stars and the use of their forces was in no way to be compared only with modern astrology – even astrology rightly understood. It was a kind of "pre-Akasha" and the basis for much of the higher magical work – especially for telepathy, auric forces and image-building.

In those days the moon was practically one with the earth or had only recently ceased to be so: the moon's times and currents were far more obvious than now in their action on physical life. There was some mind – in the adepts at least – but it was not so concentrated in the brain but worked through all the "centres". The Stellar Power influenced the "Ego" and the Will and thus its abuse produced the direst consequences. In the magical workings a stellar entity was "born" which was used for certain purposes. The planet Venus probably bore the same relation to the earth in those days as the moon does now; the great "Venusian Flame" was a very real thing, not merely an expression. The Stellar Forces will again come into use in the Aquarian Age but on a higher arc and this time they will have more effect on the Personality.

The Atlantean science of the stars dealt not only with the more esoteric aspects of astrology and the Laws of Evolution but also had reference to the Zodiac, of which the contact is in Chokmah – "The Father of the Stars". This star contact of Chokmah compares with the sea contact of Binah, and these two Sephiroth together have provided the positive and negative aspects of the basic teaching of the Mysteries from Atlantis to the present day. Their archetypes are the "Bright Adept" and the "Dark Adept" respectively – Merlin being the British Racial aspect of the former. A priest or priestess may be far from the grades of Chokmah or Binah but the major spirits among the priesthood develop under one or other of these archetypes which overshadows their Higher Self. In this connection it should be remembered that Binah has two aspects and the Dark Adept in completion works through both. When an initiate has attained a very high grade he will be able to assimilate practically the whole of the archetypal power.

To put the teaching in principle in a very condensed form it may be said that the Stellar Magic is the interrelated action of Chokmah and Binah through the Higher Selves and integrated Personalities of two very high grade Adepts.

The Hall of Images

From the Sun-Temple an underground passage down a spiral stairway led to a secret door which opened on to the Hall of Images. This Hall gave the appearance of being filled with strange purple-green vapour through which one walked as in a mist so terrific and tangible was the power concentrated there; yet the Hall was like a place of the dead – the dead who, at any moment, might rise and crowd round the visitor.

In the Hall were four separate rooms or sections which held the "power-systems" connected one with each of the Four Elements. The power-system of Water was controlled by a certain vibration of sound, the Atlanteans being skilled in the knowledge of the use of sound and of its production. The Water-chamber in the Hall of Images was guarded by an Elemental sentinel and the suction near it was almost unbearable. Knowledge of the ocean-springs and of the secret power of this Water-chamber and the controlling sound-vibrations enabled the higher planes to loose the water-cataclysm on Atlantis.

The "Keys of the Sea" (as in the legend of the submersion of Ys) were not merely a phrase but a great Symbol. The Atlanteans held those Keys and allowed the wrong people to handle them with disastrous results.

The Hall of a Thousand Faces

In the Sun-Temple was a small rock-hewn shrine containing an Image which gave off a high mystic type of "magnetism". The Image consisted of a vast Face – always veiled save to the higher priesthood – the features of which were made of hundreds of smaller faces: it had an immense magnetic pull and was a primordial image of the One God. The faces which composed the one Face were made of stone and the whole represented the One manifesting in the Many. This shrine was much used in the making of images.

After the downfall of Atlantis confused memories of this Image gave rise to the conflicting claims of religions based on one God and on many Gods; and to one God and many Gods being confusedly worshipped in the same system.

The Emerald Skrystone

The Emerald Skrystone was a rough lump of emerald matrix. It was a symbol of the Atlantean High Priestess and was kept in a Shrine as a Temple-Mystery, guarded by Inner Plane beings. Some tradition of its use has descended to the Mayan race.

Druidic Origins

In the past a nomad tribe came direct to Britain from Atlantis, in the last days of the doomed continent and founded a colony in Britain. Among them were some of the Wise Men of Atlantis for though most of the preisthood were buried in the ruins of the Temples some few escaped and of these were the "Wise Men" referred to.

From them descended the occult lore known as Druidism. They brought with them certain symbolic representations of truths and memories that we still retain; such as "The Land under the Waves", the "Caves" which contain the Mysteries of Earth and Sea, the Solar Fire and the Sun-myths of all ancient creeds, the female forces known as Moon Gods and Goddesses. All these had been in the Sun Temple of Atlantis.

In Atlantis the Priesthood developed to a very great and unsurpassed stage from which it later fell. It was in Atlantis that mediums began to be used more as now understood although there was a much greater technical knowledge and skill partly because of the supreme wisdom then on earth, and of far greater natural ease of bodily fitness for such a thing in those far-off days. "Far off" in time but very advanced in civilisation and achievement and physiological development compared with the preceding Age. Atlantis fell and colonising units took root in various places and gave birth to the "Mysteries".

The Druids had a direct Atlantean culture, there is a particularly strong stream of the Mysteries in Britain itself when that stream is really traced to its source. The Druidic element in ancient Celtic civilisation was brought direct from Atlantis by those who were the heirs of the Atlantean colonies and in that ancient contact is a very pure teaching when you trace it to its beginnings before its degenerate days. By "pure teaching" I mean that word in a very correct sense: it is not generally known that the Druidic power was at first untainted Atlantean and much of it from the better days of Atlantis before the corruption set in. For it was the better type of the Priesthood which led colonists, and those that actually survived the cataclysms that engulfed Atlantis were themselves chosen by the Higher Powers to carry the last remnants to a better place – among the very few fitted to survive.

And therefore in Druidism at its purest you get a magic equal to Egyptian but drawn yet more directly from Atlantis because slightly earlier in foundation; you get a deep spiritual understanding, a "primal" light of knowledge of the Cosmos also and, though what we mean by Compassion and Love were non-existent in the very early Races, there was a fineness of social harmony and patriotism and individual goodwill that was a very fair approximation and this was very strongly shown among the Druids.

Appendix Three
The Mystery Of Gwenevere
Wendy Berg

The Arthurian tradition is a living tradition, a growing tradition, and it therefore seems fitting to conclude with an overview of the latest esoteric research that continues within the Dion Fortune, Margaret Lumley Brown tradition, in the work of Wendy Berg. That which follows is a gloss of salient points from a long manuscript by her entitled "Red Tree, White Tree", which will be published by Thoth Publications in 2007.[1] It represents insights of an experienced esoteric student based upon a remarkable academic work by Professor K.G.T. Webster, privately published by his wife after his death, entitled "Guinevere, A Study of her Abductions" [Turtle Press, Milton, Massachusetts, 1951] in which Arthur's queen is assumed to be a supernatural being whose early history explains her later behaviour.

Of Elves and Men

Although King Arthur and Queen Gwenevere together form the central axis around which much of the mythology of the Western world revolves, there is a great deal about them and the state of their kingdom which is not as it should be. For a start, their marriage is famous not for the manner in which it upholds the virtues of that honourable state but for the fact that Gwenevere, according to most versions of the legend, was having an affair with her husband's best friend Lancelot.

As if this were not enough, the reputed childless state of their marriage rather suggests that Arthur may have had "problems", a cause for which has been suggested in Dion Fortune's script, that is to say, that his energies were consumed from consorting with faery women, although it may well be that there were other factors at work as well. But whatever the case, there can be no doubt that as a model of perfection Arthur and Gwenevere fall short. Whatever the initial grand designs were in the days when Merlin brought about the conception of Arthur through magical means, these do not seem to have been achieved.

If the status and power of King Arthur appears to diminish throughout his reign, he none the less still shines beside his wife Gwenevere, who as Queen of his Kingdom, appears to have been ineffectual right from the start. It would seem that the only notable things she achieved were to have an affair with Lancelot and get herself abducted by a variety of marauders with extraordinary frequency. Apart from these indiscretions she is otherwise described in the conventional terms of the literature of the Middle Ages, which heaps platitudes of praise upon her as the fairest woman of the British Isles, but cannot disguise the fact the she did not have a tongue in her head or a purpose to her life.

Another frustrating fact about Gwenevere is that her ancestry is virtually unknown, and this is rather odd. Who, for example, is Gwenevere's mother? Although the origins of Arthurian mythology lie far beyond the mundane world it is the way of every myth to attach its characters to various times and places. Yet while King Arthurs abound and have been "proven" to have been alive and centred in Cornwall, Wales, Scotland and the Midlands during a period which spans several centuries, there is virtually no evidence of any link between Gwenevere and an actual physical location or historically recorded character.

There is no doubt that it would have benefited Arthur to have married into the nobility in order to cement his claim to the throne of Britain. According to historians and mythographers he had to fight for his throne, and it would have been very helpful to his cause if he could have married a bride who was well endowed with land or who would have brought about an alliance with a neighbouring king. There was surely no dearth of contenders. But Gwenevere has a tenuous ancestry to say the least, and she brought neither land nor allegiance in her dowry. In fact her dowry seems to have consisted of a single piece of dining room furniture!

Some versions of the story such as the *Vulgate* cycle, suggest that her father was Leodegrance, king of a land called Cameliard, although such a country will not be found on any map. Earlier versions make no mention at all of Gwenevere's origins. Yet the Celtic belief was that the right of succession was traced through the female, and certainly Arthur's sister (or half-sister) Morgawse was not only a powerful queen in her own right but her four sons Gawain, Gareth, Gaheris and Agravaine play a prominent role in the stories and were obviously possessed of considerable status and power. It makes no sense, therefore, that Gwenevere apparently comes from nowhere. In the process by which myth earths itself into historical reality, the Arthurian stories are abundant with names and genealogies, and with eligible women, so the concensus of silence on Gwenevere's ancestry is all the more puzzling.

Turning to the matter of archetypes, it is something of a puzzle as to what archetype Gwenevere actually represents. None of the conventional roles fit her at all comfortably. There is clearly a need to make her into something, and many have attempted to do so, but the process of matching her with standard feminine roles is often little more than wishful thinking. We would like Gwenevere to be an archetypal Queen so we try to find ways in which that cloak of Sovereignty may be hung upon her but only succeed in mistaking the cloak we have woven for the figure beneath it. Gwenevere is no Sophia, nor is she a goddess, nor a mother, and she is not even a very convincing human being.

But to attribute to her an archetypal weight which she does not have, or to assume the she has some sort of problem which needs to be solved, or to ignore her altogether, are all approaches which seem rather to miss the point. If something of the real purpose and meaning of her presence within the stories could be identified then a much fuller understanding of the purpose of the Arthurian stories would result.

It is often said, particularly in the stories of the quest for the Holy Grail, that it is essential to ask the right question. The results of Percivale's failure to ask the right question after he had witnessed the Procession of the Grail were extreme: the Grail castle and all its inhabitants disappeared and it was a long time before he found them again. Once I had asked *who* Gwenevere was, the answer came very rapidly. She is neither an archetype, nor a goddess, nor an ineffectual human being, and we are wasting our time to try to fit her into any of these moulds. *She is a Faery.*

That is to say, she has an objective reality of her own Faery kind. She exists within that Faery reality and she comes from a Faery Kingdom which has its own objective reality. She will not conform to human expectations of Queenliness because she is not human. The concept and expression of Queenliness which exists in her own land is very different to that found in any human land and she cannot wear the cloak of human concepts and wisdom. Her purpose within these stories is very simple: she is a Faery amongst humans, and the entire corpus of Arthurian legend revolves around this, and around her marriage to the human King Arthur. The relationship between human and Faery lies at the very core of the Arthurian stories, and theirs was the climax of many long years of preparation.

Once this premise is accepted then so much else falls into place. For example, to take the most obvious instance of the usual translation of the name Gwenevere as "White Shadow", this does not, as is often assumed, describe a pale or ineffectual or weak human but a *shining Faery.* It is an accurate description of her physical appearance to human eyes, and of how the white light of the Faery world shone bright and clear through the physical form which she, and others of her kind, must adopt if they are to exist within the human dimension.

The implications for the evolution of both the Faery and human races in this marriage between Arthur and Gwenevere are at once profound and disturbing. If we accept that Arthur, the manly symbol of heroic leadership within the world, was married to someone who was from a different and non-physical race of beings, then our concept of reality is severely threatened. If we believe that Arthur has objective reality then we must also believe the same of Gwenevere. And if we believe this, then we are challenged to take a new and very different look at the stories in which this couple are King and Queen, because their marriage bridges two different worlds of reality in a way which affects all those of both their kingdoms, human and Faery.

In the light of all this, the message of the stories becomes different indeed. The Faery world cannot be explained or understood in human terms, and to do so has been the source of much of the misunderstanding of Gwenevere's purpose within the human, Arthurian world. But if it is accepted that the Arthurian legends are the written record of an attempt to explore and heal the relationship between the two races which inhabit the earth: Faery and human, then a way forward from apparent failure is revealed.

To look at the Arthurian legends from the Faery point of view is illuminating but not always very comfortable. Humans in general and, it has to be said, King Arthur in particular, appear to have a very limited understanding of those of the Faery race who live amongst them. During the time in which this book was written Gwenevere made herself known to the author as a loveable, endearing, characterful, curious and wonderful friend. The relationship became one of mutual exploration in which boundaries were tested, realities probed and pomposities laughed at. They reached an understanding of their differences that developed into an acceptance which in turn became creative and life-enhancing. It is upon this basis, and only this basis, that any useful work can safely be undertaken between Faery and human worlds.

The relationship between Faery and human, whether this is between the same or opposite sex (although the concept of "sex" has limited relevance to the Faery world) has to be one of mutual trust and respect in which the human partner does not become entranced by Faery glamour and lose his or her head. Neither must the human partner blunder heavy-footed, trailing clouds of stinking worldly garbage into the fragile constructs of the Faery world. The Arthurian and Grail legends are littered with many examples of just such inter-world pollution which bears only too close a resemblance to the junk-littered state of the planet Earth.

Equally, there are, or should be, restraints on those of the Faery race who seek to form partnerships with those of the human race. But the over-riding message, first from Gwenevere and then from others of her race, is that something must be done to heal the division, misunderstanding and downright denial which presently exists between Faery and human, and done urgently. One of the greatest fears of the Faery race is they will be forgotten. Their inclusion in the tide of evolution back to the source depends on the human race and, conversely, without the Faery race the human race will fall short of all that it might be.

The gradual building of any one relationship between human and Faery, particularly when they are King and Queen, serves a much wider purpose than the purely personal. Any bridge of understanding is built in order that others may then walk over it. It is likely that this is what was intended in Gwenevere's original entry into the human world as Arthur's wife but, for various reasons, the attempt achieved only a limited success.

Yet they were not isolated in their attempt. The foundations which prepared the way for their union had been painstakingly laid through many centuries of magical endeavour, and much of that magical work is recorded, albeit in disguised form, in the Arthurian and Grail legends. Within these legends is the record of the ritual work of the inner Priesthood who appear as characters in the stories, and whose actions, often inexplicable in terms of everyday behaviour, are the memory of the magical rituals they enacted, rituals which in many cases were designed specifically to explore and heal the relationship between human and Faery.

Faeries at the Bottom of the Garden

Who are the Faeries? We use the spelling "faery" rather than "fairy" not because the former has any particular merit over the latter but to reflect the recent tendency to recognise a difference in meaning between the two words. When we refer to Faery, we are not referring to "fairy stories" in the sense of the imaginative tales often written for children about the tiny creatures of the natural world. Nor are we talking about something that exists only in the imagination, although the imagination is one of the best means by which the Faery world can be contacted. By Faery we mean the race of beings, very like humans in some ways but in other ways very unlike, which inhabited the earth before the human race arrived and which now exists in parallel with, but invisible to, the human race.

This is not to say that Faeries are real and Fairies are make-believe. Both are real, but it is important to understand the difference. The Fairies' existence is closely linked to the natural, living, vegetable world. Flower-fairies, for example, have forms which are an almost inseparable part of the plant with which they are associated, and their shape, colour and distinctive vibration is closely attached to the life and form of that particular plant. By way of example one may with ease, in a dreamy mood in the garden on a hot summer's afternoon, tune in to the fairy forms which can be found dancing about the nearby flowers. The sunflower fairy will be dressed in golden yellow, not in larkspur blue or carnation pink. A lily-of-the-valley fairy will be perceived to be wearing the delicate whites and the fresh greens of spring, not the rich crimson of an autumnal chrysanthemum. The lives of the flower fairies are very much an extension and expression of the plant and their life-energy is linked to the life of the flower. They are dancing, moving expressions of the spirit of the flower. A flower fairy cannot live for long when its flower has died.

Many other fairy creatures can be placed under the broad category of pixies or the goblins, and the numerous other local names for these small beings. Like fairies, they are generally much smaller than humans and are associated with the living vegetation of the earth. Their lives are also closely linked with the natural, vegetative forms upon the planet but they are less ephemeral than the flower fairies. They are part of the planet's consciousness, an expression of the infinite varieties and moods and facets of the planetary being and they have been upon the earth since it was created. Their "evolution" is therefore intrinsically linked to the planet's rhythms and any changes or development in them is as slow and infinitesimal as that of the rocks themselves. A 21st century pixie is much the same as a pixie of ten thousand years ago. There were goblins around when dinosaurs were lumbering about the earth. They are part of the fullness of expression of the planetary being and their purpose is fulfilled simply through their existence. They have no mission in life. Understandably, they hold little truck for the human race which to them is but a brief passing phase, a blink of the planetary eye in the cosmic year. They mimic humans, certainly, in various ways, but generally speaking their attitude is one of indifference.

There is a world of truth in the adage "I'll believe in you if you believe in me." Our everyday human perception, struggling to find something tangible which the concrete mind can latch on to, tends to invent or impose a definitive shape, form, or colour when these are lacking. When tiny beings such as fairies or goblins are closely associated with natural objects then a suitable form is readily suggested by that object. Fairies are not so fixed into form as are humans; their shape is fluid and changeable and they will appear differently to different people and at different times.

Nevertheless, fairies are an integral part of the Green World which is inhabited by elementals, fairies and Faeries. Another important point is that the Green World is inhabited by the birds and animals which are also a part of our human world, and because these creatures are visible to normal human sight they form the vital function of linking between the two worlds. The appearance of a white hart, or a black dog, or a raven, will often indicate the opening of the ways between the human and the Green World, and those whose awareness is drawn to these creatures are alerted by the fact that the veil between the worlds is about to be lifted and may allow the seeker to pass through.

But Faeries are different. By "Faery" we refer to those beings of a form which is very close to human form but who lived upon this planet before human beings emerged as a separate race. They are generally rather taller than human beings and their bodies shine with light and are fluid with colours not of the physical world or the visible spectrum. There are male Faeries and female Faeries, although the difference between the genders is not nearly so pronounced as in humans and their method of reproduction is not linked to sexual organs. Their form is moderately fixed, in that they tend to choose one expression of form and stick with it through many ages. This is partly a matter of our perception, but partly their own choice. But unlike the fairies they have great intelligence, deep wisdom, humour, and a well-developed understanding of each other, of the human race, and of the planet Earth and its relationship with the cosmos. They have an understanding of Deity and of the angelic and archangelic hierarchies which they share with humans. In fact it may be said that in their fluidity and their joy and harmonious sharing in creation they are much nearer to the angels than are we.

Faeries do not use speech in the same way as humans although their appreciation of the real nature of sound and vibration is so much more developed than ours that their communication, through this means, is subtle and refined. Their speech is nearer to song than speech, although their use of sound bears no similarity to the foursquare harmonies of Western music, but relies on infinite subtleties of tone and tiny shifts in vibration. And they do not need to use audible sound perceptible to human ears, but respond to far more subtle changes in vibration.

Their mode of living is closely attuned to the shifting qualities of light. They are not elemental creatures as such: their bodies contain air, fire and water but these elements are not the same as their earthly equivalents and it is more useful to think of them in terms of light: the light of air, the light of fire, and the light of water. They use and experience light much as we use and experience the physical elements. Colour, light and sound to the Faery race are all facets of one substance, so they will for instance experience the colour violet as one vibrating sound and the colour blue as another vibrating sound.

These concepts are better experienced rather than described, and the best way to do so is through the raised state of consciousness attained through meditation. Another approach to experiencing the state of being of the Faery race is to try to develop an awareness of synaesthesia: the ability to "hear colour" or to "see sound." Those who naturally possess this ability find that without conscious effort their senses make unusual connections, and they will see a piece of music as a series of shapes, colours or physical sensations, or hear different colours as different sounds. But it is possible for many people to develop synaesthesia to a certain extent, particularly when meditating or day-dreaming, and to practice the technique is a sure way of approaching the state of being of the Faeries, for whom sound is colour and colour is sensation.

Faeries are intimately connected with the rhythms of the planet in ways that are beyond our perception and they are much closer to the processes of creation than are humans. The earth is very much their concern, and they are intimately connected to it. Yet their approach to it and their relationship with it is very different to ours, and they see its changes in a way that is far less rooted in physical reality. Their consciousness is closely linked to earth but at the same time is attuned to the vast movements of the universe. If one imagines the changes in energy which are manifested when the tides of the great oceans rise and fall, then the Faeries are in like manner tuned in to the inner tides: those of the planets, the sun, the moon and especially the stars. Also of the movement of the Ages through the signs. Because of their great age, Faeries hold within their consciousness the expression of many of the ages of the earth, and although they appreciate the broad differences between, say, the present Piscean Age and the former Age of Aries, the quality of each Age forms an equal part of their consciousness and is not lost to memory. Whereas humans tend to see things from a worm's eye view, and in small chunks, Faeries experience the much longer rhythms of the cosmic tides and the cyclic movements which take thousands of years to manifest their effect on earth.

One of the most important differences between the Faery and human races is that Faeries do not experience desire in any way which humans would generally recognise. They do not have the physical, sexual desire of humans, nor do they experience desire for anything but that which is an expression of the fullness of the light of God. The full spectrum of light contains qualities which, when unpolluted by any shadow of any kind, will only bring about the best possible good. One might say that God, light and love are three facets of the same thing, so that the fullest possible light is an expression of the fullest possible love, and this is God. Faeries' understanding of light is as far beyond our understanding as is their appreciation of colour and sound. There is as much distinction, to them, between violet and lavender as we would experience between the sound of a rock band and the sound of a harp. Vibration is the key to all.

It is not always appreciated that there is as much variety among the Faery kind as there is among human kind, and the same span of human consciousness and endeavour which produces priests, scientists, teachers and poets is also found within the Faery race, though they do not display any of the human tendency for abuse, whether of self, others or the planet. The attitude of the Faery race toward the human race is mixture of indifference, ignorance, dislike, curiosity and, from a minority, a genuine desire for understanding and synthesis born of an appreciation of our shared destinies upon earth. In other words, much the same as the human attitude towards the Faery race. The feelings humans may well experience at the thought that they share "their" planet with another race of beings are shared by many of the Faeries, especially as they got here first! But here we are concerned with the individuals of both races who are ready and willing to communicate with each other.

There are many ways in which the two races of Faery and human may interact, and there are a small number of Faeries who deliberately step down their rate of vibration in order to come closer to our world and to form a partnership with human males. It is with those such as Gwenevere, Arwen, Melusine and Etain, who have found their way into recorded fiction, legend or history, and in whose actions we are particularly interested because their actions were deliberately designed to bring about a closer relationship between the two races.

The major hurdle to overcome when looking for ways in which to work co-operatively with the Faery race is always the hurdle of belief. The first step always has to be to accept that they are still with us now even though, for the most part, the etheric body of the Earth is the nearest approach they make to our physical world of reality. Myth and legend tends to assume that the Faery race gradually disappeared underground or to another, remoter place, after the arrival of humans, but this is not the case and such tales can be misleading. Although the Faeries were once the only humanoid inhabitants of Earth it is the Earth, not the Faeries, which has changed in its rate of vibration. The Earth which we now inhabit and regard as the basis of our reality is not the same as the Earth which they inhabited. In fact they have stayed the same, while the earth and its human inhabitants have moved away.

The other major difference between the Faery race and the human race is that the Faeries are relatively immortal while the humans are born, die and are re-born many times over. This is not to say that Faeries never die, for they do undergo a sort of fading which comes through the stresses which any near-physical body in an imperfect world will experience. Although they are far purer in "body" than the human race they are not perfect beings, and any less than perfect being will, in time, decay. In fact there are many signs that the Faery race is nearing the end of its viable form and that some sort of change is imminent, albeit in terms of many human life spans. There would appear to be a growing urgency for some sort of change to be achieved, and to this end the Faery race is a good deal more forthcoming in its attempts to contact and work with the human race than has been the case for some years. They may be "immortal," but they can't go on for ever. Because their existence is so closely bound up with that of the planet Earth, the (relative) immanence of such changes is of great importance, and is also inextricably bound up with changes to the planet, and of course with human evolution.

Gwenevere's dowry

Now that we have laid the foundations we can move to those at the centre: Arthur and Gwenevere, and the relationship between them. If Gwenevere's ancestry had been of normal human parentage then she would certainly have been expected to have brought something in the way of dowry with her, whether of land, wealth or property. As it happens she was endowed with but a single piece of furniture: the Round Table.

Given that Gwenevere was a less than obvious choice, it is also curious that there was apparently no contemporaneous comment on Arthur's choice of a bride. The chief sources of information concerning Gwenevere's early life are found in the Arthurian legends themselves, particularly in the *Vulgate* Cycle. This long prose epic clearly identifies Gwenevere's father as King Leodegrance of Carmelide. (Carmelide is variously spelt, and its similarity to Camelot is noted.) Another of the distinctive Faery Kingdoms such as Sorelois or Listenois, Carmelide seems to lie to the south-west of Arthur's kingdom. One of the chief cities of Carmelide was Carohaise, which is the Cornish name for the city of Exeter in the neighbouring county of Devon. (There is also a Carhaix in Normandy.)

There are several clues to the identification of Carmelide as an "innerworld" or Faery equivalent of Cornwall. A profusion of Arthur-related sites is scattered upon Bodmin Moor towards the eastern borders of Cornwall, and there is no doubt that such a cluster of sites reflects an inner significance behind the physical location. Esoteric tradition goes further by correlating Leodegrance's kingdom with the drowned lands of Lyonesse which are said to lie off the south western tip of Cornwall. The Isles of Scilly, two of which are named Great Arthur and Little Arthur, are not the only visible remnants of this drowned land, but a comparatively recent rise in sea-level has separated islands which were once joined together, inevitably giving rise to the suggestion that the Isles of Scilly were also once joined to Cornwall.

Any drowned lands rekindle memories of Atlantis and the Isles of Scilly are no exception to this rule, although as any visitor to Cornwall will know, they fulfil their Atlantean requirements without any need for more esoteric explanations.

Viewed from Cornwall's south western tip, they lie tantalisingly upon the extreme horizon, sometimes disappearing in the sea mists for days or weeks at a time, only to re-appear not quite where you remembered them.

Carmelide will not be found on any map, but it has its own inner geography.

Leodegrance's connection with Gwenevere is very important. His name indicates "The Great Lion." He is a figure of considerable presence. He is of the same order as other great pre-Arthurian figures such as the PenDragon brothers Aurelius and Uther. Like them, Leodegrance's name also links him to an important constellation, and like them he also was closely associated with the Round Table.

In terms of linear time, the age of Leodegrance's influence is far more distant than that of the Pendragons. His name places him firmly within the age of Leo, which spanned the period 10,000 – 8,000 BC. While the PenDragons represented the period of transition between human and Faery, Leodegrance is of early, pure Faery/Elven blood. His later appearance in the stories is no contradiction in terms for we are not dealing with the linear, historical time marked out by human lives and deaths. Leodegrance is of the Immortal Clan, and as alive now as he was ten thousand years ago. His purpose, as representative of the Age and power of Leo, was to forge the connections between the Arthurian initiative and the star Sirius, and this was achieved primarily through his daughter Gwenevere and the Round Table which she brought to Arthur's court at the centre of Logres.

The connection between Leo and Sirius is best seen in the civilisation of the ancient Egyptians. Lion deities feature strongly in their early cosmology, notably in the forms of Shu and Tefnut, leonine first offspring of Atum, who expressed the ka of their mother/father. Shu was associated with the principle of space, and Tefnut with the principle of moisture. The most famous manifestation of the Leonine influence is of course the mysterious Sphinx on the Giza plateau, believed to have been constructed in the Age of Leo by those who point to the evidence of water erosion upon its sides. The sun enters the constellation of Leo at the time of the inundation of the Nile, the most important physical and spiritual event in the yearly cycle and central to the entire belief-system of the ancient Egyptians, while the rising of the waters was ascribed to the influence of Sirius which re-appears at this time, having spent 70 days below the horizon. The lion was also seen as having an equally creative fecundating power, a memory of which is found to this day in the many stone-built fountains from which water issues from a lion's mouth.

The Age of Leo was, to the ancient Egyptians, "Zep Tepi", the First Time, the age of a civilisation which they knew had preceded their own, the time in which Isis and Osiris (before his enclosure in Set's coffin) reigned. This period was also known as the Time of Return. It represented the gateway in time through which, when the appropriate funerary rites had guided them to it, they could cut through the bounds of linear time and make straight their way of return to the stars. This journey achieved, they would become as the Shining Ones, the Akhu, or People of the Stars, just as Osiris had returned to his ka of Orion. When he had achieved reunion with his body of light, Isis, now reunited with her ka of Sirius, mated with him to bring about the conception of the child Horus. Thus were the floodgates of fertility between star and earth opened.

The star Sirius lies at the centre of the Faery cosmos. Sirius is sometimes called "the Sun behind the Sun," indicating that while the star we call the Sun is related to our physical centre of Self, the Solar Plexus, and the expression of our Selves within the physical Earth, Sirius represents a centre which is more hidden. The Sun and Sirius stand in relationship to each other as the human and Faery races stand in relationship to each other.

The symbol for the stellar gateway which opened within the Age of Leo is the aker, a hieroglyph of two lions crouching back to back and forming a gateway of the present which unites yesterday and tomorrow, past and future. A more familiar interpretation of this same concept can be seen in the Tarot card Strength, where a woman is holding open a lion's mouth. The woman is Virgo, the eternal Virgin, Isis.

Translated into the language of the Arthurian mythos, Leodegrance is Lord of Sirius, the lion of yesterday and tomorrow, guardian of the gateway to the First Time. This gateway into the First Time of the race of Shining Ones is symbolised by the Round Table, which is given by Leodegrance to Gwenevere. She is the virgin Queen, representative of the powers of Sirius, the Faery Sun manifested within the court of Arthur.

Leodegrance, like the PenDragon brothers, was a Star Lord whose task it was to transmit certain stellar influences into the group soul of the inhabitants of Earth. The PenDragon brothers laid down the patterns which would link Earth with its starry serpent counterpart of Draco, initially through Ambrosius Aurelianus and the "Round Table" of Stonehenge, and then through the actual body of Uther. Once this preparation had been achieved, Leodegrance was responsible for putting the final piece of the pattern in place, through the cosmic glyph of the Round Table and his daughter Gwenevere.

The principle at work here is fundamental to all true magical endeavour. First, the connection between earth and stars is made through an enduring cosmic symbol, a properly aligned and dedicated temple built on Earth but constructed to cosmic principles. Next, the principles established within that temple are literally embodied by those who work within it.

On one level the Round Table is a meeting place for a group of like-minded souls who have been brought together by their commitment to the achievement of a common and higher purpose. But we can trace the gradual descent of the Table through various stages as it passes down through Arthur's ancestors. It is interesting to note that seven, not six, are the stages of manifestation and it can therefore be said that the Table has yet to reach its final earthly manifestation. Of this it may be said that after the dissolution of Arthur's kingdom the Table returned into Merlin's keeping until such time as it should again be made manifest.

The first Round Table is the wheel of the precession of the Equinoxes: the rising of the spring Sun against the moving backdrop of the stars and the associated cycle of movement of the Pole Star. The ultimate journey of the Solar hero is to find the way in which to travel backwards through the cycle of the Ages, to overcome the illusion of linear time, and to find the way of return. This is the archetype embodied by Amlawdd, the owner of the mill of earth and his star-white goddess, Gwen.

The next owner of the Table is Merlin. Merlin interprets the meaning of the Round Table, and will reveal whatever is appropriate to those who seek to understand its significance. Standing between the earth and the starry heavens, Merlin mediates the patterns of the cosmic Table and transmutes them into forms which may be more easily perceived upon Earth.

Merlin does not give the Table directly to Arthur, but to Uther PenDragon. During Uther's period of ownership its qualities were embedded within the deep earth in the cosmic glyph of Stonehenge.

Uther passed the Table to Leodegrance, who passed it to his daughter Gwenevere. The final transference of the Round Table from Faery to human is described in the *Vulgate* Cycle. It describes how Leodegrance and Gwenevere are invited to a celebration held by Arthur to mark his defeat of the Saxon marauders. Leodegrance has come along with his "barons", that is to say, with others of his own land, but on his arrival apparently had so little understanding of what was happening that he had to enquire which noble lord was holding the celebration, and for what purpose.

Taken at face value this lack of comprehension makes no sense. As one of the local rulers of a kingdom near to Arthur's own, how could he not know who Arthur was or to what occasion he had been invited? Yet while this meeting is described as a simple celebration of battle success, it is of course far more than this. It is a description of a magical ritual in which one level of meaning of the Round Table is embedded within another. In Leodegrance and Arthur two great cosmic forces have come together, each representatives of different ages, different times and different races, and this is indicated in the symbolic language of the story by their apparent inability to recognise each other.

The real purpose of this celebration is that an exchange of energy may be made and new patterns set in place. The gateway of the First Time of the Shining ones in the Age of Leo is transmitted through the glyph of the Round Table into the new order of the human race represented by Arthur. On a mundane level this union was marked by the conjoining of Arthur and Gwenevere. But Gwenevere's greater part in this was to bring to effect upon the physical level the marriage of her stellar background with Arthur's Solar background. Leodegrance could not himself bring this about. At an energetic level the requirement has to be that the Stellar pattern is held by a female in order that the union can properly be made, with the Solar pattern held by a male.

Gwenevere's abductions

One of the most remarkable things about Gwenevere is that she was abducted from court and castle with astonishing regularity. The total number of Gwenevere's disappearances as they have been recorded in the legends which have come down to us is no less than fourteen. This is quite extraordinary, and testifies to a consistent and determined effort on the part of the Faery world to put a stop to her life in the human world and reclaim her as its own. Also demonstrated, of course, is the equally determined effort on the part of one or two of Arthur's knights (notably Gawain) that they should not be allowed to do so.

On a more immediate level, it is rarely asked whether or not Gwenevere herself actually wanted to marry Arthur. The legends are certainly silent on this point even though we are assured that Arthur desired union with Gwenevere. And we have no reason to assume that Gwenevere, before entering the human world, had not already formed a relationship with members of her own kind and had Faery lovers who, understandably, were not very keen on the idea of her marrying a human. This dynamic is certainly well supported by the many stories in Welsh and Irish mythology in which a female Faery forges a brief union with a human man only to be taken back into Faery by her former Faery partner.

A more rational and historical explanation for these frequent abductions would be the kidnapping of the Queen by a rival petty King as a means of consolidating his claim to land or to the throne. History and myth both provide examples of a rival nation or group using a Queen as a figurehead for their own purpose, one of the most obvious being that of Mary Queen of Scots. But this does not appear to be the case with the abductions of Gwenevere.

It has been suggested that there is a correspondence between the disappearances of Gwenevere and that of goddess figures from other mythologies, notably that of Persephone, who disappeared from the surface of the earth every year to spend six months as the Queen of Pluto, King of the Underworld. Such a correlation is certainly an attractive attempt to make more sense of Gwenevere's disappearances and it furnishes her with the respectable background of the yearly vegetative cycle, personified by all Earth-mother goddesses and it would make a lot of sense if she could be equated with the nature inspired cycle of, say, the Maiden, Mother and Crone and the three-fold aspect of the Goddess, or as the Summer Queen and Winter Queen. It is true that there are stories of her going a-Maying, but the correspondence ends here, for she does not appear to have become a mother and she did not attain sufficient age to become the wise old crone. In fact she seems to have stayed a maiden all her life. Another difficulty with this theory is that Gwenevere's disappearances do not take place at yearly intervals (nor indeed at any regular interval) such as that of Persephone's sojourn in the underworld. Each disappearance is brought about by a different abductor, and not only do her abductors vary a great deal in character but there appears to be a different reason behind each attempt.

The first episode of this kind is the attempted abduction and substitution of a false Gwenevere on the very night before the wedding, when kinsmen of a false Gwenevere plot to exchange her for the "real" Gwenevere in order to inflict hurt upon Leodegrance. This is a vital moment, again involving a magical mating, when Merlin, who has been present at the court for some time, now steps forward into the action and takes control of events before it is too late. Having learnt of the planned substitution and realised that this would put all his plans in jeopardy he enlists the help of the same Ulfin and Bretel who had helped him when he brought Uther to Ygrainne at Tintagel. With their help the plot is uncovered, the false Gwenevere exposed, and the real Gwenevere rescued from the hands of the traitors and returned to Arthur's bed that their relationship may be consummated.

It would seem that all is now well, and the union between the two races of human and Faery, which had been worked towards for so long, about to take place. Yet this was not entirely the case. And although Merlin had stepped in to prevent disaster on this occasion, the false Gwenevere continued to live in close proximity to the court, where she became the focus for unrest and at least one further attempt at abduction and substitution at a vital moment.

The *Prose Lancelot* describes the second abduction of Gwenevere. By this time the love affair between Gwenevere and Lancelot is well underway, a tale which is so familiar that it needs no repetition here. The story tells how the false Gwenevere now reappears with a vengeance for she sends a messenger to the court at Camelot and claims that she is the real Gwenevere and that it was she who was joined to Arthur in wedlock at St. Stephen's. She insists that she was that very same day taken and cast out, while the "false" (i.e. "real") Gwenevere was put in her place. The reaction among those who hear this is understandably one of great shock, all that is except for one knight, Galehaut, who is on close terms with Lancelot. On receiving the news he feels sorrow for Lancelot but is at the same time joyful, because he will be able to retain his close friendship with Lancelot for a lot longer than if Gwenevere was with Arthur. It is the very human details such as this which invests these stories with moments of striking realism.

Galehaut is given some prominence in this version of the story. He is the son of the Fair Giantess, Lord of the Faraway Islands and prince of the land of Sorelois. Clearly he is not human, but is of Faery origin, and rules another Faery country of a similar nature to Carmelide. He is one of the few male Faeries in any of these or similar stories who is able to move freely in and out of the human world, an ability which is more frequently found in women. He easily forges a close friendship with another who also moves freely between the worlds: Lancelot, who was raised by none other than the Faery Lady of the Lake.

In confirmation of their shared origin we are told that Galehaut and Lancelot are actually buried in the same grave, which is another way of saying that at their death they both return through the same gateway to their country of origin. The nature of the triangular relationship between Lancelot, Galehaut and Gwenevere is of some interest, for when trouble looms in the guise of the false Gwenevere it is Galehaut who immediately steps in with some very practical help. In offering a solution to Gwenevere's plight he also provides an interesting insight into the relationship between the human and Faery worlds at this point in their development.

It would appear that Galehaut and Lancelot's shared kinship in Faery prompts Galehaut's unusual attitude towards Gwenevere's love for Lancelot. Unlike the rest of the court, and indeed the rest of the world, who raise their hands with shock and horror he appears to have an understanding of their love and finds nothing wrong, sinful or even worthy of comment in it. In fact he encourages it and offers them both his loyalty, apparently pleased that Gwenevere is no longer with Arthur, because this means that she can now openly be with his friend Lancelot.

If his attitude is indicative of that of the Faery world as a whole then it would appear that Gwenevere's union with Lancelot was considered to be far more acceptable than her union with Arthur. An odd echo of this is found in the suggestion in some versions of the story that Arthur, rather than riding to collect Gwenevere himself and bring her to court for their first meeting, sent Lancelot to do the job for him. Perhaps Lancelot was able to make the journey into Faery and escort Gwenevere from that world into the human world while Arthur was not able to make the transition. Whatever his reasons, by this action Arthur undeniably took a grave risk in making Lancelot Gwenevere's escort in this vital journey between the worlds.

But to return to the claims of the false Gwenevere, it would seem that Arthur has been completely taken in by her. When confronted by her claim to be the real Gwenevere he immediately announces her to be the rightful Queen and rejects his wife, announcing that she will be brought to trial at Pentecost. It is at this point that Galehaut, (accompanied by Gawain who also has Faery connections and is therefore a suitable accomplice in his intended course of action) steps in to take the real Gwenevere to safety by escorting her out of the human world and back to his own Faery land of Sorelois.

In fact he takes matters further than this, and it would seem that he is prompted by more than a simple desire to provide a temporary haven for Gwenevere until things are sorted out with Arthur. The land of Sorelois does not have a Queen. As soon as Galehaut has taken Gwenevere back with him to Sorelois he pronounces her to be its Queen and ensures that she is acknowledged as such and received with due homage by its people. Gawain, obviously in agreement with this course of action, waits until he has witnessed that she has been properly recognised and that oaths of fealty have been sworn, and then returns to Arthur's court, satisfied that Gwenevere is now properly established in her rightful place.

Although Galehaut and Gawain act very promptly after the sudden reappearance of the false Gwenevere, it has to be said that their actions are not what one might expect. Clearly they, at least, are able to distinguish one Gwenevere from the other, but rather than taking the obvious course of trying to persuade Arthur to respect his true wife and not be taken in by the false Gwenevere, they seize the moment to achieve with great speed what we can only suspect might have been their aim all along. The rapid installation of Gwenevere as Queen of Galehaut's Faery kingdom, when she has just been thoroughly disgraced and rejected by Arthur in the human world, is certainly over and above the call of duty on Galehaut's part, particularly as there is no hint of a physical relationship between him and Gwenevere. Galehaut and Gwenevere are not lovers, and Galehaut appears to fully accept the relationship between Lancelot and Gwenevere. It can only be assumed that he and Gawain are restoring Gwenevere to her rightful position in the Faery world, and that this is something they had planned for.

Gwenevere remains Queen of Sorelois for three years, during which time Arthur kept the false Gwenevere as his concubine. It is entirely feasible that Arthur was as happy with one Faery as another. One is even tempted to ask whether it really matters as to which Gwenevere was Arthur's queen.

Actually it mattered very much, although Arthur does not appear to be mindful of this. And here he makes a grave error, for his indifference to the consequences of his actions puts into jeopardy all that Merlin and the previous PenDragon dynasty had worked towards. The consequences of this three-year period in which the real Gwenevere was not with Arthur at the centre of the kingdom were far-reaching indeed: "everything on earth rotted." And not only did everything rot, but a great "interdict" or restraint was placed upon the land such that no body could be buried in consecrated ground during that period, unless it was done in secret. In other words, during Gwenevere's absence the land is cut off from spiritual sustenance and protection, the normal sanctity afforded by holy ground is no longer available and the creative and fertilising energy of the cycles of renewal are withdrawn from Arthur's kingdom. Logres is plunged into calamity and Arthur's disregard for what is symbolised by his marriage with Gwenevere sets himself and his kingdom apart from the Will of God and the normal healthy patterns of life, health and growth.

Arthur at times displays some of the worst of human behaviour and in this instance acts in only too human a fashion by ignoring what he knows of higher things and being driven purely from his baser instincts. The consequences of this are graphically described, and while it is easy for us to dismiss the rottenness of his kingdom as the hyperbole of the story teller, the message is an unmistakable testament to the deeper power and purpose of these legends: this is what happens when you set yourself apart from the Will of God and from your own destiny. And Arthur's destiny was to further the unity of Faery and human by his marriage to Gwenevere.

The episode reaches to the very heart of the concept of sovereignty and of the king's intimate connection with the land, and at one level it may be interpreted as an example of the anciently held belief of the connection between the fertility of the land and the fertility of the king. Something of this may indeed be found amongst the many levels of meaning to be found in the Grail legends, but here Arthur's state of fertility is not called into question: he is not the wounded Grail King, nor is he the only one whose personal failings put Merlin's plans into jeopardy. The unfortunate situation at this point in the story seems to be that the Faery woman who should have been Arthur's queen wasn't too keen on the idea, that the Faery world as a whole wasn't too keen on the idea, that the "substitute" Gwenevere was not able to function in the same manner as the real Gwenevere, and that Arthur did not care.

The question is posed as to why it mattered which Gwenevere Arthur held as his Queen. Even if Arthur was careless of his destiny, then why should not one Gwenevere do as well as the other? After all, both are Faeries, and both are the daughters of Leodegrance. Would not one therefore be as good as the other in bringing about the intended union between the races?

Chapter 16 of the *Prose Lancelot* tells us why this was not so. It describes the reappearance of Bertelay the Old, who holds considerable influence over both Arthur and the false Gwenevere. Bertelay is one of the false Gwenevere's kinsmen and played a part in the original substitution attempt on Arthur's wedding night.

The real Gwenevere was such that she was a suitable vehicle for considerable forces of creation which flowed through her and which were thus made manifest within the physical world. This concept can be more readily understood if we compare her to others who have undertaken a similar task, not least the Virgin Mary. The physical vehicle which housed and gave birth to the incoming forces of creation embodied by the Christ had to be one of very special and particular properties, hence the legends of the Immaculate Conception of Mary herself, who was as pure a vessel as might be.

This bringing through into manifestation of the highest spiritual principles has to be made within such a vessel, just as one would not pour new wine into an old wineskin. This is the difference between the real and the false Gweneveres. The *Prose Lancelot* describes how the false Gwenevere and her kinsman Bertelay secretly dosed Arthur with various drugs in order that he would not challenge her or oppose any of her wishes. There is something rather unpleasant in these hints of the practice of debased magical arts. The chronicler further describes how although Arthur took the false Gwenevere with him wherever he went, he would not sleep with her unless he was in his own room.

One cannot help but wonder why the author felt it necessary to include this odd detail and as to what significance it holds. Why could Arthur not sleep with the false Gwenevere except in his own room? Yet the author is recording a fact which he must believe to be significant even if he does not know, or does not wish to communicate too clearly to his readership as a whole, why this is so.

The act of intercourse between a human and a Faery brings us of course to the very heart of the matter, and this is where every problem and every joy comes, literally, to a climax. The first plot to substitute the false Gwenevere was intended to prevent this very moment of union from taking place. Whether the act of love takes place between two humans or between a Faery and a human it brings all worlds and all levels together for a brief moment. Any gaps in the seams, any mismatching of the levels, any lack of synchronisation between the planes, and the mesh which holds the forms together is placed under immense pressure. Perhaps the problem was not with Arthur but with the false Gwenevere: that it was she who could not permit the act of love to take place unless she was within the walls of the chamber which kept her in close proximity to her confidante Bertelay, whose presence seems to have been so necessary to her. And perhaps the herbal potions which were given to Arthur were also taken by the false Gwenevere in order to support her presence in the physical world.

This takes us into uncharted and difficult waters, but we must move through them as best we may. At root, this section of the *Prose Lancelot* is dealing with the actual mechanics of moving between one level of manifestation and another. For humans to enter the Faery world it is necessary to raise the level of vibration. For most people this is generally done by thought and directed imagination, and by the elevation of one's consciousness upon the planes so that the senses begin to function at a higher level. The persistent practice of these disciplines will eventually take effect upon the physical body, and as is well known, the health of the physical body is very closely related to the health and integrity of the subtle bodies. But for others, although such persons are in a minority, the step between the human and Faery worlds is just that: a step. Hence the stories of those such as Thomas the Rhymer who entered Faeryland whether he would or no, and for these few the veil between the worlds is not so much thin as non-existent.

For Faeries, of course, the process is very different. We have already seen those such as Galehaut or Gawain who are able to move between the worlds with apparent ease, but for Faeries to function within the human world it is necessary for them to step down their level of vibration. Some idea of what this entails may be realised if we try to imagine how we might best spend time interacting with the world of an earthworm, or a mollusc, or a fungus. The idea quickly loses its attraction! And indeed just as the habit of raising one's consciousness to the higher vibrations can only have a beneficial effect so the habit of lowering one's consciousness may have the opposite effect.

One night, after having quarrelled with some of the noblemen of Arthur's court, the false Gwenevere withdrew to her quarters. But a transformation of the most unpleasant kind then began to overtake her body. The first sign of this was that she lost all her physical strength, an indication that the vital energies which support the body are under attack. The process of withdrawal of vital energies continued so that her muscles gradually became paralysed, with the exception of her eyes. Not having the benefit of a 21st century life-support machine, her flesh then began to rot from the feet up.

One begins to wonder at this point what the origin of this "Gwenevere" is, for the graphic account of this most unpleasant decay does not accord with our normal perception of a Faery being. However, the Gweneveres are not normal Faeries but Faeries who have descended into human physicality, and while the real Gwenevere appears to have adjusted reasonably well, perhaps by retaining a certain amount of the phantom-like transparency which is reflected in her name, the false Gwenevere seems to have had more difficulty. Like the act of love, the act of death also brings a soul to the gates between the worlds, and the *Prose Lancelot* may indeed offer us an eyewitness description of the rapid decay of the physical body when the Faery spirit has left it. At any rate, when she and Bertelay have confessed to Arthur what they have done they presumably both soon die for nothing more is heard of either of them. Presumably, also, Arthur's kingdom returns to its former verdant state following the death of the false Gwenevere and the restoration of the real Gwenevere to his side. It would seem that another crisis is over and all is once more as it should be in Camelot.

The examination of the details of this episode in the life of Gwenevere has revealed many apparent inconsistencies in the behaviour of the main characters. It may be argued that as this is not a history as such, and to attempt to interpret the characters' behaviour in the light of normal rationality is bound to run into problems. But they are responding to an inner, higher truth which informs and inspires them, and fills them with a coherency and sense which cannot be ignored. These stories are above all memories of magical rituals; memories which have been many times elaborated and embellished until their inner core is all but obscured. But this magical core remains, and many of the apparent inconsistencies can therefore be taken as pointers to aspects of that inner truth.

For example, when Arthur forgets for three years that the real Gwenevere is easily distinguishable by the small birthmark of a crown on her back, this is not indicative of a lapse of memory on the part of the storyteller but that something of far greater significance is happening. Arthur, representative of Everyman, has all the knowledge he needs to enable him to distinguish between true and false, and the truth in this instance is intimately connected with his acceptance and realisation of his destiny to build a bridge between the human and Faery races. The episode of the false Gwenevere presented him with his first major test; the opportunity to choose between the more difficult path of his true purpose or the easier life with his concubine. As Arthur stands for the whole of humanity, the deeper meaning behind this episode speaks of humanity as a whole which also knows of the existence of the Faery race but chooses to ignore it. The consequences are, in a sense, the same as the rottenness which afflicted Arthur's kingdom. We and our physical world are very much the worse for our state of divorce from those who also inhabit it.

The Faery and Human conjunction

This is just the first of many more attempts on the part of the Faery race to take Gwenevere back as their own, and these attempts grow in persistence and significance. They tend to show Gwenevere playing an almost entirely passive role in the dramatic events which unfold around her. But is this a true indication of Gwenevere's state of existence in the human world, or is there any evidence to show that she might have played a more positive hand in her destiny?

Several of the lesser known stories are particularly interesting, and help us to gain a better picture of Gwenevere herself, rather than Gwenevere as mediator of archetypal forces, in that they offer glimpses of her Faery family. It is the lesser known, still untranslated chronicles such as *Diu Crone* which contain the more interesting information as regards Gwenevere's Faery background. The accounts which have achieved popularity tend to be those which emphasise the human side of the stories at the expense of the Faery perspective.

One of the better known of the abductions is that attempted by Melwas, ruler of the Summer Country, who captures Gwenevere and takes her to his City of Glass, a location which can readily be equated with Glastonbury. Melwas' stronghold is surrounded by marshland, a feature of the natural landscape which surrounded Glastonbury before it was drained, and which also appears in several other versions of the abduction stories.

Arthur searches for a year before he finds Gwenevere but manages to rescue her safely, with the help of Saint Gildas, who is responsible for telling the story. While this particular tale is interesting for its specifically Avalonian setting and for the unusual appearance of Arthur as the one who rescues his wife, it does not really provide us with any new information. However, it should be noted that the story makes no suggestion that Gwenevere was ill treated by Melwas, nor that she was unhappy with the situation, and this fact becomes increasingly more evident as we look at some of the remaining abductions.

In the *Perlesvaus* we are given one of the best indications of Gwenevere's family. Following her death, a certain Madeglans of Oriande, who lives in the "far North", claims that he is her next of kin. He therefore requests that her dowry of the Round Table should be returned to him, or alternatively that Arthur should now marry his sister, the oddly named Jandree. We are given no exact indication of the nature of their relationship but something may be inferred. Presumably Madeglans is not Gwenevere's son, nor is Jandree her daughter, or they would be named as such, which makes it likely that they are her brother and sister. But the nature of the relationship is less important than the fact that Gwenevere had a next of kin at all, and the hierarchy of human blood relationships is not applicable to Faery families, which consist of a large, interconnected group of like beings all of whom could be described as brother or sister.

The episode is also significant in raising the question of what happened to the Round Table after Arthur's death. As Madeglans is of the Faery race then his point that the Table should return to them after the ending of the PenDragon dynasty is correct, and an indication that its work within the human world was now over. The Table represents far more than a mere piece of furniture and when it no longer has an appropriate human guardian then it must return to the inner planes and the Faery realms from which it originated. His other suggestion, that Arthur should now marry another of the Faery race is also interesting for it reveals a continuing understanding from the Faery point of view of the purpose behind Arthur's marriage.

A little-known poem, the *Lanzelet* of Ulrich von Zatsikhoven also offers rare insights into Gwenevere's ancestry. This telling of the story introduces King Valerin of the Tangled Wood, who lives in a shining castle at the top of a high mountain. The castle is surrounded by mists and can only be approached by a single road through a forest that is inhabited by serpents. Clearly this is no human king and no mundane forest. Valerin appears at Arthur's court and announces that Gwenevere belongs to him, because she was pledged to him as a young girl. Lancelot, not Arthur, fights a duel with Valerin, whom he defeats. Valerin rides away, but on a later occasion when Arthur is hunting the white stag in a forest, he attacks again and this time successfully carries Gwenevere away.

However, the poet informs us that Gwenevere did not enjoy her stay at Valerin's castle. This time it is Arthur who attempts to rescue her, although he has to enlist the help of the enchanter Malduc who is able to cast a spell upon the forest and overcome the serpents surrounding the castle. Valerin has put Gwenevere into a deep sleep, although one wonders why he should. But if Gwenevere was unhappy in Valerin's care then perhaps this action was necessary to prevent her from escaping. As it is, Arthur wakes her, and kills Valerin. Malduc knowingly remarks that if Gwenevere had gone to Valerin of her own free will, his life would have been spared. It would seem that Gwenevere was happy with some of her abductors but not with others. She was apparently happy to be carried off by her own kind only if she liked them, which seems fair enough!

Diu Crone (The Crown), provides us with many more names of Gwenevere's relatives, and the author of this remarkable story has many insights into the meaning of events which normally remain a puzzle. In this version Gwenevere has a sister called Lenomie, a brother Gotegrin, and her father is called Garlin of Galore. Whilst one Gasozein le Dragoz accuses Arthur of taking Gwenevere from him and of keeping her captive in Britain, for seven years,

Gasozein is clearly of the Faery race and we are at last given an unconditional description of the situation from the Faery point of view: that it is Arthur who has abducted Gwenevere. This makes sense of the otherwise inexplicable series of "abductions" which are thus exposed as a persistent attempt to remove Gwenevere from the human world and take her back to her rightful place. Gasozein is described in some detail by Gwenevere, who obviously has known him long before Arthur meets him. She tells how he wears only a white silk shirt with red hose, that he rides a white horse, and carries a white shield and red spear. He spends each night at a ford which is marked by a black thorn tree, all the while singing songs to his love, Gwenevere. This is the ford between the worlds.

Arthur and his companions ride to the ford and meet Gasozein. He claims that he is Gwenevere's real husband, having had her love from the time that she was born. He and Arthur agree to fight a duel for Gwenevere, but just before this takes place Gasozein asks for the proceedings to be drawn to a halt and says that Gwenevere should be allowed to decide whom she would prefer to stay with. Gwenevere is unable to decide.

The stalemate is a true symptom of the underlying problem, for no amount of fighting can bring a resolution to the issue at stake: that of Gwenevere's inability to choose freely between the worlds. To the vital question put to Gwenevere: "Are you doing this (i.e. attempting this union with a human) of your own free will?" the answer, from Faery and human alike, must eventually be a convincing "Yes."

As it is, Gasozein returns to his own kind where he presumably waits until Gwenevere will one day return to him. Gwenevere returns to Arthur but produces no children. Arthur produces Mordred, who kills Arthur and is himself killed. It is rarely admitted that the Arthurian legends are a catalogue of failure, yet until this reality is acknowledged, we cannot move on. We have arrived at the same stalemate and our period of inaction has lasted too long.

The Question of the Hallows of the Grail

The unresolved fight offers a vivid image of the "fight" between the two worlds of human and Faery as represented by this stage in the Arthurian story. At this point, nothing can be resolved, nothing can move on, only acted out in a repetitive cycle punctuated by periods of withdrawal and, as things stand, this is currently how the human and Faery worlds relate to each other.

As with any stalemate, a real solution can only be achieved by an intervention from a higher level, and one which will be recognised by both sides. Although Merlin initiated these events, One greater than he must bring them to a resolution. So let us now broaden our perspective, and look for that One. To do so, we must become like the knights of the Round Table who, when their mundane tasks within the kingdom were completed, turned their attention to the higher realities of the Grail.

Much has been written about the Grail. But although the commentaries and interpretations of the original stories flow as richly as ever, the actual stories of this mysterious and sacred object were committed to paper within a very short period indeed. They appeared out of the blue at the end of the 1100s and by the mid 1200s their profuse but brief flowering was more or less complete. However, many of the Grail chroniclers insisted that they were recording an older tradition, and there can be no doubt that this is true.

The phenomenon of a sudden outpouring of a hitherto secret tradition occurs from time to time, and last occurred in the final quarter of the 20th century when a tide of revelation of information hitherto kept locked behind the doors of esoteric fraternities was unleashed upon the general public. Volumes of newly revealed information (not infrequently peppered with wild speculation) of the Western Mystery Tradition: its beliefs, its practices, its temples, its liturgy, and in particular the real identity and message of Jesus, were for the first time laid before the public.

There is a close connection between these two creative outpourings of previously hidden knowledge. The first was concerned with a vessel, the San Graal, which was said to have contained the blood of Jesus. The second was concerned with the actual nature of the blood: the Sang Real or True Blood. The first revelation set forth the stories, legends, rituals and symbolism connected with the Grail, but the second period of revelation has taken us far closer to the reality which lies behind them.

Briefly, the Grail legends may be summarised thus: the Grail is guarded by a King who lives in a mysterious castle that is hard to find. Those that do find it witness a variety of strange events including a procession that appears to be part of a ritual connected with the Grail, and a group of artefacts which usually includes a spear, a dish and a stone. The Grail King is sometimes called the Fisher King or the Rich Fisher King. He suffers from an incapacitating wound that is related to the wasted nature of his kingdom, which has been deserted by its people and in which nothing grows.

In spite of the barrenness of the King's land, the Grail itself is a source of unfailing physical and spiritual abundance, and it nourishes those who find the castle and sit at its table. Curiously, it does not feed or heal the Grail King, although no-one asks why. The healing of the Grail King depends on the actions of those who discover the castle and, on witnessing the Grail procession, ask the right question. Only then will the King be healed of his wound, the land become green, and its people return. The King will be released from his position as guardian and the "questor" will become the new Grail King. Simple!

Yet not so simple. Because the seeker, usually Percivale, eventually does manage to find the castle and ask the right question although on his first visit he is too excited to remember it. But the question is no secret: it is "Whom does the Grail serve?" And we all know the answer: "The Grail serves the servants of creation." It must have been asked, and answered, a thousand times over by those who read, ponder, and act upon the message of the legend. Yet nothing has changed! The story remains the same, the King is still wounded, the question still asked and answered, the land still laid waste and unpopulated.

At the heart of the Grail Mysteries lies a figure whose identity is vital to their meaning yet whose identity seems curiously indistinct. There is a confusion between the Grail King and the Wounded King. They often appear to be brothers, and indeed the concept of the Grail King's brother is a thread common to most versions of the story. But sometimes the two brothers seem to have merged into one person while at other times they separate into two distinct characters. Yet the wound which is borne by one of them is intricately linked with the other.

The Grail Guardians consistently suffer from a wound which will not heal, and which is inseparably linked with their guardianship of the Grail Hallows. Yet there is widespread confusion as to whether it is the Grail King or his brother who is wounded. On a purely literary level this is a clumsy device. If these stories are only fantasy then such an odd confusion would never have arisen, so we must assume that its persistence throughout the stories is because it is a vital key to the mystery, even though encrypted in ritual form. It leads to the question: Who is the King's brother?

His role is crucial. He appears in almost all the Grail chronicles, but there is considerable variance as to whether he is dead and the object of a veneration which appears to equate him with Christ, or alive and, again like Christ, possessed of a miraculous blood which brings healing and restores life. Clearly he is someone of very great significance yet he remains in the background, a mysterious and unexplained figure.

In fact there is a persistent confusion between the identity of the two brothers. The Grail Guardian is mirrored in a dark glass by his brother who is the same, yet not the same. One brother is wounded and one is implicated in that wounding, but there is disagreement as to which is which. There is a consistent acceptance and acknowledgement of the brother's existence yet a reluctance to reveal his real identity to the uninitiated reader except through tantalising clues. When we have discovered who the mysterious brother is then we will be approaching the very heart of the mystery.

But before we do there is another question: *Why were the Grail Hallows removed from Jerusalem?*

This in no manner denies the obvious and lasting benefit of the "legend" which provokes thought and questioning, and is a source of spiritual nourishment. There is no doubt that many who meditate on the meaning and symbolism of the Grail have benefited from doing so, and its inner reality is unquestionable. But it is so easy to become enticed, like Percivale, by the plethora of characters, symbols and imagery with which it is associated and by the intellectual satisfaction of cross-referencing one version of the story with another that we, too, fail to ask the right question.

The Grail question is no longer the right question, and we need to move on. The legend once designed to be a catalyst for change, is now stuck, and we are perpetuating its stuckness. We know the question and we know the answer, yet we continue to ask it. The Grail Question no longer serves us, neither are we served by the answer: "It serves the servants of creation," which serves only to send us round in circles upon a treadmill that sounds full of esoteric promise but gets us nowhere. The answer tells us "I'll help you if you help me," or "I'll believe in you if you believe in me," which of course is true, but it is also true of God, or of Isis, or of any inner plane guide, or of one's own self, or one's own consciousness. In short, it is no answer at all. If the Grail stories are to be more than a perplexing (albeit rewarding) riddle there must still be something more to be discovered.

The Grail literature falls broadly into two parts. The part with which most readers are familiar describes how the several knights set out from Arthur's court on a quest to find the Grail which is hidden somewhere in Britain. But there is an equal body of literature which describes how the sacred Christian artefacts of the Grail, along with the spear, the sword and the dish, were removed from the Holy Land and taken on their long journey West.

They eventually arrived at their destination in Logres, where they were hidden from the common gaze. But given that Christ was a Jew living in the Holy Land this was not an obvious course of action by any means. Why were the Hallows not left in the Holy Land? This early half of the story is understandably neglected in favour of the episodes which deal with the adventures of the questing knights, for it would appear to serve only as a prelude to the "real" story which starts with the challenges of the Grail Castle, but it contains much which is of great significance to us.

Boron tells us how at first, when the Emperor Vespasian visited Joseph in prison after forty years, all he could see within the cell was a brilliant light. Eventually he released him, but he destroyed the Temple of Jerusalem, an actual event of AD 70.

These two events are closely linked, for the destruction of the Temple of Solomon simultaneously marked the outward destruction of an ancient line of priesthood as far as Jerusalem was concerned, and the beginning of another, inner line of tradition which was removed from Jerusalem to be reborn in the islands of the West. The outer wheel had reached the end of its turning; the inner wheel began to move. Joseph of Arimathea and his companions left Judea, first travelling north by land to the "City of the Sun" and then by sea to Britain. Their destination, however, was not the outer, physical land of Great Britain but one of the Faery lands which can be accessed through certain gateways to be found in Britain, and through carefully constructed magical ritual: Listenois.

It cannot be emphasised enough that the Grail Castle and its inhabitants are not to be found within the physical, human world, yet neither are they "symbolic" or "archetypal" in the sense of only existing within the imagination. They are to be found in another, equally real world: that of Faery. The spear is not a symbolic or archetypal spear, but a real spear that has been taken from the human world into the Faery world, as are the cup and the sword. The answers which the Grail-seekers elicit concerning the spear and the cup do not reveal an archetypal or conceptual spear or cup, but ones which possess a particular, definite and real history, *and it is the discovery of their origin, and of the reason why they have been moved to the Faery kingdom of Listenois, that is the object of the Grail quest.*

It has been suggested that the revelation of the Christian origin of the Grail Hallows is a device employed by the authors of these tales to provide such fantasies with a gravitas they would otherwise lack. Another frequently expressed opinion is that their "Christianisation" devalues and rides roughshod over their Faery origins and, if only it were removed, their original significance would shine through. Yet the real message of the Grail stories is that the two are intimately and inextricably connected. And this leads us to our final question: *Why were the Faery race entrusted with the guardianship of these sacred Hallows?*

According to the Grail chroniclers, the deepest secrets contained within the Grail Castle, revealed onto to a very few and even then only after years of searching and questioning, were that the Grail and Spear were connected with Christ. But where can be the secret in this? Why should this knowledge have been so thoroughly removed from the sight of the questing knights when "sacred relics" abounded in the world in which these stories were written?

The revelation which awaited those who asked the catalysing questions was not that these Christian sacred artefacts existed at all, *but that they were held within the custodianship of the Faery race, and that it was to the Faery race that their quest had led them.*

In addition to the reversal of the normal initiatory sequence, here lies another mirror-like reversal of the normal sequence of events, for the removal of the Grail, Spear and Sword from the human world back into the Faery world is a reversal of the normal manner in which the Faery race offer their magically charged weapons to those of the human world.

When the sword, spear, cup and dish which had all been intimately associated with the life and death of Christ were taken back into the Faery Kingdom, they were being returned from whence they came, just as the dying Arthur arranged for Excalibur to be returned to the Lake of the Faery Priesthood of Avalon. The Grail Hallows, as with all other Faery weapons, once their cycle of use had been completed within the human world, were returned to their land of origin. The cycle of movement is from Faery to human, then back to Faery. The quest is to realise this pattern, and the goal of the Grail Quest is to realise that these particular Hallows were used within the world by Christ.

There is a strange and evocative wood cut of 1588 which shows the human Eve and the Faery Melusine linked together by the spear which has pierced the side of Christ and caused two intermingled streams of blood to flow to the ground. Two separate fluids released from Christ's body: a redemptive flow which holds equal relevance for the two races of human and Faery. Melusine had married a human, Raymond of Lusignan, and their ten sons became powerful men of renown in many countries and their descendants included Kings of the Frankish kingdom of Jerusalem.

Of the two streams of fluid, the Bible says: "But one of the soldiers with a spear pierced his side, and forthwith came thereout blood and water. And he that say it bare record, and his record is true: and he knoweth that he saith true, that ye might believe."

We find it easy to accept that one of the streams of fluid that came from Christ's side was blood, but the exact nature of the other fluid is less obvious. John's suggestion that it was water can hardly be true: Christ's veins were not filled with water. Yet they contained two different, life-supporting fluids.

Yet the only other clue to the identity of this mysterious fluid lies in the tradition that Joseph of Arimathea brought two cruets with him to Glastonbury, each containing one of the fluids which flowed from Christ's side. One of these contained red liquid and the other, a white fluid. In an expression of the highest magic rooted in earth, the two streams that flow from Glastonbury Tor and mingle in the orchard of the Chalice Well at its foot are also red and white. This entirely natural phenomenon, occurring at the very place in which it is said the young Christ once trod, has understandably supported a centre of religious and spiritual experience for many centuries.

There are many descriptions of the white, shining appearance of those of the Faery race, as if the life-sustaining fluid within their bodies was white. The image of Melusine and Eve with the Christ propounds that the two streams of blood that flow from the living Christ are equally relevant to both the human and Faery races. It suggests that whatever was achieved by Christ's death and redeeming blood was as true for the Faery race as for the human race, and the relevance of Christ is equal both to humans and Faeries. It is therefore for this reason that both Melusine and Eve hold the spear, the same spear which would hold the properties of redeeming blood for both their races and which figures so prominently in the Grail legends.

Here is the explanation for the mysterious brother of the Grail King. The Grail King's brother is Christ, as he is perceived by the Faery world.

After Christ's death to the physical world, his message and purpose, often so distorted by its human adherents, passed on into the Faery world. It may well be said that the Grail quest offers a fuller appreciation of the real nature of Christ than much that the exoteric Christian church has to offer,

Perhaps one of the most challenging problems to our acceptance of this is one of language. Does this mean that Christ is a "Faery"? When we remember that the Elven/Faery race are not tiny grotesque creatures lurking under toadstools but tall, shining beings of great beauty and grace who possess immense wisdom, knowledge and understanding and who inspire and bring light and love to all who come into contact with them, then we are halfway there, but the whole truth is that Christ was both human and Faery. He is of the original root race from which both human and Faery evolved, and it is this which makes him the avatar for the future of both races.

After Christ's death, the function of Priest after the order of Melchizedek was also released; not through the established

Christian Church but through the esoteric Christian movement brought by Joseph of Arimathea to Britain and then, coming full circle, back into the Faery race.

The long line of Grail Guardians are Priests of the Order of Melchizedek, and the Mysteries of this order are now in the safe keeping of the Guardians of the Grail. Christ, the greatest High Priest of them all, brought these Mysteries to their greatest exposure within the human world but he marked the turning point of their evolution. After his death they passed from the outer world of men to the inner world of Faery, as did the Faery weapons of Cup, Sword, Spear and Stone which had played their part so distinctively in the passion of Christ also return to the inner Kingdoms of Faery from which they had originated,

The Grail legends are the liturgy of the Priesthood of Melchizedek. Their rituals are recorded in the stories of the quests of the Arthurian knights who sought the Faery Kingdom and the Grail Castle at its centre yet struggled to accept the reality of what they witnessed there.

The last two thousand years have witnessed a curious anomaly in which these ancient rituals of interaction between Faery and human have become increasingly "externalised" and made available to the population at large, yet the very process by which they have become common knowledge has simultaneously resulted in them becoming almost completely overlooked as a source of Inner Wisdom. Even when they were first committed to paper these rituals were "occulted" and their real significance disguised. There is no doubt that Malory, Chrétien de Troyes, Wolfram von Eschenbach and their like all had access to this inner wisdom whether or not they were themselves Priests of these Mysteries. The enduring strength which underpins these stories and ensures their continuing attraction stems from the realities which lie hidden within them: they are memories of the rituals of an ancient order of the Priesthood which serves the combined Mysteries

of Faery and human. The Priests of this Order still call to
their own, and the modern day seeker, just as the Arthurian
knights of old, may hear their call and, sustained by faith and
no little grace shall find their way to serve within the heart of
the Grail Castle.

But while it is for the knights to seek out these Mysteries
and ask their meaning, it is those such as Melusine, Etain and
above all Gwenevere, who leave behind their birthright of
Immortal Clan of Faery and enter into the human world, to
cajole and inspire any who have heard the faint call of Faery
to take the first step towards the most important alliance our
planet will witness.

Postscript

In light of the conclusions of these 21st century meditations upon an ancient wisdom it seems fitting to recall the conclusion of the Chant of the Elements received by Dion Fortune and her friends on Glastonbury Tor at the Pentecost of 1926, which may thus be seen to shine light from a slightly new perspective.

From of old, and for ever, rule we our kingdom,
And we are in the depths of your being.
Awaken and come –
Awaken and come –
Awaken and come.
Come from the depths of your Elemental
Being and lighten our darkness –
Come in the name of the White Christ
and the Hosts of the Elements.
Come at our bidding and serve with us
the One Name above all Names –
The Lover of men and of the Elemental Peoples –
The Great Name –
Of JEHOSHUA – JESUS.
He who said as he descended into the Underworld:
There shall be no night where my people are –
And the night shall be as day in the
light of the eternal fire –
And there shall be peace where my people are –
The peace of the heights above the winds.
And there shall be purity.
Fire and Air –
Fire and Air –
For Power to serve the Master.

Index

Other titles form Thoth Publications

PYTHONESS The Life & Work of Margaret Lumley Brown
By Gareth Knight

Margaret Lumley Brown was a leading member of Dion
Fortune's Society of the Inner Light, taking over many of Dion
Fortune's functions after the latter's death in 1946. She raised the
arts of seership to an entirely new level and has been hailed with
some justification as the finest medium and psychic of the 20th
century. Although she generally sought anonymity in her lifetime
her work was the source of much of the inner teachings of the
Society from 1946 to 1961 and provided much of the material for
Gareth Knight's *The Secret Tradition in Arthurian Legend* and *A
Practical Guide to Qabalistic Symbolism.*

Gathered here is a four part record of the life and work of this
remarkable woman. Part One presents the main biographical
details largely as revealed by herself in an early work *Both Sides
of the Door* an account of the frightening way in which her natural
psychism developed as a consequence of experimenting with
an ouija board in a haunted house. Part Two consists of articles
written by her on such subjects as Dreams, Elementals, the Faery
Kingdom, Healing and Atlantis, most of them commissioned for
the legendary but short lived magazine *New Dimensions.* Part
Three provides examples of her mediumship as Archpythoness of
her occult fraternity with trance addresses on topics as diverse as
Elemental Contacts, Angels and Archangels, Greek and Egyptian
gods, and the Holy Grail. Part Four is devoted to the occult side of
poetry, with some examples of her own work which was widely
published in her day.

Gareth Knight was a colleague and friend of Margaret Lumley
Brown in their days in the Society of the Inner Light together, to
whom in later years she vouchsafed her literary remains, some
esoteric memorabilia, and the privilege of being her literary
executor.

ISBN 10: 1 870450 75 2
ISBN 13: 978-1-670450-75-1

PRINCIPLES OF ESOTERIC HEALING

By Dion Fortune. Edited and arranged by Gareth Knight

One of the early ambitions of Dion Fortune along with her husband Dr Thomas Penry Evans was to found a clinic devoted to esoteric medicine, along the lines that she had fictionally described in her series of short stories *The Secrets of Dr. Taverner*. The original Dr. Taverner was her first occult teacher Dr. Theodore Moriarty, about whom she later wrote: "if there had been no Dr. Taverner there would have been no Dion Fortune!"

Shortly after their marriage in 1927 she and Dr. Evans began to receive a series of inner communications from a contact whom they referred to as the Master of Medicine. Owing to the pressure of all their other work in founding an occult school the clinic never came to fruition as first intended, but a mass of material was gathered in the course of their little publicised healing work, which combined esoteric knowledge and practice with professional medical expertise.

Most of this material has since been recovered from scattered files and reveals a fascinating approach to esoteric healing, taking into account the whole human being. Health problems are examined in terms of their physical, etheric, astral, mental or spiritual origination, along with principles of esoteric diagnosis based upon the structure of the Qabalistic Tree of Life. The function and malfunction of the psychic centres are described along with principles for their treatment by conventional or alternative therapeutic methods, with particular attention paid to the aura and the etheric double. Apart from its application to the healing arts much of the material is of wider interest for it demonstrates techniques for general development of the psychic and intuitive faculties apart from their more specialised use in assisting diagnosis.

ISBN 10:1 870450 85 X
ISBN 13: 978-1-870450-85-0

THE GRAIL SEEKER'S COMPANION

By John Matthews & Marian Green

There have been many books about the Grail, written from many differing standpoints. Some have been practical, some purely historical, others literary, but this is the first Grail book which sets out to help the esoterically inclined seeker through the maze of symbolism, character and myth which surrounds the central point of the Grail.

In today's frantic world when many people have their material needs met some still seek spiritual fulfilment. They are drawn to explore the old philosophies and traditions, particularly that of our Western Celtic Heritage. It is here they encounter the quest for the Holy Grail, that mysterious object which will bring hope and healing to all. Some have come to recognise that they dwell in a spiritual wasteland and now search that symbol of the Grail which may be the only remedy. Here is the guide book for the modern seeker, explaining the history and pointing clearly towards the Aquarian Grail of the future. John Matthews and Marian Green have each been involved in the study of the mysteries of Britain and the Grail myth for over thirty-five years.

In *The Grail Seeker's Companion* they have provided a guidebook not just to places, but to people, stories and theories surrounding the Grail. A reference book of Grail-ology, including history, ritual, meditation, advice and instruction. In short, everything you are likely to need before you set out on the most important adventure of your life.

"This is the only book that points the way to the Holy Grail in the 21st century." *Quest*

ISBN10: 1 870450 49 3
ISBN 13: 978-1-870450-49-2

THE FOOL'S COAT
By Vi Marriott

The story of Father Bérenger Saunière, the poor parish priest of Rennes-le-Château, a remote village in Southern France, who at the turn of the 19th century spent mysterious millions on creating a fantastic estate and lavishly entertaining the rich and famous, is now as well known as "Cinderella" or "Eastenders". He would never divulge where the money came from, and popular belief is that in 1891 he discovered a priceless treasure; yet Saunière died penniless, and his legacy is a secret that has continued to puzzle and intrigue succeeding generations.

Since *The Holy Blood and the Holy Grail* hit literary headlines in the nineteen eighties, hundreds of solutions have been suggested. Did he find documents that proved Jesus married Mary Magdalene? Was he a member of The Priory of Sion, a sinister secret society that knew the Da Vinci Code? Did he own the equivalent of Harry Potter's Philosopher's Stone?

A literary mosaic of history, mystery, gossip and myth, THE FOOL'S COAT investigates Father Saunière's extraordinary life against the background of his times, and suggests that the simplest solution of his rise from penury to riches is probably the correct one.

Vi Marriott is a theatre administrator, writer and researcher. Her play *Ten Days A-Maze*, based on Count Jan Pococki's *Tales of the Saragossa Manuscript*, had seasons in London and Edinburgh; and she contributes regularly to three "house" magazines concerned with the mystery of Rennes-le-Château and other esoteric matters.

ISBN 10: 1-870450-99-X
ISBN 13: 978-1-870450-99-7